Praise fo...

"Rich with emotio... rich characters, *Fool for Love* is an absolute treat."
            —Kristan Higgins, *New York Times* bestselling author

"Ciotta's wit adds spark to this tale of extended-family joys and sorrows, small-town living, and complicated characters with secrets that will keep readers waiting eagerly for the next Monroe family story."
            —*Publishers Weekly* on *Fool For Love*

"Ciotta is a master of the fun-to-read romance, and this outing is no exception."
            —*RT BOOKreviews* on *Fool For Love*

"Ciotta writes fun, sexy reads with a good dose of realism. Hot romance, a little suspense and a whole lot of charm make this a fast read."
            —*RT BOOKreviews* on *The Trouble with Love*

"Ciotta writes with style, wit and heart. Can't wait for the next one!"
        —Susan Andersen, *N... ...* ...stselling author

P... ...vels

"Enchantin... ... ...fun and sexy ...
Ciotta's fan... ...utely be looking forward to the next." —*Publishers Weekly* on *Charmed*

"An amazing charmer."
                —Heather Graham on *All About Evie*

anything but love

a cupcake lovers novel

BETH CIOTTA

St. Martin's Paperbacks

ANYTHING BUT LOVE

Copyright © 2013 by Beth Ciotta.

For information address St. Martin's Press, 175 Fifth Avenue, New York, NY 10010.

ISBN: 978-1-250-00134-4

Printed in the United States of America

St. Martin's Paperbacks edition / October 2013

St. Martin's Paperbacks are published by St. Martin's Press, 175 Fifth Avenue, New York, NY 10010.

10 9 8 7 6 5 4 3 2 1

To my fellow Bards of Badassery—Cynthia Valero, Elle J Rossi, and Rachel Aukes. You inspire me, challenge me, and enrich my craft and life. BoBs rule.

ACKNOWLEDGMENTS

Some stories are easier to write than others. This was a tough one. It's also one of my all-time favorites so I feel especially blessed to have such an amazing support system.

First and foremost, I want to thank my editor, Monique Patterson, and my agent, Amy Moore-Benson. Or . . . as I've grown to think of them . . . the Dynamic Duo! They keep me sane and inspired. Thank you, ladies.

I also want to express my gratitude to Holly (Blanck) Ingraham who's all kinds of wonderful and my copy editor, David Stanford Burr, whose expertise was invaluable. Thank you to *everyone* at St. Martin's Paperbacks for creating magic and propelling the Cupcake Lovers worldwide. A personal dream come true!

I'm blessed with amazing family and friends and I thank you all for your constant support! A special shout-out to my co-workers at the Brigantine Branch of the Atlantic County Library System. Beth, John, Jean Marie,

Gina, Linda, and Bonnie . . . We've had a rough year, yet through it all you supported my writing endeavors with enthusiasm and my frazzled days with kind concern. Bless you.

I'm forever grateful for the support from readers, booksellers, librarians, bloggers, and the wonderful people I've met in cyber-land.

As if I weren't lucky and blessed enough . . .

To my husband, Steve. Thank you, always and forever, for everything. I love you.

AUTHOR'S NOTE

Though inspired by a northern region of Vermont, please note that Sugar Creek and the surrounding locations mentioned in this book are fictional. Escape and enjoy!

As an added bonus, in the ongoing celebration of cupcakes and camaraderie, we've included a few scrumptious recipes from Honorary Cupcake Lovers. My heartfelt appreciation to the amazing JoAnn Schailey and Dawn Jones for sharing their cupcake-a-licious delights!

ONE

Sugar Creek, Vermont
December 23

Luke Monroe was no Scrooge. He was all about family
and giving and good times with friends. He co-owned and
ran the Sugar Shack, a local pub and restaurant devoted to
camaraderie via top-notch food and drinks, and a cozy
atmosphere. Like every other year, this year he'd decked
the Shack's halls with boughs of holly on December 1st—
fa-la-la-la-la. He'd helped decorate two other family businesses, too. J. T. Monroe's Department Store—owned and
operated by his dad and Luke's older brother, Devlin. And
Moose-a-lotta—a kitschy café owned and operated by his
grandma, Daisy Monroe, and Dev's lady love, Chloe Mad-
ison. Lots of red and green and a good dose of silvery
white due to the latest snowstorm. Overall the entire town
of Sugar Creek looked like Santa's Vermont Village. Normally, Luke felt like a giddy kid for most of the month of
December. This holiday season, for reasons that alluded
him, Luke was bluer than blue. Fa-la-freaking-la.

Considering Luke and his entire family had a lot to

celebrate, first and foremost, his dad's ongoing recovery from a scary bout of cancer, this seasonal funk really pissed Luke off. No way was he going to rain on anyone's holiday parade, so he'd been putting up a cheery front for weeks, waiting for the funk to fade and the joy to commence. No moping. Life as always. Hence why he was with family just now instead of home alone, swigging beer and watching sports.

Sunday dinner at Daisy Monroe's was a Monroe family tradition. Only last month Gram had moved out of her longtime spacious home and Luke's sister, Rocky, and her fiancé, Jayce, had moved in. Just before that, Gram, who'd grown eccentric and reckless, had officially agreed to let Chloe (a kick-ass gourmet chef) take over the planning, prepping, and cooking. So now Sunday dinner was at Rocky's house and Chloe oversaw the meal.

In essence, nothing had changed. (With the exception of Luke's brother and sister and even his grandma now being in committed relationships.) As always, not every member of the Monroe family and their extended clan attended the traditional dinner every Sunday. As always, you never knew who you'd end up seated by at the table. Since it was the night before Christmas Eve and a really big family shindig, only a core few Monroes were in attendance. There'd been more food than people, but Luke had doubled up on portions and he'd offered to take home leftovers since Rocky's fridge was crammed with the next day's feast. Amazing that he had room for dessert, but he did. Lately Luke had had a real weakness for sweets and, in addition to other holiday goodies, there were a boatload of cupcakes leftover from the holiday party Rocky had attended earlier in the day. The annual bash for the town's number-one social and charity club—the Cupcake Lovers.

While Rocky, Dev, Chloe, and Gram laughed and fussed over last-minute decorating in the living room, Luke battled the blues and lingered over the nearby dessert buffet. He'd been lingering for a while.

"Seriously? That's your fourth cupcake, Luke."

Grinning, Luke glanced at his sister while licking sweet, tangy icing from his fingers. "Yes, but it's my first—" He glanced at the card tented near this particular batch, focused on the three words and waited until the letters stopped swirling in his brain. "—Chocolate Peppermint Surprise."

"Leave him alone, Rocky. Obviously our poor boy is eating to fill some emotional void."

That observation was a little too keen for Luke's comfort. He shifted his gaze to Gram—hell on wheels at the spry age of seventy-five. "Did you read that psychobabble in *Cosmo*? And don't deny you're reading that glam mag, Gram. I saw it sticking out of your Make Love, Not War tote bag along with a copy of *Simple & Delicious*."

"I'm trying to spice up my life," Gram said while repositioning one of three nativity scenes on the fireplace mantle.

Luke opened his mouth as did Rocky, but Dev beat them to the punch. "You recently moved out of this grand old Colonial and into a rustic log cabin with your boyfriend," Dev said while climbing a step stool to straighten the crooked tree topper. "Your life is spicy enough."

Luke was surprised that his brother left it at that. Dev had always been anal and overprotective. Although he wasn't half as bad as he used to be since hooking up with Chloe, a bit of a free spirit who went with the flow.

"It's not a log cabin," Chloe said, sticking up for Gram, who also happened to be her business partner. "It's a salt-box farmhouse."

"And Vincent is my roommate and companion," Gram said, moving in alongside Chloe to rearrange a few ornaments. "Boyfriend sounds silly considering his mature status."

"Silly, *huh*?" Luke smiled and talked around a mouthful of chocolaty goodness. "Gram, you're wearing glitzy reindeer antlers and pointy elf slippers." She'd also dyed her springy curls flaming red, and had swapped her cat-eye specs for a pair of blingy green-tinted bifocals. Oh, and she had blinking snowmen dangling from her wrinkled lobes.

"It's called being festive," Gram said as she rearranged the presents under the massive Christmas tree she and Rocky had decorated to death. "It's almost Christmas after all."

Like Luke needed a reminder. Christmas was Rocky's favorite holiday. Before her home and business had burned down, she used to decorate the hell out of her Victorian bed-and-breakfast. Obviously she'd invested some of her insurance money into replenishing her Christmas holiday décor and then some. There wasn't a square foot of Gram's, strike that, Rocky's house that hadn't been touched by an angel, snowman, snowflake, holly, garland, ice cycle, St. Nick, reindeer, candy cane, nutcracker, toy soldier, or wreath. Usually Luke was all for holiday cheer, but. . . .

Cripes. He'd almost thought: Bah, humbug.

Noting that nagging emptiness in the pit of his stomach, Luke eyed the desserts. Maybe one of these Oggneg . . . He did a double take at the printed tent card and slowed his mind. *Aw,* hell. *Eggnog.* Maybe an Eggnog Cupcake would inspire some Christmas joy. Just as Luke bit into the moist rich confection, a furry, big-eyed mutt bounded into the room. "Hey, Brewster."

"Don't feed him any people food," Rocky said. "No matter how much he begs. It's not good for him."

"Gotcha," Luke said while allowing the dog to lick crumbs from his fingers.

"Got the wood." Jayce Bello, Dev's oldest and closest friend, and Rocky's fiancé, crossed to the fireplace with a canvas tote of chopped logs. "Sorry it took so long. Brewster was wound up and I figured it was better to tire him out with a few minutes of fetch, rather than risk him going on a tear in here." He motioned to Dev. "Can you get a fire going? I need Luke's help whipping up Daisy's after-dinner cocktail."

Luke frowned. "What are we in for this time?"

"Candy Cane Cocktails," Gram said with a fist pump. "Yes!"

"Disgusting ingredient?" Rocky asked.

"Strawberry vodka," Jayce said while brushing a kiss over Rocky's cheek.

Luke's heart squeezed when his sister smiled and blushed. Must be nice to be so freaking in love and for that person to freaking love you back.

"Remember to make Chloe's a virgin," Dev said.

"Got it." Luke caught a sweet look between his brother and Chloe, who palmed her barely swelling stomach, and his heart squeezed again. Well, damn. His brother had lucked out in the love department, too, and the woman he loved was pregnant with his baby. It's not that Luke hadn't been in love. He'd been in love thousands of times. He had a way with women. In fact, seducing women was his one and true talent. But he'd never experienced the bone-deep forever love Rocky felt for Jayce or Dev felt for Chloe. Although he'd felt a glimmer of something different, something special a couple of months back with Rachel Lacey. He thought about their one ill-fated kiss, the sizzle that had damned near singed his senses, then immediately shoved that mystifying woman from his mind. Rachel had been a mistake and she wasn't even a possibility. The woman had skipped town and had moved on to wherever. Rachel was history. Jayce rapped Luke on the shoulder as he strode toward the kitchen.

"Right. Candy Cane Cocktails for six—one virgin. Let's do this. I assume I'll need candy canes," he said to

Jayce as they sailed through the dining room. "What else?"

"Crème de menthe. Cranberry juice. Here's the recipe Daisy gave me." Jayce slapped a folded page from a magazine into Luke's hand as they breached the state-of-the-art kitchen. "I located Rachel Lacey."

Luke stopped cold. His brain zapped. His heart jerked. "I thought you gave up."

"I only told you that so you'd stop hounding me for an update twice a day."

"I didn't—"

"You did."

Jayce had years of experience in law enforcement, first as a cop with the NYPD, then as a successful private investigator. Now he ran a cyber detective agency and Luke had hired him to find Rachel Lacey. Two freaking months ago.

"The reason she was so hard to track," Jayce said, "is because when it comes to hiring someone to create a false identity, Rachel can afford the best."

"What are you talking about? Rachel lived on a shoestring." She'd dressed in frumpy clothes and she'd driven a beat-up car. When she'd lost her job at the day care center, Luke had hired her as a waitress. She was desperate for the work, desperate for money. She'd said so. "*I need the money, Luke.*" Her shy, anxious gaze haunted him . . . sort of like that sizzling kiss.

"Maybe you should sit down."

Heart thudding, Luke dragged a hand through his shaggy hair. "Is she dead?"

"No."

"Dying?"

"No."

"Hurt?"

"She's alive and well in Bel Air, California. Her name

is Reagan Deveraux. She's a trust fund baby. An heiress. As of tomorrow, her twenty-fifth birthday, she'll be a millionaire."

Luke blinked then snorted. "You're kidding me, right?"

Jayce shook his head.

Luke gawked. "That's screwy. That's . . . impossible. You've got the wrong girl, Jayce."

The PI plucked his iPhone from the pocket of his leather jacket, thumbed through bells and whistles, and then showed Luke an image of Reagan Deveraux.

Holy . . . It was Rachel, but it wasn't.

Luke leaned back against the kitchen counter, willing starch into his legs and air into his lungs. "What the hell? Why the ruse?"

"I don't know."

"She lived in Sugar Creek for almost a year," Luke said. "She was a member of the Cupcake Lovers. A beloved teaching assistant at Sugar Tots. She was shy and awkward and freaking mousy. That chick in the picture, that's not mousy, that's . . . that's . . ."

"Hot. I know." Jayce raised a brow then thumbed something else on the screen. "I can't tell you why Deveraux pretended to be someone she wasn't, but I can fill you in on her background. I downloaded the report. Here. You can read—"

"No, you read it." Luke pushed off the counter, nabbed a cocktail shaker from the cabinet. "I'll make Gram's cocktails." Trying to read all that information . . . the letters would dance and swim in front of Luke's eyes and he'd end up staring at the screen looking like an idiot while he tried to get the words right in his head. Jayce didn't know Luke was dyslexic. No one knew. His family thought he'd beaten his reading disability when he was a kid. He'd just learned to hide it, to fake it, really, really well. Only one person—Rachel—had seen through his polished ploy and he had no idea how. It's not something they'd ever discussed. But in his gut he knew she knew.

"I'll hit the highlights," Jayce said, scrolling through his screen.

Luke nabbed ice cubes, cranberry juice, and the liquor. Bracing for the details on Reagan Deveraux, he mixed up the holiday cocktail without one glance at the recipe. He'd been a crack bartender for years. He could wing it.

"Her father, now deceased, was a tycoon. Her mother, a B-list Hollywood actress, has remarried three times since. Seems to have a type."

"Stinking rich?"

"You got it. An only child, Reagan was raised in a privileged environment," Jayce went on. "Private schools, lavish vacations. Rich and smart. College educated, with a master's in education."

The more Jayce revealed about the trust fund baby, the more Luke felt like a fool. When he thought about the strife Rachel had caused between him and his cousin, Sam. . . . When he thought about the way she'd abandoned the Cupcake Lovers in the midst of their big recipe book publishing deal . . . the way his sister and the other Cupcake Lovers had fretted over her disappearance . . . the nights Luke had wrestled with guilt and worry . . .

"*Dammit!*" Luke exploded just as Rocky poked her head into the kitchen.

"Everything all right in here?" she asked.

"Just mixing up some Christmas cheer," Jayce said.

"Fa-la-freaking-la," Luke said then passed the chilled shaker to his sister. "Fill martini glasses with this and garnish the rims with candy canes."

"Where are you going?" Rocky asked as he stalked toward the back door.

"To solve a mystery."

TWO

Reagan Deveraux nibbled on a Godiva truffle bar, hoping sweets would offset her sour mood. Later she'd indulge in cupcakes—delectable homemade mocha fudge with peppermint buttercream icing or maybe dark chocolate with an espresso ganache. For now the gourmet candy she'd filched from her mother's Tiffany decanter would have to do. Unfortunately, Rae was three-quarters through the creamy bar and the mood-elevating effects had yet to kick in.

She eyed the ritzy candy jar.

In order to get through the next couple of hours, she might have to chase this truffle bar with that chocolate salted almond bar.

On the other hand she wasn't sure her waistline could bear it, especially since she was definitely set on making and treating herself to those decadent cupcakes. She'd even bought a special bottle of Red Velvet wine as her beverage of choice. A sinful combination, but what the heck? It was, after all, her birthday.

Her *twenty-fifth* birthday—a legal and financial milestone.

As of today, Rae was a millionaire.

Whoop-de-flipping-do.

Finishing off the truffle, she sighed and shifted from the snow white leather club chair to the snow white leather sofa in yet another attempt to find comfort in her mother's luxurious Bel Air home. The furnishings were sparse and expensive. The decorative accessories tasteful, bordering on sterile. Not one area of casual clutter. Even the holiday decorations were meticulously arranged.

Classical music played softly in the background, compliments of a new stereo system, hidden away somewhere— otherwise Rae would've dialed up a livelier playlist. Instead, she endured the stuffy music while scrolling through real estate listings on her iPhone and fantasizing about cupcakes and better times.

She'd spent the past year living a simple life in Sugar Creek, Vermont. Then the last two months driving across country sorting through jumbled emotions and bracing for the future. She'd only been back in California and living under her mother's roof for three days, and it was two days too long.

Anxious, she glanced toward the grand stairway, wishing her mother and stepfather would dress a little faster. Rae had been ready for an hour. The sooner they got this evening's pretentious holiday dinner over, the better.

"Bah humbug."

There. She said it. She'd been thinking it all day. Rae had never been a big fan of Christmas. Mostly because it had never lived up to her expectations. As an only child of a celebrity socialite who preferred the limelight to home life, Rae had spent a good majority of her childhood keeping company with her very own TV. Holiday programming highlighted the importance of family and friends, the spirit of giving, and the magic of believing.

Rae had never lacked for presents, but there'd been no festive activities with family. No gathering around the piano to sing carols. No sleigh rides, no tree trimming, no baking of holiday cookies. Oh, there'd been decorations, but her mother had hired a company to trick out whichever mansion they were living in at the time. And there'd been parties, but they'd been the Hollywood kind or the business-related kind, depending on which man her mother had been married to, and certainly none were the kind that welcomed kids.

Christmas Eve had always been Olivia Deveraux's night on the town, bouncing from one glitzy party to another. Never mind that Christmas Eve was also her daughter's birthday. Surely the fact that Rae got presents *that* day in addition to Christmas morning was celebration enough.

This year was no different. This morning Olivia had presented Rae with diamond earrings, a special gift for her twenty-fifth. *"Really, sweetie,"* she had said, *"you're independently wealthy now. A legitimate heiress. Time to start dressing and acting the part."*

Olivia had been dressing and acting the part for years. She'd never been the real deal. Rae was the real deal. Thanks to Olivia's first husband, the father Rae had lost at age two.

Just now Olivia was upstairs with husband number four, a man Rae despised, taking forever and a day dressing for the first of three parties on their meticulously calculated social calendar. Amazingly, Olivia had invited Rae along. Although maybe not so amazing. As of this morning, Rae was stinking rich, a magnet for attention, something Olivia breathed like air.

Not wanting to insult her mother, especially since Rae was trying to forge some sort of genuine bond, she'd sucked it up, agreeing to attend the dinner party being hosted at the Beverly Wilshire. Rae had never been a social butterfly, but she could endure a formal dinner, and besides, the proceeds went to a local children's hospital. She'd simply beg off after, leaving the wilder, drinking parties to Olivia and Geoffrey while she took advantage of their state-a-of-the-art kitchen.

Rae planned to spend her Christmas Eve birthday whipping up a holiday cupcake that would make the Cupcake Lovers proud, then chowing down and drinking wine while watching a marathon of sappy holiday movies on the Hallmark Channel. Movies celebrating friends and family, old-fashioned values, open hearts, and love. Movies that celebrated the kind of Christmas Rae had always craved and—double whammy—reminded her of the down-to-earth folk she'd been surrounded by in Sugar Creek. Being filthy rich couldn't compare to being happy.

Rae eyed her mother's professionally decorated, artificial tree, weathering a wave of melancholy as her mind exploded with the visions and scents of naked Vermont pine. Over the last two months Rae had done her best to forget her attempt at lying low and living incognito in the Green Mountain State under the mousy, shy guise of Rachel Lacey. All she'd wanted was a few months of anonymity, time to assess a dicey situation with Geoffrey, time to contemplate her future without her shallow mother breathing down her neck.

Losing herself to find herself.

Hiding until she had the funds to fight fire with fire.

Being a nobody had paid off in ways she'd never dreamed. Working with the children at Sugar Tots had been a dream. Joining the Cupcake Lovers and baking cupcakes for charitable causes had been a joy. If only

Sam McCloud hadn't fallen for her. (*How could any man fall for drab, aloof Rachel?*) If only Rae hadn't fallen for Sam's cousin, Luke Monroe.

Another dicey situation.

Disappearing, *again,* seemed the best course. No one would miss her, right? People came and went all the time—at least in Rae's life.

"Stop moping, Deveraux. *Jeez.*" Disgusted with her blue mood, Rae pushed to her feet and smoothed the wrinkles of her cocktail dress. "It's your birthday. You're a millionaire."

Surely it was sinful for someone so fortunate to feel this miserable.

Time to find new happiness. Honest joy and real contentment. As for love . . .

There was always the Hallmark Channel.

"Someone to see you, Miss Deveraux."

Rae blinked, startled by the depth of her daydreaming. She hadn't heard the doorbell. She hadn't even heard Ms. Finch, her mother's latest housekeeper, enter the room. "Who is it?"

"Said he's an old friend."

That heightened Rae's curiosity. True friends were sacred, a rarity in Rae's life, and she was certain she didn't have any in Bel Air.

Ms. Finch, who struck Rae as having a broomstick up her butt, raised her fastidiously penciled, coal-black eyebrows. "He seemed harmless so I allowed him access through the security gate and asked him to wait in the foyer."

"Oh. Right. Thank you." Rae dragged her fingers through her Bordeaux-colored, newly cropped hair. In her desperate need to cut ties with Rachel Lacey, she'd invested in a stylish makeover and a chic wardrobe. Months ago she would have been wearing a mid-shin peasant dress and clunky, flat-heeled sweater boots. This afternoon she'd zipped herself into a knee-length emerald green sheath with an Empire waist and donned a pair of platform pumps. A dash of holiday spirit combined with an air of sophistication—perfect for the dinner at the Wilshire.

Rae bolstered her shoulders as she moved across the pristine living area and then through two other rooms in order to greet her *old friend*—who was more than likely a smooth-talking reporter or an annoying member of the paparazzi. She'd begged Olivia not to brag about her inheritance but that was like asking her mother not to pose for the camera. Nothing would have surprised Rae. Except . . .

"Luke." His name scraped over her constricted throat, sounding choked and raspy and, to her utter embarrassment, besotted. Rae had never considered herself shallow, but she'd fallen for Luke Monroe's boyishly handsome face and incredible body the first time she'd laid eyes on him—much like every other woman in Sugar Creek. His ornery smile and easy charm were irresistible and his devotion to family and friends admirable. The fact that he openly dated several women at the same time should have been a turnoff, except he was honest about his no-strings-attached intentions and that was oddly refreshing.

As always, he was dressed down in faded, baggy jeans and a snug tee that accentuated his muscled torso. He'd rolled up the sleeves of a blue flannel shirt that hung unbuttoned and untucked, and he was wearing heavy boots more conducive to the snowdrifts of Vermont than the sand and sun of California. Rumpled and unshaven, he looked incredibly out of place in Olivia and Geoffrey's ostentatious mansion.

Luke Monroe's presence here, now, was surreal and, though stunned, Rae couldn't suppress a giddy thrill.

"What are you doing here? How . . . how did you find me?"

"It wasn't easy."

His clipped tone betrayed his anger as did his grim expression. Luke was one of the most jovial, easygoing men she'd ever known. She'd seen him harried once, frustrated, but never angry. Well, except for the fateful night a randy college kid had grabbed her butt when she'd been taking a drink order. Luke had interceded and he'd been angry, no, *outraged* on her behalf. She'd been smitten with Luke for months, but that night she'd fallen in love.

Rae's cheeks burned while she grappled for words, while Luke dragged his gaze down her body, soaking in the transformation. She struggled not to fuss with her cropped hair or to tug up her scooped neckline. There was absolutely nothing she could do about her bare legs, and kicking off her pumps would be ridiculous and embarrassing. She'd never been one to flaunt her curves and there was nothing promiscuous about this dress, yet Rae felt naked.

Exposed.

"Born and raised in privilege," Luke said in the wake of her silence. "Exclusive private schools. Extended lavish vacations."

Rae flinched at Luke's caustic tone. He spouted the cards she'd been dealt as though she'd been lucky. As a teen, she'd been shipped off to various locations and pawned off on assorted relatives so as not to cast a shadow in her mother's spotlight.

"College graduate with a master's degree in education. A freaking *master's*," he said in a low, tight tone, "yet you worked as an assistant at Sugar Tots and then came to work for me as a freaking waitress in a freaking *bar*. You said, and I quote: *I need the money, Luke.*" He stuffed his hands into his jeans' pockets, swept a disgusted gaze over the opulent foyer then back to Rae. "What the—"

"*Hello.* Who do we have here?"

Rae cringed at her mother's sultry tone and knew without turning that the woman was shrink-wrapped in a sexy gown and no doubt slinking down the white carpeted staircase. Rae watched as Luke turned his attention to her mother, saw the moment he recognized her as the tabloid famous Olivia Deveraux, one-time starlet, all-time sex kitten. Rae waited for Luke to get that bewitched, lustful expression most men, ages eighteen to eighty, got when they saw her voluptuous and overtly stunning mother in person. Instead, he just looked annoyed.

"Friend of yours?" Olivia persisted, moving in alongside Rae, and reeking of Chanel No. 5 and fruity martinis.

"We worked together," Rae blurted, because *friend* didn't really describe their association. Especially not now.

"Luke Monroe," he expanded, while offering Olivia a hand in polite greeting. More than he'd done with Rae. "Pleased to meet you Ms. Deveraux."

"Are you *really*?" she asked in a coy tone, clasping his palm and pursing her crimson lips in a sexy pout. "You don't *look* pleased."

"Blame it on the long flight and the holiday crush," he said in a gentler tone that only made Rae feel worse. Instead of celebrating Christmas with his family, a family he was incredibly close with, he'd flown across the country . . . for what? To give Rae hell?

"You just flew in from China today?" Olivia asked, looking mildly shocked. "Good heavens, Reagan. Invite the man in for a drink. I'll join you." She looped her arm through Luke's and guided him toward Geoffrey's well-stocked bar.

Rae's heart pounded as she hurried after them, wondering how she was going to wiggle her way around another colossal lie. Wondering what Luke was thinking just now and wishing she'd booked herself into a hotel rather than buckling under Olivia's invitation to stay here while seeking a new home suited to her birthday inheritance.

"Maybe Luke will tell me more about your volunteer work abroad," Olivia said over her shoulder to Rae before turning her wide, kohl-lined eyes on Luke. "Every time I ask her about her work with those poor children, she declares those days the best days of her life then changes the subject. It must have been *horrid* working in such a remote location," she said to Luke then pointed out the premium back bar. "I don't suppose you know how to mix up an appletini?"

"I think I can manage," he said with an enigmatic glance at Rae. "Vodka or gin?"

"I'm a vodka girl. And as Bond would say . . ." Olivia winked and purred. "Shaken, not stirred."

Just as Luke reached for Grey Goose and vermouth, Geoffrey swaggered into the reception room in a dapper Armani suit, his salt-and-pepper hair slicked back from his handsome, aging face. "Olivia, sweetheart, what the hell?" he asked while checking his gold watch. "We're late as is and . . ." He noticed shaggy-haired Luke in his rumpled tee and flannel shirt mixing drinks behind the Italian marble bar and frowned. "Do we know you?"

"This is Luke Monroe, dear," Olivia said with a beaming smile. "A friend of Reagan's."

"Really."

Rae couldn't tell if Geoffrey was frowning because he didn't like the idea of Rae entertaining a virile, young man or because he was peeved about the way Olivia was ogling said virile, young man. Knowing the way her mother's mind worked, Olivia was no doubt mentally comparing Luke to one of Hollywood's young hunks, in this instance Ryan Reynolds, and imagining herself starring alongside him as the mature love interest. Olivia was constantly lamenting how Sandra Bullock was stealing all of her roles.

Instead of acknowledging Luke, Geoffrey eyed Rae. "Dinner starts promptly at five."

"Maybe Luke could join us," Olivia said.

"There's a dress code," Geoffrey said. "Reservations for three." He spared Luke an annoyed glance. "No offense."

"None taken," Luke said, but he didn't take the hint and leave either. Instead he poured sour apple liquor into the shaker then reached for the lemon juice.

Clearly he meant to have his say with Rae and it wasn't a discussion she wanted to have in front of Olivia and Geoffrey. In a way, Rae was grateful for Luke's obstinacy. The less she had to endure Geoffrey's company—the man who'd threatened her in this very house *last* Christmas—the better. Also, Olivia was already three sheets to the wind. She wouldn't miss Rae for long, if at all.

Feigning nonchalance, Rae moved behind the bar and stood beside Luke. Her skin tingled, her pulse tripped. He'd only held her once, kissed her once, yet she recalled every detail of that tender, searing encounter—a brush with passion that would haunt her for the rest of her life. "Actually," she said, speaking past the lump in her throat, "I've decided to skip the Wilshire in favor of spending time with Luke. He flew all this way and—"

"You're going to waste a five-hundred-dollar plate?" Geoffrey asked.

"No waste," Rae said, holding the industry kingpin's intimidating gaze. "All proceeds go to charity. You two go on. Don't give me a second thought," she said, unconsciously leaning into Luke. "I'm in good hands."

"Do tell," Olivia said with raised brows.

Geoffrey worked his clean-shaven jaw. "What is it you do, Monroe?"

"You mean aside from mixing a mean appletini?" Luke asked, shaking and pouring.

While Olivia sampled his creation, Luke snaked an arm about Rae and held Geoffrey's cold gaze.

Rae's heart pounded. Because of Luke. Because of Geoffrey. Because she was trapped in a web of lies.

"Sweet heaven, this drink is *orgasmic*!" Olivia moaned in ecstasy. "You *must* try it, Geoff."

"Pass. Could I have a word with you, Reagan?"

Rae's stomach turned as the walls closed in. This situation had just gone from awkward to intolerable. The last person she wanted to be alone with was her so-called stepfather. "Aren't you running late for dinner?" she asked. "I know we are." She looked up at Luke, her panicked heart in her eyes. "Ready?"

Hand at the small of her back, Luke prompted her from behind the bar. "Nice meeting you, Ms. Deveraux. Mr.—"

"Stein. Geoffrey Stein. Of Stein & Beecham Industries. And you're Luke Monroe."

"Of the Sugar Creek Monroes," Luke said as he escorted Rae toward a temporary reprieve. "We're in the book."

THREE

"A cab?"

"Had to get from the airport to your place somehow and since I don't know the area and my time was limited, I opted for a cab."

Rae shifted anxiously on her heels as Luke opened the rear door for her—mad as hell but still a gentleman. Heart pounding, she eased inside. "But a taxi from LAX to Bel Air? And you asked him to wait? We're talking a lot of money, Luke."

"Don't talk to me about money right now, Rachel . . . Reagan . . . whatever the hell your name is. Not now." He closed her door and rounded to the other side.

She swallowed hard as he slid in and buckled up. As supportive as he'd been inside where Geoffrey was concerned, in private he'd reverted to the angry man she'd greeted at the door. Six feet of hunky fury. "Rae," she managed.

"What?"

"Call me Rae."

Luke glared then shifted his attention to the driver. "Back to the airport, please."

Rae blinked. "Flying in and out of LA in one day?"

"Skipped out on my family for Christmas Eve," Luke said. "Need to be back for Christmas."

"Why did you skip out at all?"

"Because I only just learned of your whereabouts and I had to know if . . ." He shook his head then dragged both hands down his face.

The man's frustration crashed over Rae in suffocating waves. Unsettled, she cracked open the window and reminded herself to breathe. "Why are you here, Luke?"

"I need to know why you lied to us Rach . . . *Rae*. I need to know why you pretended to be someone you aren't. Why you played us . . . me, Sam, the Cupcake Lovers . . . for suckers."

"I didn't—"

"You did."

"It might seem that way, but it wasn't intentional."

"I'm all ears."

Rae worried the handle of her purse, averted her gaze. She'd never been one to talk about her troubles. Luke's scornful attitude wasn't much of an enticement to change her ways. "How are things between you and Sam?"

"Not great."

Luke's cousin, a man who'd been smitten with Rae, had walked in on the one kiss she'd shared with Luke. Sam was above making a scene, but she'd felt the ferocity of his disappointment. It hadn't been pretty. "I wrote him a letter. I apologized—"

"I know. He told me. It's the only reason I knew you weren't dead in a ditch somewhere."

Rae's heart warmed even as her stomach clenched. "You were worried about me?"

That whipped Luke's head around. "Are you serious? You lived in Sugar Creek for a year. You were part of the community. A Cupcake Lover. A beloved teaching assistant. Maybe you didn't care about us, but we cared about you!"

Another stab to her gut. Except they hadn't cared about Rae, they'd cared about Rachel.

"So what?" he plowed on. "We were some kind of joy ride? Or maybe you lived in Sugar Creek on a dare? Wait. Let me guess. You were slumming. Seeing how the yokels live. Why Sugar Creek?"

"I threw a flipping dart at the map." Rae was seething now. She'd had enough of Luke's venom. If she wanted ugly, she would've hung back and joined her mother and Geoffrey.

He cast her a fiery glance.

Angry? Confused? Intrigued? Disgusted?

Rae couldn't read Luke and she wasn't sure she wanted to. Where was the charitable playboy she'd fallen in love with just months ago?

This cynical man jammed his hand through his already messy hair. "I need a drink."

"Join the club." Furious, disillusioned, Rae crossed her arms over her chest and stared out the window. She wished Luke would have stayed away. Her memories of Sugar Creek and the people who lived there were sacred. Luke was tainting the best year of her life. Plus, warping her vision of him as her knight in shining armor. The only man who'd ever defended her was now attacking her. The luxury homes lining Stone Canyon Road blurred as Rae fought back tears. She refused to cry. *Do. Not. Cry.*

"What's up with your mom's friend?" Luke asked in a tight voice.

"Geoffrey's her husband. Her fourth husband. Don't you read the tabloids?"

"No."

Still facing away, Rae closed her burning eyes and cursed her flippancy. Of course he didn't read the tabloids. He probably skipped respected periodicals as well. Luke had a reading problem. She didn't know to what extent. She'd picked up on the signs when she'd applied for a job at the Sugar Shack, his popular pub and restaurant. He actually had a keen knack for disguising the disability, but she had a stepbrother who'd suffered with dyslexia and she'd also studied learning disorders while earning her teaching degree.

"Is he always a dick?" Luke pressed. "Or did I just bring out his worst?"

Rae's stomach knotted. She didn't want to talk about Geoffrey. "How's Daisy?" The eccentric but lovable matriarch of the Monroe family had been the first member of the Cupcake Lovers to praise Rae's baking talents. The senior member's glowing compliments warmed Rae to this day. If only Olivia had been half as nurturing.

"Gram's fine," Luke said. "She moved in with Vince."

"They make a cute couple. Speaking of, how are your brother and Chloe doing?"

"If you'd bothered to stay in touch with any one of us you'd know," Luke snapped. "Why the hell did you tell your mom you spent the last year in China? Volunteering with underprivileged children in a remote area." He snorted. "Quite the story. What are you? A chronic liar? Disconnected with reality?"

Rae finally turned and, eyes now dry, glared at Luke. In all his scenarios he hadn't once given her the benefit of the doubt. Yes, she'd lived in Sugar Creek under an assumed identity, but she'd lived a good life. She'd been a good person. Inheriting a fortune didn't change who she was inside. How could Luke think so little of her? How had she thought so highly of him? "Better a chronic liar than a judgmental jerk." Rae bolstered her shoulders then turned and beckoned the driver. "Pull in up ahead, please. The Hotel Bel Air." She'd be hanged if she'd spend another minute in Luke Monroe's irritating company.

"What are you doing?" he asked as she dug in her purse.

"Thank you for saving me from an awkward moment with Geoffrey. Have a safe flight home, Luke."

Rae leaned forward and passed the driver two fifties then shoved open her door and swung out with as much grace as she could muster. Apparently she was doomed to a lifetime of crappy birthdays. This was the worst by far. To hell with Luke. To hell with going back to her mother's mausoleum of a house. She'd treat herself to a night of pampering. A deluxe room with a flat screen TV and a stocked minibar. Dinner at Wolfgang Puck. A full body massage. Maybe a swim. She could purchase whatever she needed in the Boutique. Her fortune couldn't buy her happiness, but it could certainly buy her comfort.

"What the hell?" Luke watched as Rae strode toward the doors of the luxury hotel. Stunned by her hasty exit. Mesmerized by her sensual body. Call him a dog, but Luke had a longtime obsession with the female form. Rachel Lacey had hidden her considerable assets beneath baggy ankle-length dresses, whereas Reagan Deveraux show-cased her curves. Not in a slutty way, but that almost made things worse. *Rae* was class on designer heels.

And she just called him a judgmental jerk.

"Son of a—"

"LAX?" the driver asked.

"What?"

"Still going to the airport?"

"Yes. No. Not yet." Luke unbuckled his seat belt.

"Want me to wait?"

"Yes." Luke noted several taxicabs parked near the lobby. "No." He hadn't flown all this way to get the bum's rush. "How much do I owe you?"

"Your lady covered it."

"She's not my lady."

She'd duped Luke and all of Sugar Creek. *She'd* run off

and left them all to worry. Where did she get off giving Luke attitude? She hadn't given Luke a straight answer to any one of his questions. "How much did she give you?"

"A hundred."

She'd paid his entire tab. As if he couldn't afford it. Luke's pride reared. He passed the man a generous tip, nabbed his backpack and jacket, and hit the pavement. He blew through the doors of the swanky hotel feeling severely underdressed.

Damn.

So this was how the other half lived. Even though the lobby had a cozy vibe—hardwood floors, comfortable furniture, raging hearth—this hotel reeked of sophistication and money. Similar to Rae's house. Or rather her mom's house.

He'd been so angry when he'd first confronted Rae, he hadn't paid much mind to her posh digs. He'd been too focused on the gorgeous redhead with the kickass curves and impeccable style. He still couldn't believe the extent of her physical transformation. Jayce Bello, Luke's almost brother-in-law and an ace private eye, had not only, *finally,* traced this woman to Bel Air, he'd also filled Luke in on her real background and had shown him a "pre-Rachel" photo. Luke had barely recognized the stunning woman. Reagan Devereaux was *hot.* Even more so in person. Luke hated that he'd noticed and kept on noticing. On their short cab ride it was all he could do not to stare at her sexy legs. And now those sexy legs had taken her . . . where?

Luke did a three-sixty. No Rae. He approached the concierge. "I'm looking for a woman who just came in. Gorgeous redhead in a green dress?"

The man raised a brow and Luke realized he probably sounded like a stalker.

"Reagan Deveraux," Luke added. "I was supposed to meet her in the lobby."

"I believe the woman you're looking for went into the lounge."

Luke thanked the man and headed toward where he pointed. He found Rae sitting at the bar throwing back a shot of tequila. He had no idea she did shots. He'd only ever seen her sip beer. Now she was licking salt from her hand like a pro. He watched, transfixed, as her red lips closed over a wedge of lime and sucked.

He wasn't the only man watching.

Luke felt a jab of jealously when a designer-suited dude eased in and offered to buy her a drink. Then a surge of relief when Rae turned the man away. Luke cursed his whacked-out emotions. He shouldn't be feeling anything for Rae aside from betrayal and confusion.

He joined her at the bar. "What are you doing?"

"Treating myself to a birthday drink." She barely cast him a glance while attacking her second shot.

Luke clenched his jaw as she repeated the ritual. Salt, tequila, lime. Lick, drink, suck. Not overtly sexy, but sexy all the same. He gestured to the bartender. "Two Coronas, please." Then he looked back to Rae. "Drinking alone on your birthday is sort of pathetic."

"I'm not alone." She met his gaze. "Unfortunately."

Luke searched her eyes, his gut clenching when he caught a glimpse of Rachel Lacey, the same vulnerability that had intrigued him all those months ago. He had a weakness for women in need. Hell, he had a weakness for women period.

The bartender served two longnecks.

Luke waved off the glasses.

"Put it on my tab," Rae said.

"It's on me." Luke paid cash for two of the most expensive beers he'd ever bought in his life. "As for the cab," he said to Rae, "thank you, but I can manage." He pulled five twenties from his wallet and when she refused, he shoved the money in her purse. "Three months ago you were desperate for money. Or so you said. Jayce called you a trust fund baby. You might not have inherited your fortune until today, but you must have had access to a monthly allowance."

"I didn't want to touch that money."

"Why not?"

"I can't believe you had me investigated."

She sounded somewhere between hurt and outraged. Luke knew the feeling. "I had you tracked, which I wouldn't have done if you had had the decency to say good-bye."

Gaze averted, she sipped her beer then ordered another shot. "I felt awful about hurting Sam. Plus I was compromising the success of the Cupcake Lover's recipe book by refusing to participate in any publicity."

"So you ran away?"

"I didn't think I'd be missed."

What the freaking hell? "Are you *that* insecure or *that* oblivious?"

"People come and go all the time, Luke."

"You're missing the point, Rae." He nabbed her wrist as she reached for the salt shaker. Her pulse raced beneath his thumb. His own heart bucked. He'd always had a talent for reading and finessing women. He had no clue how to handle Rae. Did she have the tolerance to withstand a third shot? He didn't want to take the chance. He grabbed her shooter and downed the Cuervo himself. "Why don't we sit at one of those tables and talk?"

"Why aren't you on your way to the airport?"

"Why won't you tell me why you paid for a false identity?

She glanced away, picked at the label on the beer bottle. "I needed to be someone else for a while."

"Why?"

"It's personal."

One thing hadn't changed. Reagan Devereaux was every bit as aloof as Rachel Lacey. Luke wanted to shake the crap out of her. Kissing her came to mind, too. He'd never been so angry and turned on at the same time. He told himself it was because she was smoking hot and he'd been celibate for weeks. Aching to jump her bones was natural. It wasn't because he was jonesing to re-create the magic he'd felt the one and only time they'd locked lips. Who needed that kind of misery? Having a thing for a woman beyond his reach. A woman of privileged birth. A woman who'd earned a master's degree. A woman worth a freaking million!

Hit the road, Monroe.

He wasn't getting the answers he wanted so why was he wasting his time? As it was he'd be lucky if he got home before Christmas morning. Part of him had been desperate to see for himself that Rae was okay. She was more than okay. Except for her obsessive lying and the tension between her and her mom and that dickhead Geoffrey Stein. Every family had drama, right? The Monroes certainly had their fair share. More often than not, Luke played mediator. He should be home making peace, not here waging war. Besides, reasoning with this woman was a losing battle.

Luke reached down for his backpack and when he straightened the infuriating enigma was finishing off another shot.

For the love of . . .

He couldn't leave Rae in this bar. What if she drank herself under the table? What if one of the several men watching took advantage?

"Do you think your mom and Stein left the house yet?"

"I'm sure of it. God forbid they miss a moment of the party."

"Then come on. I'll drop you home before I head to the airport."

"I'm not going home." She flashed a key card. "I'm staying here tonight."

"Then I'll walk you to your room."

"Not necessary." She stood, swaying a little on those sexy four-inch heels.

Luke groaned. "Humor me."

She wasn't drunk, but she was buzzed. The longer Luke had sat next to Rae, the more she'd wanted to numb her senses. He made her ache for Sugar Creek and the simple life she'd created there. She missed her friends in the Cupcake Lovers. She missed the children she'd bonded with through Sugar Tots. She mourned the fact that she'd probably never find the kind of love that existed between Chloe and Dev, Rocky and Jayce, Monica and Leo. She'd had the misfortune of falling for Luke Monroe, who clearly thought the worst of her and who wasn't at all who she'd built him up to be.

He expected her to spill her guts, to share her most intimate problems as though he were her friend. A friend wouldn't make her feel like the most selfish person on earth. Christmas Eve, her birthday, was always difficult. Luke had made it intolerable.

To make matters worse, all she could think about was their one spontaneous kiss and what might have happened if they hadn't been interrupted. Luke's presence rekindled the burning desires she'd worked weeks to snuff.

"This is it." The number on the door was a little fuzzy, but she heard a click when she swiped the key card and the handle moved, so good. This was good. She'd found her room. He could go and maybe she'd be able to breathe. She turned to say good-bye, only her heel caught in the carpet and she teetered and knocked into the hard chest of Luke.

Tall, sexy, handsome-as-sin Luke.

He steadied her and . . . *bam*.

Suddenly they were kissing. She wasn't sure who started it but no one was ending it. The kiss was frenzied, impassioned. He backed her into the room and against the wall.

The door snicked closed, shutting out the world, muting reality. Not the heiress and the bartender. Just two people in crazy blind lust.

He dropped his bag and coat.

She ditched her purse and shoes.

Her senses exploded as they grappled and soul-kissed.

The same spark as before, only *more*.

More was not enough.

Rae shoved Luke's shirt off his shoulders then fumbled with the fly of his jeans.

He unzipped her dress, unhooked her bra.

His palm seared the bare skin of her back while his other hand smoothed up her thigh, under her dress.

His lips, his tongue . . . *Heaven*.

But then he broke off. "Tell me to go."

She couldn't. Not yet.

"Dammit."

She backed him against the opposite wall, her actions frantic as she tugged at his clothes and ate him up like a starving sexaholic.

Feel me. Take me.

Pent-up yearning and frustration overshadowed rational thought.

They had no future.

But I can have now.

His mouth was magic, his touch perfection. Skilled. Seductive. The earth moved. No, *she* moved. Luke spun their position, pinning her between his hard body and the solid wall. She nearly lost it when he tugged at her thong. When the tip of his shaft grazed and . . . *God*.

One swift thrust. Luke was inside her, filling her, rocking her, taking her hard against the wall.

Her heart nearly burst through her ribs, her lungs burned. Every fiber of her being vibrated with heady pleasure. So primal. So perfect.

Rae shuddered with a mind-blowing orgasm. A wondrous sensation that echoed through her being like a never-ending aftershock. Luke peaked with her. It was powerful and amazing, wonderfully amazing.

Until he froze.

She felt the tension in his shoulders, sensed a rising darkness.

He still held her close, was still inside of her, but his forehead banged to the wall. "Christ."

The horror in his tone twisted her heart into a bleeding knot.

"Why didn't you stop me? Why . . ." Another head bang. "Dammit!"

Rae was too stunned, too dazed to speak. Why was he so upset? So they'd had sex. So it was a onetime thing. Luke Monroe was a notorious hound. He typically juggled three girls at a time. He was no stranger to casual sex. She knew his motto. Everyone in Sugar Creek knew his motto. *No strings attached.*

"Are you protected?"

Her reeling mind glitched. "What?"

"Christ, Rae. No condom."

Her heart and brain stuttered back to life. Her stomach churned. "I'm on birth control."

"Great. Good. That's something."

His attitude was less than romantic. All she sensed was remorse on his part whereas she was still semiflying from

the greatest orgasm of her life. Why was that anyway?
She refused to attach it to love. Loving Luke would only
end in heartbreak. He'd already done a pretty good job of
crushing her tender feelings.

Suddenly, *painfully* aware that her dress was hiked to
her waist and his jeans were around his ankles, Rae tried
to disentangle herself from Luke with some modicum of
dignity.

Earning her master's had been easier.

Luke—handsome-as-sin, confident, jovial, playboy
Luke Monroe—looked at Rae as if she were a two-headed
monster of seduction. "Why—"

"Maybe I just needed to get you out of my system.
Thank you for that. Happy birthday to me."

She wasn't sure why she'd been so flip, so crass. It
wasn't like her. Except her pride was smarting. She hated
that Luke was looking at her like she was the biggest mistake of his life when he was her bona fide favorite.

Drawing on her mother's questionable acting skills,
Rae rolled her eyes. "It was sex, just sex, and not even
great sex at that. Go home, Luke."

She slipped into the bathroom and locked the door,
fighting tears, fighting nausea. Now, in addition to thinking she was a lying, selfish rich bitch, he also thought her
a slut. People were always labeling her something or another based on stereotypes. She shouldn't care.

She cared.

Don't cry. Don't cry.

Luke knocked on the door.

Rae turned on the shower.

When at long last the outer door finally opened and
shut, Rae cried.

FOUR

"Ah, come on. They can't be that bad."

"No offense, Luke, but these are quite possibly the worst cupcakes I've ever tasted."

Luke raised a brow at his sister's blunt assessment of his chocolate cupcakes. Rocky always shot straight from the hip. Usually he liked that about her. But not right now. A little encouragement would be nice.

"I don't know about the worst," Chloe said. Although she was still grimacing after swallowing.

"Don't sugarcoat it, kitten," Daisy said. "He'll never learn if you do."

"I'm not sure he *can* learn." This from Ethel Larsen, one of the senior members of the Cupcake Lovers and one of Daisy's closest friends. "Luke, honey. Just because your grandma, sister, and cousin have a gift for baking, that doesn't mean you automatically do."

"Sam's the one who told me to get a hobby," Luke reminded them. Apparently, Luke had been driving his friends and family crazy for several weeks. Not on purpose, but he was bored. He wasn't dating anyone and he didn't like being alone. He could only work so many hours at the Sugar Shack, so he'd been volunteering to help folks with various projects or trying to rope them into social activities. When Sam had suggested Luke take up a hobby, Sam had been on his way to the weekly Cupcake Lovers meeting and Luke had thought, *what the hell*. He'd been working hard to mend bridges with Sam, and maybe they could man-bond over man cakes.

Casey Monahan, part of the younger set of this club, regarded Luke with strained patience. "If Sam were here tonight, I'm sure he'd tell you he was thinking of a hobby along the lines of a poker club or bowling team."

"You know we love you," Monica said, "but this is your third meeting, Luke. The third batch of cupcakes you've shared with us and every batch has been worse than the one before."

"Who substitutes maple syrup for vegetable oil?" Casey asked.

He'd been out of oil so he'd improvised. That's what he did when he mixed drinks and it usually worked. "The consistency seemed right," Luke said in his defense.

Daisy thunked her hand to her forehead.

Luke frowned. He couldn't even count on his own grandma to defend him. He looked at the women seated around Dev and Chloe's dining room table. He'd known all of them, with the exception of Chloe and Monica (transplants from the Midwest) all of his life. The Cupcake Lovers had been around since World War II. They were presently in the process of having their very own recipe and memoir book published—which was sort of exciting if you asked Luke. Baking was out of his realm, but he liked the social aspect of the club and the charitable causes. Plus, he liked cupcakes. He'd been eating a lot of them lately. Just not his own.

"Listen. Just tell me where I went wrong here." He gestured to their plates and his barely sampled cupcakes. "You told me to keep it simple. I did. Plain ol' chocolate as opposed to the Chocolate Cherry Cola with Red Licorice or the Spicy Double Dark Chocolate."

"Someone who's never baked before shouldn't be getting their recipes from *Cupcake Wars*," Judy said.

Since the Cupcake Lovers prided themselves on unique cupcakes, that TV baking show had seemed like the perfect source to Luke. Also it was easier and faster to watch and listen than to search a printed book or the Internet. But, whatever.

"This one came straight from a cookbook I checked out of the library," he said. "Monica helped me pick out the recipe." Monica, who was Chloe's best friend, worked part-time at the Sugar Creek Library. Luke went in there a lot to check out audiobooks. Getting her to help him choose an actual recipe book without betraying his reading disorder had been pathetically easy. When it came to hiding his lifelong dyslexia, Luke was a master of deception.

"I honestly didn't think he could screw this one up," she said.

"Where did I go wrong?" Luke leaned back in his chair and crossed his arms. "Go on. I can take it."

"They're too salty," Judy Betts, one of the senior members said.

"And gooey," added Helen Cole, another senior and crackerjack baker. "What kind of flour did you use?"

Luke shrugged. "The white kind."

"Self-rising?" Gram asked. "Or all-purpose?"

"There's a difference?"

"Sweetened or unsweetened cocoa powder?" Chloe asked.

Luke furrowed his brow. He thought he'd bought the right one, but maybe he'd misread. When it came to reading, letters typically swirled and flipped. Patience was key and he didn't always have it. "I didn't look specifically," he lied.

Everyone groaned then traded cryptic glances.

Luke braced. Because he loved people, people usually loved him. He was always the life of the party, the guy everyone wanted to hang with. He'd never been kicked out of a club or any other circle but he had the feeling the CLs were about to give him the boot.

His sister, who was also the president of the Cupcake Lovers, braced her forearms on the table and leaned forward. "Here's the thing, Luke," she said with a gentle smile.

Oh, yeah. He could almost feel Rocky's boot heel on his ass.

"As you know," she went on, "we're coordinating several overseas cupcake care packages. We're also struggling to hold on to that publishing contract. It doesn't bode well that they put our project on hold."

"I'm almost sorry Tasha moved to Arizona," Casey said. "She had a great relationship with our editor. If she were still acting as our liaison, she could probably persuade Brett to keep the release date on track."

Luke wasn't one bit sorry about Tasha and Randall Burke's unexpected move. Although she hadn't been directly responsible, Tasha had played a role in the destruction of The Red Clover—Rocky's former bed-and-breakfast. His sister's home and all of her belongings had been lost in a fire set by Randall's son, Tasha's stepson—who was now serving time in jail. Tasha had tried to make amends, but that hadn't gone so well and Randall hadn't appreciated living in the fallout of the scandal.

He'd retired early, giving up his position as town mayor and packing up his trophy wife (whom he really seemed to love, for reasons that eluded anyone who knew the catty woman), trading one million-dollar home for another. Randall was richer than that Facebook dude.

Sort of like someone else Luke knew. Although he didn't really *know* Rae at all and tried very hard not to think about her.

"Tasha's absence factors in on multiple levels," Chloe said. "Even though she's still an honorary Cupcake Lover, she's not a *local* member. It puts a kink in the overall package considering she contributed so many recipes and stories."

"Not to mention she's featured in photos and the publicity video," Monica said.

"Also," Chloe went on, "Brett wasn't lying when he said there's a glut in the cupcake market. Between that, Tasha leaving, and the whole Rachel snafu, I can see where we've lost some of our appeal.

"If we only had a gimmick," Ethel said.

"I hope they don't cancel our deal altogether," Helen said.

"Would we have to give the advance money back?" Judy asked. "How would that work?"

"I know I was never a fan of this project, but there's no denying the extra income would benefit our special causes," Rocky said. "Take Sugar Tots for instance. I still can't believe Gretchen closed the day care center and moved on just because she lost her grant money. We could have helped. A little anyway."

"Every time I think of Sugar Tots I think of Rachel," Casey said. "I mean Rae. Anybody heard from her again?"

"Just that one letter," Chloe said. "The same one that everyone else got a few weeks ago."

Everyone but Luke.

One good thing had come out of his disastrous visit to California. He'd made Rae feel guilty enough about fleeing Sugar Creek in the middle of the night that she'd finally written a letter to each and every member of the Cupcake Lovers apologizing for her abrupt departure. She'd also apologized for pretending to be someone she wasn't, explaining she'd been desperate to escape the limelight and certain pressures associated with her family. She hadn't meant to hurt anyone and hoped that in time they'd forgive her. She'd then personalized each letter and wished each person well, saying she'd be the first in line to preorder *Cupcake Lover's Delectable Delights—Making a Difference One Cupcake at a Time.*

The only reason Luke knew all this was because Rocky had shown him her letter and, of course, Rae's true identity had dominated the gossip portion of the CL meeting two weeks back—Luke's first meeting. Everyone, including Sam, had been stunned that Rachel was actually *Reagan,* and that she was the daughter of the famous starlet Olivia Deveraux. Stunned, confused, curious, but not angry. Luke didn't get that. How could they *not* be angry? She'd lied to them. For a year.

Then again, they'd each gotten an apologetic letter.

Every time Luke thought about it his blood burned. He'd flown across the entire freaking country and Rae hadn't confided spit. Sure, she hadn't given the CLs details, but she'd given them *some* semblance of an explanation. All Rae had given Luke was a hard-on and a guilty conscience. Oh. And *bonus.* A freaking complex.

He still couldn't believe he'd had sex with her. Especially since she'd been drinking. He'd never taken advantage of a woman like that. He'd meant to walk her to her door then walk away. But she'd wobbled and he'd steadied her. The moment they'd touched . . . *Pow!* She'd kissed him or maybe he'd kissed her. He didn't even know. It was all a blur. A spontaneous carnal mating that dogged his conscience and dreams.

"Yo. Luke."

Luke blinked and focused on his sister. "What?"

"Chloe asked if you wanted more tea."

Rattled, he shifted in his chair. "Uh. No. Thanks." Considering he was in the company of eight ladies, one of them his grandma, three of them as old as his grandma, he was more than a little embarrassed that he'd been fantasizing about nailing Rae. "So am I in or out?"

They all gawked.

"Of the club," he clarified.

They traded another round of those cryptic looks.

"Here's the thing, sweetie." Daisy pushed her blingy cat-eye glasses up her nose then reached over and patted his hand. "We don't think you have a real passion for baking and that's the number-one requirement for being a Cupcake Lover."

"I don't believe this. You're kicking me out of the club."

"We wouldn't do that," Judy said.

"Especially given your state," Helen said.

Luke frowned. "What state is that?"

"Depressed."

"Bored."

"Lonely."

"Single."

Luke blinked around the table. What the—

"To my recollection," Ethel said, "You've always had two or three girlfriends at a time."

"You don't have any now," Casey said. "Haven't had since . . . when?"

"It's been months," Monica said with an ornery twinkle in her eye.

He blamed Rae.

"It was sex, just sex, and not even great sex at that."

Every other woman he'd ever been with had declared him a god in bed. Then again, he hadn't even made it to the bed with Rae.

"You're off your game," Chloe said with a sympathetic smile.

"And so close to Valentine's Day," Helen said. "Doubly depressing."

"Have you thought about Ellie Tate?" Judy asked.

"You know," Daisy said. "Bert Hawkins's granddaughter. She recently moved back to town, fresh out of college. Doubt she's ready for anything serious."

"Young. Unfocused. Right up your alley," Casey said.

Heart pounding, Luke gawked. Oh, hell, no. This same crew has been trying to match Sam up with a soul mate for weeks. Luke had caught a glimpse of that hell and wanted no part of it. "Can we get back to my status in the club, please?"

Rocky took pity on him. Sort of. "We're not kicking you out, Luke. Just . . ."

"Don't make any more cupcakes," Daisy said.

"Unless supervised," Chloe, his ever-kind someday sister-in-law, added.

"Speaking of Valentine's Day," Monica said to Rocky, "your wedding day is around the corner. Are you excited or what?"

And just like that the conversation turned to wedding plans—gown, flowers, honeymoon. As if that wasn't bad enough, someone brought up bridesmaids' dresses, which spurred mention of special fittings for Chloe, who was six-months pregnant, and Monica, who was newly pregnant and eating for three.

Baby talk.

Luke eyed Dev's expensive wine rack, jonesing for a cheap beer and sports talk. He should have joined a damned bowling league.

FIVE

"Thanks for picking me up, Sam."

"No problem."

"You didn't tell anyone I was coming, right?"

"You asked me not to. Won't take long for word to get out though. You know Sugar Creek."

Yes, she did. A tight-knit community. The tourist element notwithstanding, everyone knew everyone's business—mostly. Amazing that she'd maintained her ruse for an entire year. Then again, Rae had worked very hard at being invisible. She was done with that now. Ready to attack life as Reagan Deveraux. She intended to use her semicelebrity status and money to help the Cupcake Lovers and to resurrect Sugar Tots. But that wasn't the only reason she'd returned to Sugar Creek.

Rae pulled up the fur-trimmed hood of her down-filled coat, shivering as a gust of frigid air blasted her face. February in Vermont.

"Colder than Los Angeles," Sam teased as he relieved the pilot of her baggage.

"Just a little." Juggling her purse and a rolling tote, Rae followed Sam across the tarmac to his truck. When she'd flown out of LAX, it had been in the low sixties. When she'd landed in Burlington it had been a brisk twenty-eight degrees. From there she'd rented a plane and pilot to take her to Starlight Field—a small airfield about thirty miles outside of Sugar Creek. It was dark now, after eight, and she'd wager the temperature was closer to twenty with a windchill of less. She didn't mind the cold or the snow. She only wished she'd arrived during the daylight so she could've been welcomed by the beauty of the surrounding mountains.

"Let me take that." Sam placed her tote in the backseat of his extended cab along with her two burgeoning suitcases.

"I'm sorry I made you miss the CL meeting tonight," Rae said as Sam opened the truck door and helped her climb in.

"I'm not. I needed a break." He shut the door and rounded the hood then climbed in, revved the engine, and cranked the heat. He did not, however, shift into gear.

Rae squirmed in her seat, shoved off her hood, and fastened her seat belt. "You're staring."

"Yeah. Sorry. Your hair."

"Really short and really red. I know."

"I like it."

"Thanks." She dragged an anxious hand through her cropped do and tried to acclimate to her new relationship with Sam. It had been easier long distance.

He'd been the only Cupcake Lover to write her back. Then again, she hadn't included a return address on any of her letters and hadn't openly invited a reply. It had been her way of putting the past to rest and moving on. Sam had gone out of his way and had finally obtained her PO Box information. His letter had been so kind and, at the time, she'd been in a bad place. His words had proved balm for her anxious soul. She'd felt compelled to call in response.

They'd spoken a few times over the last two weeks, mostly to clear the air. But in those conversations they'd also struck up what Rae tentatively thought of as a friendship.

"You sure about this?"

Rae nodded. "Absolutely."

"You don't look sure."

She shifted and, by the light of the moon on the dash, she caught the concern in Sam's eyes. Concern and . . . a flash of desire. The latter was disconcerting. She thought they'd moved past that. They'd certainly discussed it. She'd made it clear she wasn't interested in an intimate relationship. He'd said he had no intention of pushing. She thought that meant he'd given up the pursuit. Now she wasn't sure. It was troubling and flattering at the same time. Sam didn't have a problem with her being an heiress. And he wasn't intimidated by her college degree. His confidence was attractive. If only she were *attracted*.

She searched his ruggedly handsome face wondering why she couldn't have fallen for him instead of Luke. Sam was grounded and successful. He had two great kids—Ben and Mina—whom she adored. He'd been attracted to Rae even when she'd been doing her best to look as drab and frumpy as possible. That was admirable, right? They'd had a date, one date, but she hadn't felt a spark. Not then, not before. Certainly not after. Mostly she'd felt awkward.

Kind of like now.

"I'll admit," she finally said. "I'm a little apprehensive about reconnecting with everyone." Luke's reaction to her ruse was a bitter pill she'd yet to swallow. Would others lash out in kind? "After all, I lied about who I was. *Am*."

"You had your reasons."

"Yeah, well." She blew out a breath. "I'm glad you told me about Sugar Tots. I can definitely help there. And I think I know how to get the CL publishing date back on track."

"I didn't share our troubles expecting you to use your money to rectify things."

"I know that, Sam. You told me because you knew I'd care." She smiled then. "Thank you for that." At least someone had given her the benefit of the doubt. Sam hadn't bought into the trust fund baby clichés assuming she was spoiled and manipulative. Someone who'd go *slumming* in Sugar Creek on a dare or a whim, just to see how the *yokels* live. Luke's presumptions still stung.

"I know you have personal issues. Things you don't feel comfortable talking about. I'm not a talker either," Sam said. "But I am a good listener."

He'd proven that on the phone.

"Just saying."

Rae nodded then broke Sam's gaze, swallowing past a lump in her throat. If only Luke had taken a more tolerant approach rather than pushing and badgering her into lashing back then closing down. She regretted how they'd parted. The ugly things she'd said. When they next spoke, she promised herself she would take the high road, no matter what. She couldn't control Luke's behavior, but she could certainly monitor her own.

"Where am I taking you?" Sam asked as he put the truck in gear.

"What? Oh. The Pine and Periwinkle Inn." She'd made an open-ended reservation.

"How long are you staying?"

"I'm not sure."

"An extended stay at a resort . . . could get expensive," he said as he pulled out onto the dark country road. "The kids and I, we have an extra room."

The lump in her throat swelled to the size of an orange. "Thank you but, not to sound pretentious—"

"Money's not an issue. Right. So, just curious, and you don't have to elaborate, but making due on what little you made as a day care assistant when you were used to an opulent lifestyle . . . that must've been a challenge."

"There's something to be said for living by your wits and seeing what you're made of."

Eyes on the road, Sam shook his head. "I was wrong about you."

Her stomach clenched. "How so?"

"I didn't give you enough credit. You're a warrior, Rae."

"Who'd of thunk it, *huh*?" She smiled a little. "Let's just say I've decided it's time to control life rather than allowing life to control me."

Sam pulled into his driveway, struggling with a tangle of conflicting emotions.

Had he tipped his hand? Did Rae sense his stubborn infatuation?

He didn't want to scare her off. He wanted to win her over.

When she'd stepped out of that private plane his heart had swelled. Yes, she was more polished than the last time he'd seen her, but the attraction went beyond her new so-phisticated style. Through letters and on the phone they'd formed the kind of easy relationship he'd yearned for when she'd been living in Sugar Creek. Something had clicked between them—*genuine friendship,* he thought.

They could build from there.

Sam prided himself on being a grounded, rational guy. There was nothing sensible about pining for a woman who had no interest in him sexually. So he'd decided to get proactive. To woo her. Seduce her. Subtly. Based on mutual respect and common interests. Might take some time, but Rae was worth waiting for, worth fighting for. The perfect mother for his children.

Patience, he'd once told Luke, was not just a virtue, but a weapon.

The first step was to lure her back to Sugar Creek. He didn't know a lot about Rae, but he knew she had a gentle heart. He knew her Achilles' heel. Kids. He knew she'd be concerned about the lack of a local day care facility. And he knew she had a genuine fondness for every member of the Cupcake Lovers. He knew she missed Sugar Creek. She'd said so. So he'd given her a reason to return.

Sam flexed his hands on the steering wheel and stared through the windshield at his moonlit house, the home he'd built with his wife, Paula. The home in which their two kids now slept. When Paula had died, she'd taken a piece of Sam with her. She'd been his soul mate and he was damned sure he'd never love again.

Rae gave him hope. She made him feel. Yearn.

He'd once thought her a tortured soul. He still sensed she was damaged somehow, guarded. The soldier in him wanted to save her. But tonight he'd also gotten a glimpse of her fighting spirit. A quiet confidence. And under and through it all, that gentle heart. The entire package was a turn-on.

As for his hound-dog cousin, Luke had sworn to Sam that he didn't have feelings for Rae. That she'd been upset that night and the kiss Sam had walked in on had been Luke's lame way of trying to comfort her. Which sounded like Luke, balls on. The younger man viewed sex as a cure-all.

If Luke had lied, if he *was* hot for Rae, then he and Sam were going to butt heads in a big-ass way. He wouldn't feel great about kicking the shit out of a family member— literally or figuratively. But he wouldn't shy from it either. Luke had never made a serious commitment to a woman in his entire life.

Sam was ready to go all out.

SIX

Luke woke up the next morning just like every other morning these last few months—alone and broody. He'd bailed on the Cupcake Lovers meeting early. Yes, he was happy for Chloe and Monica—Chloe's baby would be his niece or nephew and Monica. . . . Hell, Monica and her husband, Leo, had been trying for a baby for almost a year and then when they stopped trying, *bam,* she'd conceived. *Twins!* Everyone in Sugar Creek had celebrated that news.

Luke was also thrilled for Rocky and Jayce. Theirs had been a long and stormy relationship. That they'd finally settled in the love zone and were actually getting married was a big deal. He just wasn't up for hearing the gory details. Who knew his tomboy sister would turn all sappy girly when it came to planning her wedding?

Overall the night had sucked. His cupcakes had flopped and the Cupcake Lovers had pegged him as depressed, bored, and lonely. Never mind that it was true. It's not like this was a permanent state. He'd bounce back. At some point.

Maybe he *would* call Ellie Tate.

For the time being, he'd driven home and thrown back a couple of beers while watching late-night ESPN. He'd gone to bed thinking about Rae. He'd woken up thinking about her, too. So when the stylish redhead walked through the front door of the Sugar Shack just shortly after opening, he was certain she was a figment of his imagination.

Until Kane Brody whistled low.

His brother, Adam, looked to where Kane looked. "Holy . . . Is that . . . *Shit*."

Luke, who'd been pouring cups of coffee for the Brodys, carefully abandoned the glass carafe before he dropped it. He was *that* shocked to see Reagan Deveraux.

In Sugar Creek.

In *his* freaking pub.

The last time she'd been in this room, a randy college boy had grabbed her ass and Luke had gone ballistic. The unwanted attention had reduced Rae to tears and Luke had hustled her into his office. He'd meant to comfort her. He'd ended up kissing her. Sam had walked in and that's the moment Luke's happy-go-lucky existence started swirling down the toilet.

He relived the entire scene twice by the time she made it through the maze of tables to the bar. Except that night he'd been defending and falling for Rachel Lacey—a shy, self-conscious, and supposedly down-and-out teaching assistant. This was Reagan Deveraux—the heiress who'd screwed him just to get him out of her system.

In the words of his bud, Adam . . . *Shit*.

The Brodys swiveled full around to greet her.

"Hey, Rachel," Kane said.

Adam elbowed him.

"Sorry. *Rae*."

"So you guys know my real name. My background," she said in an even tone and without looking at Luke.

"Whole town knows," Adam said.

Not from me, Luke wanted to say, but bit his tongue.

"I heard it from Nash, who got it from Leo, who heard it from—"

"Monica." Rae smiled a little as she unzipped her coat. "I know how it works, guys."

The brothers fell quiet, appreciating a glimpse of the curves beneath the coat. Luke knew exactly what Kane and Adam thought of Rae's figure. They'd ogled her lush breasts and trim waist the first night she'd shown up in her waitress uniform. Since she'd been keen on making big tips, Luke had suggested she ditch her preferred baggy style for something more formfitting. At the time he hadn't been aware her form was so fine.

Now he knew.

Even better than Adam and Kane.

Luke's hands had been all over that hot body.

"Buy you a drink?" Adam asked.

"Coffee?" Kane offered.

Luke's mouth went dry as he imagined Rae shooting tequila. *Lick, drink, suck.*

"Water would be nice. Thanks."

Luke turned away and reached into the fridge. She probably liked sparkling or mineral as opposed to spring. Then again, anyone who slammed back shots wasn't exactly a beverage snob.

"Why are you back in Sugar Creek?" Adam asked.

"Business."

"Staying long?" Kane asked.

"That depends," she said just as Luke returned with Perrier and a glass. "Could I speak with you?" she asked, meeting his gaze head on. "In private?"

Which meant his office. The cramped, messy room where they'd shared their first kiss. Not that Adam and Kane knew. No one knew, aside from Luke, Rae, and Sam. And no one knew about their disastrous shag in L.A.

Unless Rae had spilled the beans. It's not something Luke was inclined to talk about. If only he could forget.

Their fingers brushed as she reached for the uncapped bottle. Luke cursed the tingle that zipped up his arm and tightened his chest. Maintaining a casual expression, he called over to Willa, the only waitress on the schedule this a.m., and asked her to cover the bar. "Be right back," he said to the Brodys who were looking at him like he was the luckiest shit in town.

Yeah, right.

"She's new," Rae said, referring to the petite blonde waitress as they made their way to his office.

"You know how it goes," Luke said as he opened the door. "People come and go all the time."

He thought he heard Rae sigh, but she didn't comment. She set down the Perrier long enough to shrug out of her expensive-looking down coat. He automatically helped her with it. He'd been raised to do stuff like that. Help women in and out of their coats, open the door for them, pull out the chair for them. Most women, at least all of the ones he'd dated, appreciated the courtesy.

Rae thanked him, although that sounded sort of automatic, too. "Mind if I sit?" she asked while gesturing to his secondhand couch.

"Knock yourself out." Luke, however, perched on the corner of his desk. He was wired. He was curious. He was wary. "What kind of business?"

She blinked then focused. On him. Gaze steady. Four months ago, she'd gone out of her way to avoid eye contact. With Luke and most everyone else. He'd assumed it was because she was shy. Now he knew it was because she'd been living a freaking lie. Eyes were the window to the soul and all that.

"Without going into great detail," she said, "I'm here to save Sugar Tots. And, if they'll let me, I think I can help the Cupcake Lovers with their publishing date glitch."

"How did you—"

"Sam told me."

"He called you in California?"

"He wrote back in answer to the letter I wrote to all of the Cupcake Lovers. Then I called him. We've talked a few times."

That bothered Luke more than he cared to think about. "Did you tell him about—"

"Of course not. I haven't told anyone. It's not the kind of thing you brag about."

"Right. Because the sex wasn't all that great."

Her color rose and her eyes sparked, but she didn't snap. She sighed. "I only said that because . . . Never mind. Could we keep this civil? I know I disappointed you. I know you think the worst of me. I can't help that, but I'd like to get past it."

"Why?"

"Because I'm going to have your baby."

Rae hadn't meant to blurt the news. She'd lain awake half the night on her rented pillow-soft bed rehearsing how she was going to drop the bombshell. None of her scenarios had gone like this. They'd all been more eloquent. But she was nervous. She hadn't anticipated the rush of desire when she'd walked in and saw Luke standing behind the bar. The man was at his most confident and charming when he mixed drinks and bantered with his patrons. Adam and Kane were two of his closest friends. Thank God they'd been there to break the ice, because swear to God, Rae had frozen up. She'd sworn her heart was dead as far as Luke was concerned. How could fate be so cruel?

Just now Luke was looking at her as if she'd just spoken Greek. "Come again?"

"I'm pregnant, Luke."

He angled his head, blinked. "And you think it's mine?"

"I don't think. I know."

"How?"

What, he thought she slept around? Yeah. He probably did. "Because of the timing." *Because there hasn't been anyone else.*

"Are you sure?"

"Yes, I'm sure." Rae bore his insulting attitude with hard-won calm. She refused to lose her cool. She refused to get emotional. She'd been wrestling with this unexpected twist for two weeks. Once the shock had abated, she'd experienced a spark of wonder and joy. She refused to allow Luke to warp this miracle into something ugly. That said, she thought he deserved to know. "If you don't believe me, I'll submit to DNA testing, although I'm not far enough along yet."

He shoved his hand through his shaggy hair. The same hand that had smoothed down her back, up her thigh, under her dress. "You said you were on birth control."

"I was. But the pill isn't fail-proof. Nothing, aside from abstinence, is."

So far, Luke was responding exactly like she'd anticipated. Doubting her. Blaming her. Except he wasn't yelling. He was, in fact, oddly calm. It made Rae uneasy. She swigged a quarter of the water, rolled back her shoulders. "Listen, Luke. I don't want anything from you. I'm not expecting a marriage proposal or asking for financial support. I just . . . I wanted you to know. I thought you'd want to know."

"Are you going to keep it?"

"*It?*"

"The baby."

"You think I'd give her up for adoption or . . ." She couldn't even say it.

Luke stood and paced to his file cabinet and back. Frowning, he dragged his hands down his absurdly handsome face. "I can't believe this."

Resenting his misery, even though she'd expected it, Rae swigged more water then set aside the bottle and forced herself to stand. "This isn't the life I planned either, Luke, but I'm not going to run from it. I'm going have this baby. I'm going to love this baby. If you want to be a part of her life, I'll stay on in Sugar Creek. I'll make a life here. If not, we'll settle someplace else."

He cast a suspicious glance. "Why not in California? Near your mom?"

"I have my reasons."

She saw him tense. She understood why he was bothered by her evasiveness, but he'd given her no reason to trust him with her problems. She'd thought her troubles would be over once she inherited her fortune. She thought she'd be able to lure her mom away from Geoffrey with the promise that Rae would look after her financially. She'd been wrong. She thought her own money would mean freedom and respectability. She thought it would open doors, which it did, but not doors she wanted to walk through. She'd never been more miserable and lonely.

And then she'd learned she was pregnant.

Now she had someone else to worry about. Someone to protect and nurture. Raising her child anywhere near Olivia and her toxic environment was out of the question.

"Think it over," Rae said as she nabbed her coat. "I'm staying at the Pine and Periwinkle. Do you have my cell number?"

Caught somewhere between flustered and angry, Luke

fumbled with his phone. "I don't. . . . No. Not your current one."

Rae grabbed Luke's cell and quickly thumbed in her information. She needed to get out of here. She couldn't breathe. Couldn't think. She handed him the phone then turned to leave. "I know you don't like me," she said, "but please do me this one favor. Don't tell anyone yet. Dev. Rocky. Anyone. I'm only six weeks along. The first trimester . . . it's iffy." Just saying it out loud made her queasy. But she'd listened to her doctor and she'd researched on her own. Once she reached the ten to twelve week mark, the risk of miscarrying would greatly diminish.

"You keep saying *her*," Luke said when Rae was halfway out the door. "Isn't it too soon to know?"

"Just a feeling." Heart pounding, Rae crossed the threshold and moved calmly toward the front door with a wave to Adam and Kane. Part of her wanted Luke to follow her, but she knew he wouldn't. She'd just put a serious kink in the life of Sugar Creek's biggest playboy.

SEVEN

Rocky Monroe couldn't remember when she'd ever felt this happy. She kept waiting for the sky to fall. For her recent good fortune to tank. It's not that she was a cynic or a defeatist, but she had a history of rotten luck. She'd spent years seething over her love gone wrong with Jayce Bello. *Years.* She'd experienced multiple and increasing financial setbacks. The absolute worst had been watching her bed-and-breakfast, her home, her *dream,* go up in smoke. Along with all of her personal possessions.

Oh, yeah. Losing everything sucked big time.

Only, when her senses had cleared, she'd realized she hadn't lost *everything.* Certainly, not the things she cherished most.

Her family. Her friends. Her dog, Brewster.

Jayce.

She'd also retained her confidence and drive, and her toehold in a new career as an interior decorator. Over the last three months, Rocky had settled into her new home, Daisy's old house, with Jayce and Brewster. She'd reveled in planning her wedding along with her mom and Daisy, and her two closest friends, Chloe and Monica. She'd embraced the challenge of her new business—Red Clover Renovations. It was a slow build, but she also held a part-time job at Maple Molly's Antique Barn—a job she loved—and Jayce had struck gold with his cyber detective agency. Financially, she, *they* were set. Emotionally, Rocky was riding a never-ending wave of love. Jayce rocked her world and Rocky gave as good as she got. Life was good. Life was great!

Except for the delay in the release of the Cupcake Lovers recipe book, and the woman who was fast becoming the new bane of Rocky's existence, her client from hell—Harper Day.

Rocky shook her head in wonder as she pulled her jeep into her cousin, Sam's, drive. Tasha Burke had left town and Harper Day had moved in. Not permanently, but due to her excessive texting and e-mails, she was always "present." It was like trading one pain in the ass for another. It's not that Rocky couldn't handle the high-maintenance publicist from the West Coast. She just needed a reprieve for the next few weeks so she could focus on herself and Jayce. On their wedding.

That's where Sam came in.

Hopefully.

Bundled against the frigid cold and mounds of snow, Rocky made her way across Sam's shoveled sidewalk and knocked on his front door. She'd always loved that it was painted bright red. That had been Paula's influence. She'd loved bright colors and everything cheery in life—flowers, pop music. She'd been Sam's opposite in so many ways and yet his perfect mate. Rocky's heart still ached when she thought about the awful way Paula had faded from this world. No one blamed Sam for mourning his lost love so deeply, not that he ever talked about his grief or loneliness. But everyone wanted him to find new happiness. Everyone had laid their money on Rachel Lacey, but that hadn't worked out, and now Sam was back to closing himself off to dating.

The door swung open and Rocky's tall, rugged, former military cousin greeted her with a teddy bear under one arm and two Miss Kitty pocketbooks slung over the other. Rocky smothered a grin as she moved inside what was usually a tip-top house. "What happened in here?"

"Babysitter couldn't get Mina to go to bed last night. Neither could I. In an effort to tire her out, I endured a fashion show. It lasted an hour. This was the fallout."

Rocky pressed her lips together as she surveyed the damage. Strewn about the living room were random piles of coats, feather boas, bright-colored shoes, hats, tiaras, and what looked to be about thirty fuzzy friends.

"Her audience," Sam said, indicating the rows of rag-tag stuffed animals. "Along with me."

"Where was Ben?"

"In bed. Pretending to sleep. He doesn't think I know, but he reads those anime books under the covers every night by flashlight."

"You don't want him reading graphic novels?"

"I don't want him reading period after lights out."

Rocky unzipped her jacket and perched her hands on her hips. "I never realized how many clothes and toys Mina has."

"That's because I, we, keep them pretty organized in her bedroom and playroom."

Rocky swept up one of the boas. "Haven't seen these before."

"New fascination. Boas and princess crowns."

"Why so many?"

Sam turned away, scooping up a purple elephant wearing a raspberry pink tiara. "She wanted them."

Rocky raised a brow. Sam loved his kids more than anything in the world, but he wasn't one to spoil them.

Unless . . . "Mina still crying every morning when you drop her off at school?"

"Frickin' torture. It's all I can do not to swoop her up and hit the road."

Rocky's heart jerked when she caught the miserable look on Sam's face. The rough-and-tough solider turned brawny carpenter, felled by a five-year-old's tears. "So what? You've been bargaining with Mina? Don't cry tomorrow and I'll buy you this or that? How's that working out?" she teased gently.

He turned now, smirking. "You see all the boas and crowns?"

"I'm sure it's just a phase. The crying thing. I don't know about the boas and crowns. I was never into all that girly stuff."

That drew a slight smile out of Sam. "I remember your fondness for Tonka trucks and Legos."

Now Rocky frowned. "When the time comes, I hope Jayce and I have boys." Rocky had always been a tomboy. Tailing after her brothers and boy cousins . . . Jayce.

"Boys come with different challenges," Sam said. "It's all good." He dropped an armful of toys into a jumbo plastic pink bin. "You mentioned needing a favor. Want to talk about it over coffee?"

"Sure." Rocky followed Sam into his spic-and-span kitchen, draped her jacket over the back of a kitchen high-back chair, and took a seat. "How booked are you right now?"

"What, with custom orders?"

Sam crafted beautiful furniture. Painted it, too. Intricate stenciled and freehand art. A beautiful pine armoire he'd made for Rocky had burned up in the fire. She shoved that depressing thought aside. "That and carpentry work."

"What do you need?"

"It's not for me. Well, it is for me. In a roundabout way.

I need to get a client off my back for a few weeks, turn her focus to something other than *the* perfect décor for her vacation home."

"I take it she's picky."

"More like anal."

"And you want to turn her loose on me and my designs?"

"Actually, the house needs a few interior repairs before we decorate in earnest."

"What house?"

"The old Rothwell Farm."

Sam raised a brow.

"You've always been fascinated with that place," Rocky pressed. "Here's your chance to make your mark."

"Your client's not spooked by the legend?"

"She's too pragmatic to believe in ghosts."

"Anal and pragmatic. Fun."

"She'll pay cash."

Sam sipped his coffee.

"More money for boas and crowns."

His lip curled. "Smart ass."

"So you'll do it?" Rocky whooped. "Thanks, Sam. This way I can distract Harper with another kind of renovation. Just until I get past my wedding. She's really not that bad. Just used to a faster pace than we are. Although this job *has* been dragging on since November. She purchased the farm as a second home and, so far, she's only flown in for a few days here and there. She's a bit of a workaholic and easily distracted by phone calls. I take it back. She is that bad." She smiled. "But she's nice!"

"Molly described her as a flake." Sam shifted his weight. "Last time I dropped off a piece of furniture at the Antique Barn, your client had just left."

Crap. "Would it help if I said Harper is a *nice* flake?"

"She's from California, right?"

"I think she's Canadian, but yeah, she's been living in L.A., working as a publicist. Speaking of L.A., did you hear the gossip?"

"Can you narrow it down?"

"Rachel's back in town. I mean Rae. Damn. I have to get that in my head. Not sure why she's back, but she called me a little earlier. Asked if we could meet this evening. I have to say, I'm dying of curiosity. Hey, do you think she knows Harper?"

"Why would you think that?"

"They're both from L.A. Harper's a Hollywood publicist. Rae's mom is a Hollywood star."

"More like a tabloid curiosity," Sam said. "Famous for being famous."

"And gorgeous. If you go for that sort of overt sex kitten look. Olivia, I mean. Not Rae. Hard to believe they're related."

"Not so hard," Sam said with an enigmatic expression.

Rocky narrowed her eyes while Sam refreshed their mugs. "So have you actually seen Harper Day?"

"Nope. But I heard she's pretty hot." Sam angled his head. "This carpentry gig. You're not trying to set me up, right?"

"Trust me. This is a purely selfish on my part." Rocky's suspicions continued to flare. Something was up with Sam. "You haven't given up on Rae, have you?"

Sam slid a plate of homemade pastries between them and pulled up a chair. "Haven't been inside the Rothwell house in years. We talking minor repairs? Or major?"

EIGHT

Luke had lingered in his office a good ten minutes after Rae left. It had taken him that long to catch his breath, to slow his bucking heart. For a minute he thought he might be having a panic attack. He'd never had one of those before but he'd heard it resembled a heart attack. At thirty-two, he was too young for a coronary, right?

Pregnant.

Rae was pregnant.

With *his* baby.

Unless she was lying about the paternity part, although why would she? Like she said, there were tests.

Two hours later, Adam and Kane were long gone—thank God—and Luke was still tending bar while absorbing the mind-blowing news. Rae had been eerily calm. It had forced Luke to keep his own cool. God forbid he come off like an immature ass. She'd already pegged him a judgmental jerk. He'd unwittingly pissed off some women in his time but, in lashing back, they'd never struck a sore spot. Not like Rae.

Rae pressed Luke's buttons regarding self-esteem. No one had pressed those buttons for years. Not since he was in grade school and some kids made fun of him for not being able to read a comic book. Rae had gone to all the best schools. She had bachelor's and master's degrees. She'd traveled abroad. She was freaking independently wealthy, as in filthy rich. *And* she was only twenty-five!

All the background info Jayce had dug up on Reagan Devereaux had played out in Luke's mind as she'd sat across from him in her stylish skinny jeans and classy, soft clingy sweater. She was unlike any woman he'd ever slept with. Completely out of his league.

Of course she wasn't expecting Luke to do the right thing by stepping up and offering marriage or at the very least financial support. She didn't need his money and why the hell would she want to marry a bartender who was only half owner of a business. Half owner because Luke didn't have a head for numbers and finances, unlike his smart and savvy older brother, Dev. Plus, she didn't even seem to like Luke much. It had just been sex . . . *not even great sex at that.*

Damn.

He couldn't get over how unemotional she'd been.

"I thought you'd want to know."

Hell, *yes*. The thought of having a kid in the world and not knowing about it rubbed Luke every way wrong.

"I know you don't like me."

Not exactly true. To be fair, he didn't know Rae enough not to like her. He was pissed because she'd roused his interest as shy, vulnerable Rachel Lacey. Frustrated because he'd felt something special when they'd kissed—*both* times. He resented that she'd bailed on him and everyone in Sugar Creek who cared about her, leaving them clueless and worried. He resented being manipulated then sent away on Christmas Eve. And he damn well hated the fact that Rae was a tangled mess of secrets, evasiveness, and lies. Although she'd been pretty freaking straight forward today.

"*I'm going to have your baby.*"

He'd always been so careful. Always prepared. Always covered. Even if the woman was on birth control, Luke used a condom. *Always!* He still couldn't believe how he'd lost his wits and control with Rae. One screw up and *bam*! Luke had never thought about being a dad now; maybe when he was in his forties. Now it was all he could think about.

"Um. Luke?"

Luke blinked up at Willa. "What?"

She slid a full cocktail glass back across the bar. "I asked for a gin and tonic. Customer said this tastes like vodka."

Damn. His third mistake of the afternoon. When it came to mixing drinks, Luke never made mistakes.

"You okay?" Willa asked as he poured a new drink. "You seem a little, um, distracted."

Willa was new in town. She was sweet and pretty and she'd needed a job. In the past, Luke would have flirted with her and probably dated her within the first couple of weeks that he'd hired her. She'd been employed at the Shack for two months now and he hadn't even made a casual pass.

Chloe had nailed it. Luke was off his game. And now because of one spontaneous, bonehead hookup, he wasn't sure he'd ever get *back* in the game. Yes, he wanted to play some part in his child's life. But how the hell could he go on with his own life—casually dating a string of women, hanging out with his sports buddies, working long and late hours at the Shack—with his son or daughter, and Rae, for Christ's sake, living right here in Sugar Creek? Like he wanted his kid to think he was a skirt-sniffing, absentee dad! On the other hand he didn't like the thought

of them living in another state or, God forbid, overseas—
out of sight, out of reach.

"Luke?"

He blinked back to Willa. "Yeah." He garnished the
glass with a wedge of lime. "Here you go, hon. Sorry. Tell
your guy it's on the house."

She nodded and moved away.

It wasn't even Happy Hour yet and the Shack was already crowded. Though a small town, Sugar Creek had a
bustling tourist contingent. Especially in the summer and
winter. When Luke had invested in the Sugar Shack he'd
wanted to offer more than greasy burgers and wings. He'd
hired a gourmet chef, which had proven a brilliant move.
A cozy atmosphere, stellar menu, widely stocked bar, and
friendly personnel made the Sugar Shack a local hot spot.

Luke loved this pub. But right now he could feel the
walls closing in.

Since his longtime, number two bartender had just
showed up, Luke considered stepping out. Maybe a brisk
walk would clear his head. But then one of his several
cousins came strolling in, shaking off a dusting of fresh
snow and heading straight for Luke.

Sam.

Well, hell.

"Talk to you a minute?" he asked while nodding toward Luke's office.

Privacy. Right. "Sure." Yeah, boy. Why did he get the
feeling his day was about to go from bad to worse?

"Given the way this town works," Sam said as soon as
they were behind closed doors. "I'm guessing you've
heard Rae's in town."

Luke dropped into his worn desk chair feigning nonchalance. "She stopped by a while ago. Wanted to clear the air."

"How'd that go?"

"Fine."

"Did she tell you why she's in town?"

Luke bit the inside of his cheek, shrugged. "Something about saving Sugar Tots and the Cupcake Lover book deal."

Instead of sitting, Sam leaned back against the door and folded his arms over his chest. It was a dominant stance, not that Luke was intimidated. Although maybe he should be. Sam had six years on him, some bulk, and several years of combat duty. Luke had been on the business end of Sam's fist back in October and, hell yes, he'd seen stars. Still, the fact that his older cousin seemed to be settling in for some sort of lecture chafed.

"Depending on what all's involved," Sam went on, "Rae could be in town for a while."

"So?"

"I think you should drop out of the Cupcake Lovers."

Luke frowned. "Why?"

"Because Rae plans to get involved with the club again."

"So?"

Sam raised one brow looking at Luke like he was dense. "You don't think it might prove awkward, the three of us being in on those meetings?"

"What, because of that kiss you walked in on?" Luke stood now and rounded his desk, perched on the corner and matched Sam's stance. "I explained about that."

"So you don't have any feelings for Rae."

Luke didn't know how he felt about Rae, but he was getting pretty ticked at Sam. "This your way of telling me you're going to pursue her?"

Sam angled his head, a contrary gleam in his eye. "You're the one who told me not to give up."

"That was before—"

"Before what?"

Before she was carrying my baby. Except he couldn't

say that. He'd promised Rae. Well, technically he hadn't promised. But she'd asked him not to tell yet for reasons that were sound. Plus, he hadn't worked out in his head how he wanted to handle things between them. *Dammit*.

"Before when she was Rachel," Luke backpedaled. "She's not who you fell for, Sam."

"Money doesn't change who she is on the inside."

"She's the most secretive woman I've ever known," Luke said. "How could you possibly know . . ." Rae had mentioned recent phone calls with Sam. Luke burned wondering if she'd struck up an intimate relationship with the man. Sam was grounded, successful. An experienced and kick-ass dad. "Did Rae confide in you? Offer details explaining why she lied to us for a freaking year?"

Sam pushed off the door. "Quit the Cupcake Lovers, Luke."

"You're the one who told me to get a hobby."

"Your baking skills suck."

"Maybe they'll get better."

"Maybe you should take up bowling."

It was the exact wrong thing to say.

Luke sat stone silent as Sam left the room. He knew two things in the wake of his cousin's hit-and-run throw-down. He had no intention of quitting the Cupcake Lovers and he'd be damned if he'd sit still while Sam initiated some strategic attack aimed at winning Rae's heart. Not that Luke wanted to win her heart, although maybe he did. It would help if he knew her a better. Hell, it would help if he knew her at all.

Luke shoved off his desk and nabbed his jacket. Knowing Sam, he'd take things slow, which allowed Luke plenty of time to get a jump start. He still didn't have a handle on his feelings or a clue as to how to approach the future, but he damn well wanted a chance to get to know the mother of his child before some other man swept her off her feet.

NINE

Rae had never been a fan of unwanted attention. Unfortunately, it came with the territory when you were the daughter of Olivia Deveraux. It didn't matter that Olivia hadn't landed a decent acting gig in two decades. She'd enjoyed a spurt of fame in her early twenties and had been riding that wave ever since, somehow managing to appear in the tabloids time and again.

So naturally the citizens of Sugar Creek were curious about the famous sex kitten's daughter. Naturally they stared and whispered as Rae went about her business, navigating town in order to meet with a few local businessmen. What made matters more intense was the fact that Rae knew most of the locals, only she'd known them as shy, mousy Rachel Lacey. No one asked, but she knew they all wondered. Why had she pretended to be someone she wasn't? Why had she come back? How long did she plan to stay? Embellished with the usual curiosity attached to her infamous mother . . .

What was it like growing up as the daughter of Olivia Deveraux? Did Rae also hobnob with celebrities? Had she ever been on the red carpet? Did she know George Clooney or Ryan Gosling or Leonardo DiCaprio? Had she ever dated a Hollywood hunk? And on the subject of her inheritance . . .

Just how much was she really worth?

Honestly, Rae was surprised no one had questioned her outright. Then again maybe they were too shell-shocked by her return. Or maybe they felt bitter like Luke, too angry about her deception to broach the subject.

By the time Rae got back to the Pine and Periwinkle, all she wanted was a relaxing bath and a fortifying meal. Unfortunately, she only had time to freshen up. After leaving Luke at the Shack, she'd visited the real estate agent connected with the building that housed, or used to house, Sugar Tots. She'd visited the bank that held the mortgage and had spoken to her high-powered lawyer based in L.A. She had one last but very important appointment. A six p.m. meeting with the president of the Cupcake Lovers, Luke's only sister, Rocky Monroe. The prospect was daunting. Although Rae had never been close friends with Rocky, they'd most certainly been friendly acquaintances.

And Rae had deceived her, along with everyone else in town.

Most especially Rae dreaded facing those she'd spent the most time with—the Cupcake Lovers. Although she supposed since she'd survived the confrontation with Luke, she could survive anything.

After splashing her face and reapplying her makeup, Rae finger-combed her choppy hair and changed into a sparkly cashmere sweater combo and knee-high boots with a heel. A little flashy, but she wanted to impress upon Rocky that she could look the part of a celebrity. An angle Rae hoped would work to the advantage of the Cupcake Lovers. It didn't matter that she didn't feel comfortable in the skin of a socialite. She was doing this for the friends she'd wronged. She'd just have to dig deep, drawing on years of watching Olivia in action. Although hopefully Rae would be able to flaunt her wealthy status with grace.

She grabbed her coat and purse and left her room, rehearsing her pitch to Rocky as she rode the elevator down to the lobby. She was deep in thought as she made her way to the elegant pine carriage doors, gasping when someone stepped into her path.

Luke.

"Can I speak with you?" He noted the crowd of seasonal guests drinking hot beverages around the stone hearth. "In private?"

Rae blinked, stunned and unsettled by his presence. She honestly thought it would take him a day or two to seek her out. Not a measly few hours. "I have an appointment," she blurted, trying desperately not to admire his handsome face or to fantasize about the amazing physique beneath his coat. Talk about shallow.

"I only need a minute."

She glanced at her watch. "I can't. I need to catch a cab and—"

"I'll drive you. We can talk in the car."

He took her coat and held it open, pushing his agenda. She didn't have the energy to argue and besides she was curious. Had he already made his decision? Did he want her to stay in Sugar Creek? Leave Sugar Creek? Did he intend to fight her for custody? *Could* he? She hadn't thought of that.

Mind racing, Rae slid her arms through the puffy sleeves. Luke even helped with the zipper. Unnecessary and unnerving. His touch was gentle and deliberate, so unlike his impassioned grappling during their wham-bam coupling. Yet Rae's heart pounded just as fiercely and her stomach flipped with the same intense lust. She tempered her breathing and cursed the orgasmic sensations firing throughout her body while Luke cupped her elbow and guided her outside. How could she be so turned on by a guy who was so miserably her mismatch? A guy who'd treated her with contempt since learning her true identity? She cursed herself a thousand times over as Luke escorted her to his car, although it wasn't one she recognized.

"New?" she asked.

"Women shop for clothes when they're bored," Luke said. "With men, it's vehicles or sports equipment. I also have a new set of snow skis."

Rae almost smiled at that. Was Luke trying to strike a truce by sharing something personal? He'd been bored. That seemed unusual for a man who had dozens of friends and maintained close contact with his family. From all she'd seen and heard, Luke was always on the go, always involved with one or another social event. Always juggling multiple girlfriends. He also put in more than forty hours a week at the Sugar Shack. His life was full. How could he be *bored*?

Filing away the notion, Rae acknowledged another surge of heat as Luke helped her up into the dark blue Honda SUV. She was surprised by the brand. Most locals bought American. She was also surprised to see an iPod connected to an USB audio interface. Luke wasn't much of a gadget guy. "Stocked with your playlist?"

"Audiobooks. Prefer listening to reading." Stone-faced he closed the door and rounded the hood.

Rae's chest tightened. They'd yet to address his reading disorder. She knew he was touchy about it. Most anyone afflicted was. She also knew he suspected she knew but she was determined to allow him to be the one to broach the subject. The last thing she wanted was to make him feel self-conscious or judged.

"Here's the thing," Luke said after climbing in and buckling up.

Rae waited. And waited. After what seemed like a lifetime she lifted a brow. "What? What's the thing, Luke?"

"I don't know."

She blinked at him.

"I don't know, dammit." He keyed the ignition and adjusted the heat. "You blindsided me with this baby news. I need to wrap my mind around it."

"No surprise there. No problem. Take your time and get back to me when you have a handle on your . . . thoughts." The mention of the baby rattled her. She'd been in business mode all day, and she had this pending meeting with Rocky. She wanted to get it over with, wanted to know where she stood with the club. She did not want to be focused on the fact that she was pregnant with Rocky's niece or nephew. Things were awkward enough. "My appointment?" Rae prompted.

"Right." He shifted into reverse. "Where am I taking you?"

"Daisy's house. I mean your sister's house. I want to talk to her about the Cupcake Lovers."

"Care to fill me in on how you think you can help them with their book deal?"

"Sure."

"Really?"

"You look shocked. It's not a secret."

"Maybe not, but you have to admit you're not the most forthcoming person in the world."

"Guilty as charged." Rae settled her purse in her lap and focused through the windshield as Luke pulled out of the snow-drifted lot and onto the plowed road. He'd offered a little something about himself. Maybe she should do the same. He was, after all, the father of her child. Even though they'd known each other for a year, they barely knew each other at all.

"Here's the thing," she said, borrowing Luke's phrase. "I'm guarded. I've been guarded for a very long time. Because of my background, the life I've led, the people

I've dealt with . . . I don't trust easily. I'm not big on shar-ing my feelings because they usually end up getting tram-pled. I'm not fond of sharing personal information or even general opinions because they almost always end up twisted or manipulated or in the tabloids. That's my story and it's not likely to change anytime soon."

She waited for him to jump all over that. *You're pull-ing the poor-little-rich-girl card?*

He glanced over. "You're also the most complicated woman I've ever met." His eyes sparked with something she couldn't quite discern. Curiosity? Wariness? "Sam came to see me."

Hello, mental whiplash. "And?"

"He's still hot for you, Rae. You have to tell him you're off-limits."

Luke's revelation was unsettling on two levels. Rae addressed the latter. "Why?"

"Because you are. Because you're pregnant. With my baby."

"I know my situation, Luke."

"He's my cousin for chrissake."

"Is that why you're upset? Because Sam's family? What if Adam asked me out? Or any other guy in town— local or transient? I'm a free agent, Luke. Just like you. Just because we hooked up—"

"If you say, it was just sex—"

"Well wasn't it?" Rae worked hard to keep her heart out of her eyes as she met Luke's gaze. She couldn't deny to herself that she was infatuated with Luke, even though he'd been a jerk back in Bel Air, but she wasn't about to admit her tender feelings, unless. . . . Was it possible he felt something, too?

Luke dragged a hand down his face then focused back on the road. "Getting back to Sam. Don't you think it's unfair to give him false hope? Thinking he might have a future with you, only to learn a month down the line that you're pregnant with another man's baby? *My* baby?"

Rae wasn't altogether sure why Luke's observation ticked her off. He was right about Sam. Not that she intended to lead the man on. "For what it's worth, I told Sam I'm not interested in an intimate relationship. He promised he wouldn't press the issue."

"He doesn't have to press. He's patient."

"What's that supposed to mean?"

"It's his secret weapon. Patience."

Rae rolled her eyes. Luke made it sound as though Sam was a crafty Casanova. A game player. The man was, in fact, a straight shooter. Calculated seduction wasn't his style.

Luke on the other hand . . . Luke Monroe was the biggest flirt in town. He loved women and women loved him. He had a long history of maintaining simultaneous casual sexual relationships. No doubt *he* had a playbook of various seductions. Rae was beginning to rethink her willingness to permanently relocate to Sugar Creek. She'd been thinking about how much she loved the area, the people. She'd been thinking this would be a nice place to raise her child and that her child deserved to know the love of her/his father.

She *hadn't* been thinking about what it would feel like watching Luke carrying on as always with his revolving girlfriends.

Rae's temples throbbed. She was fatigued. She was hungry. And she was more than a little frustrated with the situation. "Listen, Luke. I know how devoted you are to your family." It was one of his most attractive qualities. "I'm not going to hurt Sam, if that's what's worrying you. My focus is on reestablishing Sugar Tots and hopefully helping the Cupcake Lovers. That, and reaching some sort of understanding with you regarding my baby."

Luke steered the SUV into the driveway of the magnificent old Colonial that Rae had known as Daisy's home. Thank God. She'd reached her emotional limit for today. Three-quarters to numb, at least she wasn't as worried now about her meeting with Rocky.

"I'd mind," Luke said as Rae unbuckled her seat belt. "If you went out with Adam," he added when she cast him a questioning look. "Or anyone else. I can't help it. It bothers me. You're pregnant with my baby."

Rae's stomach knotted. She was picking up a theme here. A theme that revolved around her behaving in an expected manner. Not because Luke had feelings for her, but because she was the mother of his child. Period. She shouldn't have expected more, but dammit, she'd hoped.

"If you think I'm going to be celibate for the rest of my life, think again." She plowed on, needing him to know she wasn't a doormat or easily manipulated. "I'm not saying I'm looking to get involved with someone now, but if an attraction happens to flare, I'm not going to ignore it." She pushed open the door, heart pounding as she issued a parting plea. "Please don't come inside and please don't wait. I'll call a cab when I'm ready to leave. And Luke," she said, willing every fiber of dignity and calm, "don't seek me out again until you've thought this out. Either you want to me to settle in Sugar Creek so you can play an active and constant role in your child's life, or you don't. This isn't about us. There is no us." He'd made that pretty clear as far as Rae was concerned. "This is about the baby."

"Wait." Luke reached across the seat and caught her wrist. "I need a favor."

She couldn't imagine.

"I was hoping . . . I need a mentor."

As in someone to help him conquer his reading disability? Was he seriously confiding in her? Admitting he had a problem? Reaching out for help? She couldn't believe it.

"I'm this close to getting kicked out of the Cupcake Lovers."

"What?"

"I joined the club a few weeks ago. Sam didn't tell you?"

"No." Shocked, Rae frowned. "You bake?"

"Not well. Hence the upcoming boot. I thought . . . If you could come over, give me some lessons."

"Why me?"

"I'm too close to everyone else."

She thought about that. "Harder to take offense when being advised by a stranger. I get that." Sad that it made her feel even more distant from the father of her child. "Regardless, I'm not sure it's a good idea."

"You think spending time together, getting to know one another better given the circumstances, is a bad idea?"

It was in fact a brilliant idea. Luke had found safe common ground. *Cupcakes.* Either they'd hit it off as friends, discover they were, against odds, a good match, or . . . they'd end up despising each other. At least they'd know how to proceed instead of lingering in this wretched limbo. Rae nodded. "Fine. I'll drop by tomorrow. What time?"

"Noon. I'll pick you up. We'll do lunch, then bake." He squeezed her hand. "Sound good?"

It sounded dangerous. "See you then." Rae slid out of the SUV, feeling more rattled than she'd felt all day and that was saying a lot. Even though she had to trudge through snowdrifts and freezing winds to get to Rocky's house, Rae's skin still burned from Luke's touch. She couldn't teach him to bake in a day. It could take weeks. And a good dose of one-on-one time. The prospect was daunting and thrilling and somewhat suspicious. She couldn't shake the feeling that she was being manipulated by Luke—the Charmer of Sugar Creek—Monroe.

But to what end?

TEN

"*Wow.*" Rocky Monroe leaned against the doorjamb and blatantly stared.

Rae bristled. She'd been in town less than twenty-four hours and she was already over the gawking and whispering. She was tired and hungry and emotionally spent from two rounds with Luke in one day. She'd waited until he'd pulled out of the drive before knocking on the door. She'd counted to ten while collecting her wits. Wits Rocky had scattered with a simple "*Wow.*"

Forcing what she hoped was a friendly smile, Rae summoned patience while dragging her fingers through her choppy locks. "The color and cut are extreme, I know. That's what happens when you tell a stylist you want something drastically different and give them carte blanche."

"And I thought I was being adventurous when I let Jayce cut my bangs. Maybe *I* should spice things up and get a makeover."

"You don't need a makeover, Rocky." Rae was pretty sure Jayce and every other man in Sugar Creek would agree. Rocky was a natural stunner. She typically plaited her long golden curls into two braids or pulled them into a high ponytail—simple styles that suited her down-to-earth personality and athletic lifestyle. Instead of chasing trends, she opted for T-shirts and jeans and sneakers or clogs. Even with no more than tinted lip balm, Luke's sister was Hollywood gorgeous. Olivia, who compared all people to movie stars, would dub Rocky the Scarlett Johansson of Sugar Creek. "Besides, you wouldn't want to do anything drastic so close to your wedding day. Congratulations, by the way."

"Thanks."

A frigid wind cut though Rae's weary bones. Frowning, she hunched her shoulders and shook off a chill. "Mind if I come inside?"

"Sorry. To think I used to work in hospitality." Rocky stepped back and waved Rae inside. "Give me your coat. Would you like some tea, coffee, wine?"

"I'm good." The sooner they got this meeting over with the better. Rae was feeling more lightheaded by the minute. Skipping lunch hadn't been smart, plus she was already drained from a full and emotionally awkward day. "Thank you for meeting with me on such short notice."

"I confess I'm curious." Rocky draped Rae's coat on an antique coat tree then turned. "About a lot of things."

Rae wasn't surprised by Rocky's wary tone and expression, but she was disappointed. Rocky, like her grandmother, Daisy, had always treated Rae to a smile and an abundance of good will. A small, no, a *big* part of Rae had hoped her written apology had smoothed any ruffled feathers regarding her abrupt departure from Sugar Creek. Just now, Rocky looked pretty ruffled.

"Where's your dog?" Rae asked as they moved into the warm and cozy living room. An appearance from that furry bundle of joy might help ease the tension.

"Brewster's had cabin fever lately, what with all the snow. Jayce had business in Pixley so he took Brewster with him. Good thing," Rocky said while inviting Rae to take a seat. "I wouldn't want fur-boy getting hair all over your nice clothes."

"I wouldn't mind," Rae said, ignoring the light jab at her stylish attire. She'd dressed to impress for a reason, although maybe that hadn't been the best idea.

Rocky dropped into an opposing matching chair. She shook her head. "I can't get over how much you've changed."

"Only on the outside. Speaking of change," Rae said, bulldozing forward, "Sam told me about the fire and how you lost everything. I'm so sorry, Rocky. I know how much you loved the Red Clover."

"I've come to terms." Her clipped response indicated she wasn't going down that personal road. "You've seen Sam?"

Clearly the spotlight was on Rae. "He called me a couple of weeks ago. We've talked a few times since. He was also nice enough to pick me up at the airport last night."

"I spoke to Sam earlier today. He didn't mention—"

"I asked him not to. I wanted to settle in and get my bearings before letting anyone know I was back in town."

"Were those Sam's taillights I saw heading out when I opened the door?"

"Actually Luke was kind enough to give me a lift tonight."

"So you've already seen Luke, too. *Huh*."

It was all Rae could do to maintain eye contact with Rocky. Luke's sister. Her baby's aunt. How would she feel when she saw Daisy or, God, Luke's older and slightly intimidating brother, Dev? Sam had also mentioned that Luke's parents would be back in town for Rocky's wedding. The Monroes were the most influential family in Sugar Creek aside from the Burkes. Although, also according to Sam, the former town mayor—Randall Burke—had recently moved away, taking his wife and former Cupcake Lover, Tasha, along. Rae had only been away three months, yet so much had changed. Everything had changed.

Okay, maybe not *everything*.

Even though this was now technically Rocky's house, it still looked like Daisy's home. The Cupcake Lovers met every Thursday and many of those Thursdays they'd gathered right here. Daisy might have moved out but she'd left all her furniture behind. Rae tried to take comfort in the familiar surroundings, but there was no comfort to be had. She was as good as a stranger to Rocky and everyone else in Sugar Creek. Like any stranger, she'd have to earn their trust and respect.

"Are you all right?"

Rae blinked.

"You look pale."

"Jet lagged."

"Ah." Rocky pressed the heel of her hand to her forehead then sighed. "I have to tell you, I thought I was more sympathetic to your plight—whatever that is. I didn't think I'd feel this—"

"Betrayed?"

"We all got the letter you sent—thank you for that—but you didn't suggest we'd ever see you again. In fact, that letter read to me like an official good-bye."

"It was."

"So why are you back?" Rocky asked plainly. "Why did you leave in the first place? Why did you pretend—"

"Personal issues were at play. I wanted to escape certain pressures. I wanted . . . I needed to be someone other than me for a while. I never meant to hurt anyone."

"So you said in your letter. But just now all I can focus on is that you played us for chumps for a year. Was any part of Rachel Lacey real?"

"All I lied about was my name and background. I don't expect you to believe me, but, aside from the money aspect, Rachel and I are one in the same. I'm quiet. I'm guarded. I have a brother, although he is a stepbrother, serving overseas in the marines. The son of my mother's second husband. We're quite close. I'm also certified to work with children. That's part of the reason I'm back. I heard about the closing of Sugar Tots. Whether anyone believes it or not, I loved working there. Working with the children. I miss them and . . ."

Rae massaged her throbbing temples, stunned that she was babbling but unable to stop. "Every town should have access to affordable, high quality day care. A safe and developmentally appropriate environment for preschool and school-age children. An establishment staffed with nurturing professionals who promote education and each child's social, emotional, and cognitive development. Gretchen's heart was never in the right place," Rae plowed on. "She cared more about advancing her personal goals than investing energy into the children's programs. Honestly, I'm glad she's gone. Although I'm sorry she closed the doors. I'm here for those children and for their parents. I'm here to make a difference. I'm qualified and emotionally invested and—"

"Okay. Okay." Rocky held up her hands. "Slow down. Damn. I never knew you were so passionate."

"That's because I suppressed my feelings and opinions while living here." Rae blew out a breath, lowered her voice. "Who am I kidding? I've been suppressing my feelings and opinions for most of my life no matter where I lived. It's safer that way. I'm learning, however, that some things are worth fighting for. Like Sugar Tots and the Cupcake Lovers and . . ." She palmed her queasy stomach.

"And what?" Rocky shifted to the edge of her seat.

Rae tensed. She was dangerously out of sorts—in mind *and* body. She reached into her purse in search of her phone. "I'm sorry, Rocky. I'm not feeling well. The jet-lag thing," she lied. "Excuse me while I call a cab. I'll share my idea regarding the Cupcake Lovers while I wait."

"No need for a cab." Rocky shoved out of the chair. "I'll drive you."

"I don't want to put you out."

"You're not. Come on. You can tell me your idea in the car. You're staying at the Pine and Periwinkle, right?"

"Yes. Thank you." Rae followed Rocky into the hall, feeling weary and embarrassed. She'd taken on too much for one day, her first day. A fortifying meal and a good night's sleep would work wonders. An ally in the Monroe camp would also help. "I don't know how long I'll be in town," Rae said as they pulled on their coats. "I might even . . . There's a chance I might move back for good."

Rocky raised one brow while looping a scarf around her neck. "Aside from Sugar Tots and the Cupcake Lovers . . . does this move have anything to do with Sam?"

"No."

"Luke?"

For the first time this day, Rae pulled a Rachel and averted her gaze. "It's complicated."

"*Mmm.*" Rocky opened the door then paused and turned. "Are you and my brother involved in some way? Did he come on to you when you worked at the Shack? Is that why you blew out of town? Things have been tense between Sam and Luke and I wondered . . ."

Rae flushed and she knew in that moment that she'd verified Rocky's suspicions.

The woman sighed. "I love Luke, but you do know he's a player, right?"

"We're not involved."

"Then why do I sense trouble?" Rocky waited a tense full minute then grunted and ventured outside.

Rae followed and climbed into her jeep. She had no intention of confiding all in this woman. Not yet. But she was desperate to strike some sort of truce. "Can I ask you something? Was it easy for you and Jayce?"

"God, no."

"But worth the fight?"

"At the risk of encouraging you, worth every battle scar." Rocky keyed the ignition and cranked the heat. "The thing is, Rae, we were in love. We'd been in love for years. Are you saying you're in love with Luke? I mean, I get it. Women fall for his boyish charm all the time. And Luke, Christ, if you ask him he'll tell you he's been in love a hundred times."

Rocky wasn't telling Rae anything she didn't already know. And she didn't have any illusions where Luke's feelings were concerned. Her own feelings, however, were a bit of an enigma.

"Sam probably wouldn't appreciate me saying," Rocky said, "but I'm pretty sure he's still carrying a torch for you."

"I told Sam I don't feel that way about him."

"That doesn't negate *his* feelings. You're the first woman he's expressed any interest in at all since Paula," Rocky went on. "I don't have to tell you what a good man Sam is. If you're attracted to my brother, you should tell Sam. Please don't let this thing blindside him."

Rae rubbed an ache in her chest. It seemed pointless to deny what she'd already hinted at. "I've been . . . infatuated with Luke for a long time. It's a mess and I'm not sure it can be fixed, but you're right, I should let Sam know my heart is elsewhere."

"With Luke." Rocky sighed. "You could have any guy in the world . . ." she said as she backed out of the drive.

Rae smirked. "Because I'm rich?"

"And beautiful."

"Believe it or not, that's not always a blessed combination."

"You're also smart and kind."

Rae cut her a glance.

"Like you said, you've only changed on the outside." Rocky smiled a little, the way she used to smile at Rachel. "Just took me a minute to get that."

ELEVEN

By the time Jayce got home, Rocky was stripped to her undies and a cami and snuggled under the covers with a fashion magazine. She'd bought a copy of *In Style* and two others like it on her way home from dropping off Rae. For the first time in her life she was seriously contemplating a *makeover.*

She tossed aside the shallow periodical when Brewster jumped on the bed and muscled in to snuggle. "I missed you, too, fur-boy." Rocky hugged the mixed breed then smiled into his big dopey eyes. Brewster was a rescue dog, a gift from Jayce, and her biggest source of joy—aside from Jayce himself. She glanced at her sexy fiancé while ruffling Brewster's lopsided ears. "How was your meeting in Pixley?"

"Interesting. How was your meeting with Rae?"

"Enlightening."

Jayce eyed Brewster with a scant smile then jerked his thumb. "Off."

The dog leaped to the hardwood floor then curled up in his own pillow-soft, fleece-lined bed along with his plush stuffed tiger. Brewster was a tad spoiled.

Sitting on the edge of the bed, Jayce leaned over Rocky, eyes sparkling. "Hey, baby."

"Hey." The sight of Jayce Bello always tripped her pulse, but the nearness of the man scattered her senses to the four winds. It had been like this ever since she was ten.

The sinfully gorgeous bad boy nodded toward her abandoned copy of *Vogue*. "What's up with the glamor mag?"

"I was thinking about a makeover."

"Why?"

She shrugged. "How do you think I'd look as a brunette?"

"Hot."

"What about a redhead?"

"Hot."

She narrowed her eyes. "What if I shaved my head bald?"

He angled his head as if conjuring the image. "Wildly fuckable."

She gave his shoulder a playful thump. "A lot of help you are."

He grinned. "Babe, I'd have a hard-on for you if you had a blue Mohawk—although that wasn't a suggestion." He kissed her then, a deep kiss that fired up her girly parts.

She smiled when he eased away, traced her fingers over his sexy goatee. "You should be naked when you kiss me like that. Makes me want to jump your bones."

"Hold that thought." He pushed up and leaned over to unlace his boots. "So what did Rae have to say about the Cupcake Lovers?"

"She thinks she can use her celebrity status to respark the publisher's enthusiasm for our project."

"Makes sense."

Rocky nodded. "Except I don't get the feeling she's all that comfortable with drawing attention to herself."

"I thought that was Rachel's MO. Shy, modest."

"Believe it or not, obscene wealth and fashion taste aside, Rachel and Rae, are pretty much the same."

Jayce angled his head as he unbuckled his belt. "You think so, *huh*?"

Rocky shifted to pull his T-shirt over his head. "You know different?"

His silence spoke volumes.

She jerked her thoughts from his muscled torso and focused on her new theory. "Remember that night I walked into the kitchen and interrupted a discussion between you and Luke?"

"The night before Christmas Eve."

"Luke was angry and blew out the back door without saying good-bye to anyone. Then he skipped out completely on Christmas Eve. So not Luke. He said it was a personal emergency with an old friend. I asked you if you knew anything about it and you said—"

"I said, I wasn't at liberty to comment." Jayce glanced over his bare shoulder. "That's still the case, Dash."

She warmed at his pet name for her, but stayed the course. "I assumed Luke confided in you and you promised to keep whatever he told you under wraps. I thought maybe it had something to do with an old girlfriend. God knows he has hundreds. And he's the biggest sucker in the world when it comes to a friend, especially a lady friend, in need."

"You going somewhere with this?"

"I've reassessed my assumption. I think Luke hired you to find Rae. That's why you can't tell me anything. Professional confidentiality."

"If that's what you think, why are you asking?"

"I'm not asking. I'm surmising." She watched as he shucked his jeans and boxers and climbed over her, buck naked, into bed. "You're trying to distract me."

"I always sleep in the raw."

"Yeah, but you've got an ornery look in your eye."

"You're the one who got all hot and bothered by a simple kiss."

"There was nothing simple about that kiss."

He rolled into her. "Allow me to complicate matters further."

She braced her palm on his chest. "Hold that thought."

Sighing, Jayce rolled back to his own pillow and placed his hands behind his head. "Go on. Surmise."

"Rae admitted she's been infatuated with Luke for a long time and that things are now a mess. I think they had a thing."

"As in an affair?"

"He does boink his waitresses on a pretty regular basis."

"Nice way to talk about your brother."

"Just saying. Anyway, maybe it wasn't an affair. Maybe Luke just flirted with Rae and Sam caught wind of it. Maybe Sam confronted Luke and they had words. Think about it, Luke had a black eye the day after Rae disappeared."

"He said he was distracted and walked into a door-jamb."

"Maybe he walked into Sam's fist."

"That's a lot of surmising, Dash."

"None of which you'll confirm or deny."

"I can honestly say I'm not privy to any of your conjecture."

She frowned. "Really?"

"Really."

"So Luke didn't hire you to find Rae? He didn't fly out to California on Christmas Eve to . . . I don't know. Talk her into coming back?"

Jayce reached over and tugged on one of her curls. "You need to let this go, babe."

"Why?"

"It's none of our business. Whatever it is, it will work itself out."

"Like us?"

"If they're lucky." He rolled back on top of her, pinning her between the soft mattress and his hard body. "About that makeover. Maybe we should start with some wigs. A couple of costumes."

Every intimate part of Rocky throbbed. "Costumes?"

"The redheaded nurse. The tight-bunned librarian."

Rocky pushed and shifted, reversing their position. Quirking a naughty grin, she shoved Jayce's hands above his head and squirmed against his erection. "What about the raven-bobbed dominatrix?"

Eyes dancing, the natural dominator feigned submission. "Works for me, Dash. With or without the wig."

TWELVE

Sam's morning started like every morning. Waking up alone. Staring at the ceiling. Listening for activity.

Rarely did he hear a sound, mostly because he woke before the kids roused. He'd always been a light sleeper, part of his combat training. Ever since he'd become a single parent, he was even more on guard.

What if Ben or Mina woke up sick or with a nightmare? What if one of them walked in their sleep and fell down the stairs?

In the hour to two before sunrise, his mind turned to the upcoming day. Making sure they were up in time, dressed, fed, and off to school. Mental reminders regarding any homework or upcoming events. Did he need to book a babysitter? Had he agreed to any playdates or sleepovers? What was he making for supper? Did he need to stop by Oslow's?

Sometimes his mind would slip to the past. How it had been before Paula died. How she'd handled the kids and managed the household with such fricking joy. Sam wasn't keen on dusting or vacuuming or folding laundry. Paula had tackled domestic chores with a smile. She'd taken pride in their home the way Sam took pride in his carpentry. He missed her infectious laugh, her shitty taste in music, the smell of her fruity shampoo. He missed her touch. Her company.

After two long years of grieving, Sam was ready to move on. He wanted a woman in his bed, in his life. A companion. A lover. A mother for his children.

His mind was set on Rae.

She loved kids. Was great with kids. She already had a comfortable relationship with both Ben and Mina. She was quiet, kind of like Sam, and she was kind. Kind and pretty. She was also loaded. If he thought she was a snob, the money thing would bug him. But he didn't get that vibe. There was plenty he didn't know about Rae, but one thing was certain—she had a gentle soul and a good heart. If she gave Sam half a chance, he was certain he could make her happy. Except he'd promised he wouldn't press.

That was the only reason Sam was on his way to the Rothfield Farm instead of the Pine and Periwinkle. He'd told Rocky he'd meet up with Harper Day. He'd agreed to tour the woman's house, assess what needed to be done and how much he could do. If he could help his cousin prepare for her wedding by taking the flaky publicist off her hands for a couple of weeks, he figured, what the hell? After multiple tours overseas, Sam was certain his and Rocky's idea of "bad" were two different things. He'd weathered active combat, he could handle Harper Day.

Just as Sam turned off of 105 onto 236, his cell rang. "Yeah."

"Are you on your way to Harper's?" Rocky asked.

"You thought I'd back out?"

"No, but, how long do you think you'll be?"

"No idea. Why?"

"I'm calling an emergency meeting of the Cupcake Lovers."

"This about the recipe book?"

"During our talk last night, Rae pitched an idea that could get us back on the fast track. Then again you probably know that since you two have been yakking on the phone the past couple of weeks."

"Your point?"

"I don't want to you to get hurt."

"That makes two of us."

"Sam—"

"Leave it. What time's the meeting and where?"

"Moose-a-lotta. Just after closing."

Ben and Mina spent every other weekend with Paula's parents. Sam wouldn't have to worry about returning home at a certain time or preparing dinner or bribing Mina for her nighttime bath with a bottle of Mr. Bubble. Plenty of time to work magic on the old Rothwell house before driving back to Sugar Creek. "I'll be there."

"Great. That makes almost everyone."

"Who bailed?"

"Casey's out of town until Monday and Luke's already committed. Can't blame him," Rocky said. "It's Saturday after all. You know Luke."

So his cousin was bartending at the Shack or showing a woman a good time. Or . . . he'd taken Sam's suggestion about leaving the Cupcake Lovers. "See you then," Sam said.

He disconnected just as he turned onto Swamp Road. Even though the two-lane roadway had been plowed at one point, Sam's tires rolled over at least three inches of packed snow and ice. Nothing he didn't manage on a daily basis, but he was accustomed to winters in Vermont. He was wondering how Ms. Day, who'd been living on the sunny West Coast, fared the frosty elements just as he approached the side road that—"Fuck!"

Sam swerved, narrowly missing the car that barreled out of Fox Lane, fishtailed across his path, and rolled on to its side. Adrenaline spiking, he braked and catapulted out of his truck. At least there were no other cars on the road. It could have been worse. Still, who drove that fast on ice when coming up on an intersection?

He assessed the situation while crossing the road. The four-door rested on the passenger side, face down in a snowbank. He had to scale the chassis to get to the driver's side. He smelled gas. Not necessarily ominous, but no reason to take chances. He wretched open the door and spied a woman curled in a ball and plastered against the passenger window.

Her long dark hair covered her face and she was swaddled in a long furry coat. He couldn't tell if he knew her. She was alone and she wasn't moving. Heart pounding, he reached in to key off the ignition. "You okay, miss?"

She groaned and stirred. "I think so." She shoved her hair out of her face—a beautiful, unfamiliar face—and palmed the side of her head. Wincing, she shifted and grappled on the floor then, cell phone in hand, started texting.

What the—

Perched precariously on the upended side of the car, Sam tempered his frustration and stretched out his arm. "Give me your hand."

"Just a sec." Focused on her phone, she continued to thumb in a message.

"You better be texting 911."

"A client. Hold on."

Leaning in, Sam nabbed the phone and tossed it over his shoulder.

"Are you crazy?"

"I was wondering the same thing about you, lady." On the other hand, her sky-blue eyes were glazed and her hands were trembling. Maybe she was in shock. Sam swooped in and hauled her out. It wasn't that far of a drop to the ground, but she squirmed and Sam lost his footing. He shifted, taking the brunt of the fall as they hit the road hard.

Sam lay there a second, more stunned by his reaction to the woman in his arms than the bone-jarring impact. He'd never been much of a talker, but he was speechless. Even though they were both dressed in layers, he was well aware of her curves. *And her face.* She was gorgeous. Model gorgeous. Like one of those fantasy chicks in the bathing suit issue of *Sports Illustrated*. Her lush mouth incited a rush of wicked thoughts and a raging hard-on.

Her blue eyes widened and Sam knew she felt the enormity of his desire pressed against her belly. "What are you, a pervert?" she asked while rolling off of him.

Assuming that was a rhetorical question, Sam pushed to his feet and watched as she scrambled around in search of . . . ah, yes. Her phone. "Let me guess," he said as anger loosened his tongue. "You were texting while driving."

"Thank God," she said while dusting off her screen. "It still works."

The woman was oblivious. A drop-dead gorgeous flake.

And she'd come straight from the direction of the Rothwell Farm.

Hell.

Frowning, Sam took out his own phone. "Yeah, Leo? Sam McCloud. Need a wrench, maybe a tow. Swamp Road across from Fox Lane. Car flipped in a snowbank. No. No injuries. Thanks."

Miss *Sports Illustrated* glanced over and held his gaze. "Sam McCloud? Rocky's cousin?"

He jerked a thumb behind him. "There's a stop sign at the end of that road, Ms. Day."

"I tried to stop but the road was slick and—"

"You were texting."

"It was important."

"As important as your life?"

She glared as if he'd just issued the gravest insult. Her phone rang and she shoved back her bountiful hair to press the high-tech cell to her ear.

That's when Sam noticed the goose egg swelling at her temple. He moved in to inspect the damage just as she started yakking to some guy named Chico.

She slapped at Sam's hand, trying to push him away, but not losing a conversational beat. "I told you before, Chico, you can't punch a member of the paparazzi. I know they're a nuisance, but they're necessary."

"You're bleeding." It wasn't bad, but now Sam wondered if she had sustained any other wounds—possible contusions hidden beneath her shaggy red coat. He pulled a wad of tissue from his coat pocket and gently pressed the compress to her small cut. "Hold this in place," he told her. "I'm taking you home."

"In a minute," she said to Sam then went back to admonishing Chico. Some shit about TMZ (whatever that was) making the guy look like a self-righteous asshole.

Sam eyed her car, in the ditch and out of the way of anyone who might drive by. Leo would arrive within the half hour. Meanwhile, it was fricking freezing and Harper Day was bruised and bleeding. Only one way to handle a stubborn, reckless, and injured woman.

Sam hauled her over his shoulder and carried her to his truck.

Meanwhile, she continued to admonish her Hollywood client while simultaneously stroking the dude's ego. "Don't worry, love, I'll spin this crisis by noon. Hold on."

She glanced at Sam with those killer baby blues as he placed her in the cab. "Would you mind going back for my purse?" Holding the tissues to her temple, she flashed a quick smile. "Thanks. You're a doll. No, not you, Chico. I mean . . . What? No, I can't pop over for a drink. I'm out of town. Now listen . . ."

Everything about this woman rubbed Sam the wrong way. Why the hell he still had a hard-on for her was a mystery. Except she frickin' *oozed* sex and Sam hadn't had any in a long while. Yeah. That was it.

Crossing over to Harper's upended car, he visualized cooling his dick in the snowdrift while sending a text of his own to Rocky:

YOU OWE ME

THIRTEEN

Regardless of the icy roads, Luke broke the speed limit and ran a couple of stop signs in his haste to get to the Pine and Periwinkle.

In anticipation of having Rae over for a baking lesson, he'd spent the morning cleaning his house. Sure Rae had maintained a frugal lifestyle the year she'd spent in Sugar Creek, but he assumed she typically lived in places as posh as her mom's Bel Air mansion. Luke lived in a modest three-bedroom Colonial on a ten-acre plot southwest of town. He couldn't do anything about the rustic décor, but he could collect rogue chip bags, beer bottles, discarded T-shirts and socks, and, as much as he hated the chore, he scrubbed the downstairs john. He'd been drinking coffee and surveying his baking supplies when he'd gotten the troubling call from Rae.

"Luke, I—"

"You're not calling to cancel, are you?"

"No. Yes. I'm sorry. I'm sick. I'm . . . I'm worried."

She'd sounded weak and shaky and her earlier warning rang in his ears.

The first trimester . . . it's iffy.

"On my way." Luke grabbed his coat and hauled ass. He'd never been a pessimist, but he kept thinking the worst. He would've been concerned for any woman and any baby. But, dammit, even though he didn't wholly trust her, Luke had a soft spot for Rae. And apparently, his feelings ran deeper than he'd imagined regarding her baby. *His* baby. He felt a whole new kind of sick as he jumped in his SUV and peeled onto the road.

Ten minutes later he skidded up to the Pine and Periwinkle Inn. Two minutes later he stood on the fourth floor in front of her door.

He knocked. "Rae, it's Luke."

Silence.

Chest tight, he tried her cell.

No answer.

"Dammit." He glanced across the hall, eyed the stocked housekeeping cart and the wedged open door. He peeked inside. Viv Underwood was making up a guest's bed. "Viv. Hey."

She looked over her shoulder, ponytail bopping. She smiled. "Luke. You aiming on coming in here and taking advantage of me and this bed?"

He forced a smile of his own. "Nice thought, but no." Luke had dated Viv awhile back. She was fun in the sack, but too clingy. He'd eased out of the relationship, wanting to spare her feelings before she was in too deep. "I need a favor, hon. Can you let me into room 412?"

"Is it registered to you?"

"To a friend. She's not feeling well and she's not answering her phone or door. I just want to check in. Make sure she's okay."

Viv frowned. "A woman friend, *huh*?"

"It's not what you think."

"*Mmm*." She moved into the hall and around her cart. "I could get fired for this."

"I won't tell a soul."

She inserted a master card key.

Luke turned the knob. "Thanks." He gave her cheek a peck then slipped inside and shut her out. He eyed the spacious, elegant suite, the empty queen-sized poster bed.

His fricking heart rammed against his chest. "Rae!"

"In here."

Luke found her in the bathroom, curled on the tile floor in between the tub and the toilet. His gut knotted as he stooped and palmed her pale face. "Did you faint? Are you hurt?"

"Just resting."

"What?"

She met his gaze, wet her lips. "Woke up sick in the middle of the night. Dizzy, nauseous. I've been puking and . . . stuff . . . all night and morning. It stopped a while ago, but . . . weak. Thought I'd rest here awhile."

He spied her cell phone, on the floor, within her reach. "Why didn't you answer when I called?"

"You called?"

He thumbed on the screen. "You lowered the volume."

"I did?"

Was she delirious? Luke pocketed her phone, adrenaline racing. She looked small and vulnerable and, short hair aside, a helluva lot like the dysfunctional woman who'd roped his interest back in October. The woman who'd fallen apart when that jerkwad college student had grabbed her ass and caused a scene. Luke weathered a swarm of emotions, most of them tender. Pulse kicking, he finessed her into his arms.

"Where are you taking me?"

"I'm putting you to bed then calling a doctor."

"Researched on-line while I was still vertical. Symptoms indicate food poisoning. I think I'm okay now. Just weak. I wouldn't have called, but then I got worried." Her voice caught. "What if the baby—"

"I'm sure the baby's fine." He wasn't sure at all, but he wanted to calm her. He laid her on the rumpled comforter, smoothed away her shaggy bangs, and felt for a fever. Her brow was clammy but cool. "Why do you think it was food poisoning? What did you eat?"

"Sweet and sour chicken. Had it delivered from that new Asian place. I was starving. Wolfed it down. If it tasted odd, I didn't notice. But that had to be it."

"You're probably right. Haven't heard the best things about King Chow's." Not that Luke considered every new restaurant as competition for the Shack, but he did take note. King Chow's had opened their doors a month ago. Knowing how popular Chinese food was, Luke had asked Anna to add three Asian dishes to their menu. Those additions had paid off in spades. Then again, Anna was a gourmet chef.

Luke eyed a quart of bottled water on the nightstand. He poured a glass then eased Rae up against the pillows. "You need to hydrate. I know that much."

She took the glass with both hands, sipped.

Luke sat beside her, nabbed his cell, and speed-dialed Doc Worton's office.

"So much for keeping my pregnancy secret," Rae said.

Luke's call rolled to hold. He listened to sappy elevator music while watching Rae sip water. She'd scrubbed away the meticulous eye makeup and bold lipstick of Regan Devereaux. She'd dressed down in baggy pajama pants, a bright green hoodie, and fuzzy slippers. She didn't look like the daughter of a Hollywood celebrity. She didn't look filthy rich. She looked real.

And *sweet.*

His heart jerked just as the receptionist answered. "Doctor Worton's office. How can I help you?"

"Hi, Leslie. Luke Monroe. Can I get a quick word with Doc?"

"He's with a patient, Luke."

"I need some medical advice."

"Nurse Dunlap's available."

"Great. Thanks." Jane Dunlap was a registered nurse and practiced alongside Worton. She was also another ex of Luke's, although they'd never slept together. "Yeah. Hey, Jane."

"Luke. Everything okay?"

He froze for a second wondering the best way to approach this while honoring Rae's reputation. If he was too cryptic about a "friend" in need, Jane might pry and even if he skimped on details, he'd be setting himself up for gossip. Sugar Creek thrived on juicy dirt—real or embellished. "Here's the thing. I think I got slammed with food poisoning. Spent the night gushing out both ends, if you get my drift."

"Loud and graphically clear. Anything else?"

"Dizzy, sweating."

"Classic signs. How are you now? Still throwing up?"

"No. All that ended about a half hour ago."

"Feeling feverish or chilled."

"Feverish or chilled?" he repeated.

Rae shook her head.

"Nope. Just weak as hell."

"That's to be expected," Jane said. "When did it start? Did it last more than twenty-four hours?"

"About half that."

"Sounds like a mild case of food poisoning or a plain old bug. Rest, drink lots of water, and try to keep down some chicken broth."

"That's it?"

"Based on what you've told me," Jane said. "If the symptoms lasted longer than two days or if you had a high fever or if you were a child under three or a pregnant woman, I'd suggest seeking medical attention just to be safe. Doctor Worton has a full schedule today but if you're worried—"

"No. I'm good. Thanks, Jane." Mouth dry, Luke disconnected and glanced around for Rae's suitcase. Not seeing one, he made a beeline for an antique bureau. Unlike his drawers at home everything was neatly folded, even her underwear and socks. He bypassed the silk and lace bras and thongs, opting for one of those cami tops and a pair of wool socks. Long-sleeved pullover, jeans . . .

He dumped his haul on the bed and peeled off her thin pajama bottoms.

"What are you doing?"

"Getting you into some warm clothes."

"Why?"

"I'm taking you to the hospital." He met her panicked gaze and tempered his own misgivings as he helped her into the jeans. "Just to be on the safe side."

His heart did another funny jerk when she blinked back tears and said, "Okay."

The closest hospital was in Pixley—a thirty-minute drive on a clear day. Given the icy conditions it would take longer. Rae was glad Luke was driving and not her. Not that she was capable of driving.

Rae couldn't remember ever being this sick, feeling this weak. After helping her to dress (something she didn't want to think about right now) and grabbing her purse, Luke had carried her to his car. She hated the way people stared as he whisked her through the lobby, but it would have taken them twice as long if she had tried to walk. At this point, she wanted to get to the hospital as quickly as possible. She needed to know that she hadn't put her baby at risk because of a stupid food craving.

Fear and guilt caused her to blurt her mind. "Admittedly, I only scanned one article on food poisoning last night, but it didn't mention anything about a pregnancy risk." Heart heavy, she slouched against the passenger door as Luke veered onto the main highway. "I should have called for help sooner. I just . . . I didn't realize it was going to get so bad."

"Shouldn't you be traveling with a personal assistant or a bodyguard or two?"

She frowned, perplexed by the turn of conversation. "Why would I do that?"

Luke shrugged. "Paris Hilton. Ivanka Trump. Don't heiresses typically travel with an entourage?"

Amazingly, she didn't detect sarcasm in his tone. The Luke who'd rushed to her rescue today reminded her of the charming man she'd initially fallen for, not the angry man who'd tracked her to Bel Air. "The last thing I want is an entourage. Yes-men. People who cater to your every whim while taking advantage of your prestige and fortune. Olivia's cup of tea, not mine."

"Then what about a bodyguard?"

"*Why?*"

"To protect you. Watch over you. You're worth a lot of money. What if someone tried to kidnap you for ransom?"

"I don't think that's an issue."

"What about the paparazzi? We've all seen how they hound celebrities. Look at what happened to Princess Di."

"I'm not royalty. And I've made it a lifetime mission to avoid the paparazzi." In spite of her anxiety, she managed a small smile. "I'm actually pretty good at it."

Eyes locked on the road, Luke grunted.

"Are you worried about me?"

He caught her gaze and her heart fluttered. "Yeah," he said. "I am."

"Because of the baby."

"That's part of it." He focused back on the road. "Hell, Rae. Seeing you down for the count, knowing you suffered through the night alone. Considering some of the more seedy ramifications of your new social status . . . I'd be worried about any woman in your position. You're vulnerable."

It wasn't what she wanted to hear. She didn't want pity. Nor did she want to be smothered by unwanted attention. "Sam said I'm a warrior."

"Sam's trying to get in your pants." Luke held up a hand before she could protest. "Sorry. I won't go there."

"You already did." Rae shifted her focus to the passing scenery. The snow-covered mountains, the occasional farm. She tried to lose herself in the beauty and serenity of the rural landscape, but there was no comfort to be had. Not with Luke tangling up her nerves and senses. How could he be so kind one second and a jerk the next? Although when she thought about it, almost every man in her life had treated her with a duality that made her head spin and her heart ache. She always ended up disappointed or hurt. Part of the reason she didn't trust easily. Since their confrontation in Bel Air, she definitely didn't trust Luke.

Yet he'd been her first cry for help.

Not Sam. Who'd only treated her with respect and kindness.

Luke.

"You okay, hon?"

"I wish you wouldn't call me that."

"What?"

She kept her gaze on the cold mountains, hoping to somehow freeze her heart. "Hon. You call every woman hon."

"I do?"

"All the time."

He fell silent for a moment then asked, "You think that's chauvinistic?"

"I think it's . . ." She closed her eyes, trying to wrangle a sensible argument. Right now she couldn't come up with anything better than it made her feel ordinary. As if there was nothing special to set her apart from any other woman he'd ever flirted up or slept with. Which was sort of needy and pathetic on her part. "Never mind."

They fell into a tense silence.

Luke turned on the radio, though he kept the volume low.

Alison Krauss.

Rae had always liked Luke's taste in music. At the Shack he pumped in classic rock and country pop. She tried to focus on the soothing ballad, but her mind was fixed on her baby. Was she all right?

"How you feeling, Rae?"

Rae, not *hon.* A lump lodged in her throat. "Lousy."

"Need me to pull over?"

"No. It's not that."

"Stop thinking the worst."

"I'm not . . ." She shook off the lie. "I can't help it."

"Think about something else. Tell me what's up between you and your mom. Why are you on bad terms? What's up with her husband?"

"I don't have the energy."

"All right then I'll talk. Back in Bel Air, you asked about my family. How about I bring you up to speed?"

Weary, queasy, she sighed and relaxed against the leather seat. "Okay."

"You know about Gram and Chloe's café, Moose-a-lotta. It caught on like wildfire. Aside from themselves, they now have a staff of five. Chloe and Dev have been living together now for almost five months. She still hasn't agreed to a wedding date, which drives my brother crazy, but she's got some sort of superstition thing going on with her pregnancy and his past."

Rae swallowed. "Chloe must be about six months along now."

"*Mmm.*"

"And Monica's expecting now, too. Sam told me. I'm so thrilled for her."

"Everyone's thrilled. Happened when Leo took her to Paris as a way of resparking their marriage."

"And in the process they made a baby. Twins. How romantic."

"You know Leo. Not a hearts-and-poetry guy, but yeah. What you said. Speaking of happy endings," Luke said, skating over baby talk. "Rocky and Jayce are getting married—day after Valentine's Day—and Gram and Vince are living together in Vince's house. Daisy's still copping to the 'just friends' living together for companionship thing. No one believes it, but no one pushes. Especially family." He frowned. "Who wants to think about their grandma getting it on? Not me."

Rae smiled a little. "Understandable." She thought about Daisy Monroe, a feisty eccentric, and Vincent, the mild-mannered operator of Oslow's General Store. They couldn't be more opposite, yet somehow they clicked.

"Did you know my dad was diagnosed with prostate cancer?"

Rae blinked. "What? No."

"Thought Rocky might have mentioned. Or Sam."

"No. No one . . ." She tried to sit straighter and failed. She did, however, home in on Luke's expression and tone. "How is he?"

"Recovering. Thank God. The proud bastard kept it to himself. Given he's a workaholic, we all thought it was fishy when he retired early to move down to Florida with

Mom. Turns out there's a specialist down there. Dad underwent radical treatment and, though it wasn't easy, he's beating it. Dev found out first and finally let Rocky and I in on the news not long after you left."

He flexed his hands on the wheel. "They came up for Christmas. Dad looked thin and worn but he never complained and declared the topic off-limits. Mom seemed in good spirits, but a little twitchy. It was hard seeing them like that. Thinking how they'd weathered the worst part alone. Pisses me off just thinking about it."

"I'm sure your dad had his children's best interest at heart. Withholding as a way of shielding."

"I'm a big boy, Rae. I may have a carefree approach to life but that doesn't mean I'm incapable of handling hard truths and challenging situations."

Rae's pulse kicked. Was he still talking about his dad?

"I just want you to know, I'm here for you." He glanced over. "And the baby."

It wasn't a formal commitment. Certainly not a declaration of love. More like an offer of friendship. She didn't know what to make of it. Or Luke. Every time she got a whiff of his devotion to family, her insides went all squishy. "You don't know how lucky you are, Luke. Being part of a big nurturing family."

"Not all sunshine and roses, trust me."

She'd take it, thorns and all. Squeezing back tears, Rae palmed her stomach. "This baby is my family."

He reached over and placed his hand on hers. "Mine, too."

FOURTEEN

The Rothwell Farm.

It had taken less than three minutes to drive from the intersection of Swamp and Fox to the property now owned by Harper Day. Tucked away in a portion of the woods and butted up against a now-barren cornfield covered with snow, the two-story farmhouse looked nothing like the last time Sam had seen it—which had been almost a year ago.

Beside him Harper yammered on her phone. She hadn't shut up since he'd buckled her into his truck, only now she was arguing with someone at her PR firm—not that he was paying attention. He could care less about some B-list celebrity bailing on rehab. Why would anyone care?

After parking, he swung out of the cab, desperate for a breath of fresh air. Harper's perfume had been doing a number on him, a sexy scent that danced up his nostrils and shimmied through his blood. Too bad she was so damned annoying. She had to be hopelessly single. He couldn't imagine any man withstanding her shallow preoccupation with celebrities, not to mention the incessant phone chatter. When he opened the passenger door she was still at it. He tuned her out and focused on the ground and the house as they carefully navigated her poorly shoveled walkway.

Sam had been intrigued by this property ever since he was a kid. At first, because of the haunted history. Later, because of the house itself. Originally built in 1880, even subsequent renovations hadn't diminished its charm. The last time he'd been here, the place had been abandoned. *Again.* The roof had been minus random shingles and the gray clapboard siding had been faded and cracked. Since acquiring the property, Harper had had the roof replaced and the exterior painted—federal blue with snow white trim. Pleasantly historic. The floor of the deep porch that ran the length of the house had been stained red. A bold touch that had Sam itching to detail the stark white eaves with a splash of color. He wondered if Harper would be open to suggestions. Although that would entail spending more time here. With her. Couldn't say he was up for that.

As impressed as he'd been with the exterior renovations, the interior was a different matter. The walls and floors were bare. Furnishings were a step below sparse. Sam took it all in, holding his tongue as he followed Harper through one unfinished room after another. Rocky had been working on this project since November, yet there was barely any evidence of her presence.

They came to the stairway leading to the second floor. Still talking on the phone, Harper paused, examined the clump of tissues she'd been holding to her head then stuffed them in her pocket and started climbing. Sam assumed the woman wanted him to follow. She didn't wave him off or ask him to wait. Then again she was so damned focused on her call, maybe she'd forgotten he was even there.

As they ascended to the second floor he mentally catalogued everything in need of—what were Rocky's words? Oh, yeah. "A little work." For one, the stairway needed an overhaul. That entailed ripping up worn carpet, sanding and staining the steps, replacing the balusters, handrail, newel post, and newel. At present, this main stairway was not only butt-ugly but a safety hazard.

"Whatever, Cecelia," Harper said into her phone. "I have to go. What? No, I didn't forget . . . I'm on it. I will. I have to go." She signed off as they breached the last step. "I forgot, dammit." She spun around, nearly knocking Sam back down the stairs.

He rooted himself, rooted her.

They were close enough to kiss. Yeah, boy, if he angled in, that lush mouth would be his for the taking. His heart pumped like a mother. Lust ravaged his calm. Casual sex wasn't his style. Something told him it was hers, though.

Damn.

"I need a ride into town," she said with a manipulative smile and a pat to his chest. "That's where I was headed when I wrecked. My cable's out and I have to watch a show that's airing at noon. I had dinner at the Sugar Shack the other night and there were plasmas hanging above the bar. I thought . . ." She faltered and frowned. "Is my lipstick smeared or something?"

"No."

"Then why are you are staring at my mouth?"

"It's a mouth worth staring at."

"Was that a come on?"

"A compliment." An observance he should have kept to himself. An observance that knocked her silent.

Miracle of miracles.

It was one of those moments when clocks stopped and time froze. When heartbeats were audible and skin prickled. Sam hadn't experienced anything like this in a long while. He should've been thrilled. He wasn't.

She stepped back, breaking the connection, angling her head and studying Sam as if seeing him for the first time. "What's a man like you—"

"What kind of man is that?"

"The kind who could take on an action star's role." She eyed him like a prized bull. "If a spot opens in the *Avengers* or *Expendables,* I've got their man. So what's a Rambo like you doing with tissues in his pocket? The soft lotion-y kind, no less?"

"I've got two young kids. Tissues are mandatory."

"I wouldn't know. I don't do kids."

"I'm not surprised."

"What does that mean?"

"You don't strike me as maternal."

"What do I strike you as?"

Sex on a stick. Self-involved. Manipulator. Control freak. "Career oriented."

"Funny, but that sounded like an insult." She smirked. "So are you driving me into town or what?"

Sam resisted the urge to haul her into his arms and kiss her senseless. What the hell was wrong with him? "I'm not driving you anywhere until we clean that head wound. I guess that qualifies as 'or what.'"

"I guess it does." Looking irritated now, Harper turned on her heel and headed down the hall. "Fine. Follow me. I've got some peroxide and Band-Aids . . . Rocky said you're handy. Does that extend to electronics? Maybe you can determine what's wrong with my cable. When I called, those idiots said they'd be here between nine and five. Hello? Anything after eleven thirty is too late."

"I'll take a look."

Ignoring her sexy figure as she peeled off her coat, Sam focused on where she was heading. As a kid he'd sneaked into this house with his cousins during the numerous times it had been abandoned. They crept though every room, recanting the haunted tale of Mary Rothwell, one of the original Cupcake Lovers, a woman who, according to legend, had died of a broken heart. Exploring the second floor had been especially creepy because the master bedroom, the room where Mary had spent her last years staring out the window and pining for her MIA husband, the room where she'd died, was located at the end of this hall. Sam was more than a little surprised when Harper pushed open that very door, revealing the one and only room in the house that was totally and beautifully furnished and decorated.

"Make yourself comfortable," she said then ducked into a connecting bathroom.

Sam did a quick sweep of the spacious room. A combination bedroom, office, and gym. He noted the array of fitness equipment, the twenty-inch plasma screen, laptop, copy/fax machine. State-of-the-art. High-energy. A techno-freak's wet dream.

Considering the ultramodern equipment, one would expect contemporary furnishings and bold accents. Instead, there was a softer retro look. Coordinating muted colors of lavender and green. A plush, solid-colored area rug. A floral-pattered sofa. An antique mahogany bedroom set. An antique desk. The paintings on the wall, the knickknacks, the furnishings . . . the entire vibe was reminiscent of the WWII era, the decade in which Mary and Captain Joseph Rothwell had made this house their home.

Odd that Rocky hadn't mentioned restoring this room to how it would have looked when the Rothwells lived here. Because, hell, this was creepy.

Harper stepped out of the bathroom and Sam's senses spiked. Dressed in a chic dress and black leggings, she looked equally at home amid the high-tech media equipment and retro 1940s décor. In that moment, Sam sensed a mysterious duality to Harper Day.

"Since purchasing this place, I've only visited a few times," she said while handing Sam a medical kit. "I prefer living on property during renovations as opposed to a hotel. So I picked a space and made it my own."

"You've got a thing for vintage Americana?"

"Not really. But in this case, it felt right. I like what Rocky did. Don't you?"

"Sure." He perched next to her on the small sofa, damning the intoxicating effects of her exotic perfume.

Her phone blipped and she shifted her focus, reading and texting. Reading and texting.

Sam opened the kit, soaked a cotton ball with peroxide then attended the scabbing bump near Harper's temple. He shook off a wave of déjà vu. He'd tended bumps and scratches and much worse in his lifetime. *Of course,* he'd done this before.

"For the . . ." Harper texted like a fiend. "I leave town for a few days and all hell breaks loose."

Since she seemed adept at multitasking, Sam spoke over her lightning-speed thumbs. "I assume you know the history of this house."

"That's why I bought it. This house, this room was lonely. Now it's not."

"Rocky said you don't believe in ghosts."

"I don't. But I believe in kindred souls."

Sam didn't ask what she meant by that because he was afraid she'd break into a ramble about psychics or some other metaphysical bunk. She probably represented some semifamous TV medium or an actor who played one. She probably believed in that woo-woo shit. Probably practiced yoga on the beach and subexisted on tofu and pine nuts. He kept ticking off West Coast stereotypical attributes while she compulsively texted. He kept waiting for his sexual interest to wane.

His nads twitched, telling him that wouldn't be anytime soon.

Damn.

"Are you going to check my cable, Rambo, or what?" she asked without looking up.

A ballbuster and seductress rolled into one.

For a split second, Sam thought about taming that sass. Except Harper struck him as a wild card and, because of the kids, he needed to play it safe. Moving toward the plasma screen he conjured visions of nuns and puppies and sweet-natured Rae. Yeah, *that* cooled his jets. As did the realization that he'd never once fantasized about hot and dirty sex with the woman he hoped to marry. Lovemaking, yes. No-holds-barred sex, no.

Not that he was having second thoughts, but he was.

He cursed the kink in his strategic plan.

He blamed Rocky.

FIFTEEN

Luke hated hospitals. He especially hated cooling his heels in the waiting room. Waiting to learn if a friend or family member was okay. A prognosis on a surgery or the verdict on an injury.

The last time he'd been here had been in October. Daisy had been transported to Pixley General after pedaling a rented bicycle down a steep hill for the thrill of it. Although she regretted losing control and skidding into a tree, she didn't regret the adrenaline rush. Even though that rush had cost her a broken ankle, fractured ribs, scrapes, bruises, and a gash on her forehead. The winter before Daisy had taken Rocky's snowmobile for a joyride. She'd fared better than the mangled Artic Cat, walking away from that wreck with several bruises and a broken wrist. Because of Luke's grandma's advanced age, the doctor had held Daisy overnight for observation.

Some of Luke's uglier memories were tied up with Sam's wife, Paula, who'd endured an invasive operation and extensive chemo treatments before ultimately losing her battle to ovarian cancer. The family had lost Grandpa Jessup, Daisy's husband, to cancer as well. If Luke's dad hadn't hightailed it to Florida, the family would have been haunting this hospital every time the old man, who wasn't even all that old, came in for treatment. But no. Jerome Monroe had spared his children and assorted relatives that misery. Rae had praised the man's good intentions, but Luke damned his pride. Luke's mom shouldn't have had to bear that weight on her own. Not wanting to cause tension over the Christmas holidays, Luke had held his tongue. But, damn, he resented the way his dad had handled the situation.

"Just be glad he's coming out of it," Dev had said.

What would his big brother say about this situation with Rae? Dev's first wife had miscarried scarcely five months into her pregnancy. Dev hadn't even known for certain that Janna had been carrying *his* child, but he'd grieved the loss all the same. Luke had only been living with the idea of being a dad for two days and Rae was only a few weeks along. Still, he felt emotionally invested.

It was damned uncomfortable.

Wired, Luke left the crowded, stale-smelling room. He needed air. Except midway down the hall he spied his grandma and Vince Redding coming his way. *That* he didn't need. He tried ducking through the nearest door, but . . .

"Luke?"

Busted.

Slapping on a smile, he faced the senior couple—hugged Daisy then shook Vince's hand. "What are you two doing here?"

Daisy pushed her blingy glasses up her nose. "I could ask you the same."

"I asked first," Luke said.

"My ticker," Daisy said.

"What's wrong with it?"

"Nothing," Vince said. "Just time for her checkup with Doctor Beane."

"Couldn't you see Doc Worton for that?" Luke didn't like the idea of Vince driving all this way on icy roads. He seemed spry enough for seventy. Still, why take chances?

"I could," Daisy said. "But Doctor Beane was the one who treated me when I had that mild heart attack a while back."

"The heart attack you didn't tell anyone about," Luke said. "What is it with this family lately?"

"You think I'm happy my son kept his illness from me?" she said. "But I understand Jerome's motives. Same reason I kept my brush with death to myself. It's personal. Stop holding a grudge, Luke."

"I'm not . . . How'd you know I was thinking about Dad."

"Do I look like I was born yesterday?"

"No, ma'am." She didn't look her age, either. In finding herself (in her seventies, mind you) Daisy Monroe had chucked her conservative wardrobe in favor of clothing more suited to a late sixties hippie. She'd also adopted a habit of coloring her springy curls in various bright colors (this month red—in honor of Valentine's Day). She was wearing velvety overalls, fuzzy purple boots, a lime green coat, and blingy cat eye glasses. "Don't let me hold you up," Luke said after glancing at his watch. "I'm sure Beane's on a tight schedule."

"I'm sorry," she said, sidestepping his observation. "Why are you here?"

Hell. "A friend of mine got food poisoning."

"Who?"

"Rae."

"Ray Howard?" Vince asked.

"Rae as in Reagan Devereaux," Daisy said to Vince. "Formerly Rachel Lacey. I told you about her and the false identity thing."

"That you did. Right out of a mystery show, that one. Don't understand why she'd fib like that, but I'm sorry she's sick," the older man said to Luke.

"I've known lots of people struck by food poisoning," Daisy said, "They didn't land in the hospital."

"Must've been a severe case," Vince said then frowned. "Hope it wasn't caused by any food purchased at my store."

"King Chow's," Luke said.

"Thank God." Vince coughed into his hand. "I mean—"

"I know what you mean," Luke said.

"We should pop in and say hello," Daisy said, looking one way then another. "Where is she?"

Damn. "I, uh, don't think that's a good idea, Gram. She was feeling really lousy and—"

"But you're waiting to see her."

"I drove her here and I'm driving her back. Just waiting to hear if they want to keep her overnight."

"Why did you give her a lift? Why not Sam? And what do you mean *friend*? You were never friends. Except for the Cupcake Lovers, Rachel kept to herself. And she only worked at the Shack a few days before disappearing and . . ." Daisy shifted her wiry weight and narrowed her eyes. "Lucas Monroe. Did you mess up the sheets with Rachel?"

"Rae," Vince reminded her quietly. "And that's none of our business, petunia."

"You did, didn't you?" Daisy asked Luke. "How could you? She's Sam's girl!"

"She's not—"

"You can go in now, Mr. Monroe."

The nurse who'd taken Rae into an examining room was now standing next to Luke. Her expression betrayed nothing, yet his heart hammered.

"We're late for our appointment," Vince said while urging Daisy forward. "Give Rae our regards."

Daisy waggled her bony finger in Luke's face. "We'll talk later."

Of that he had no doubt.

Luke followed the nurse down a side hall. She motioned him into a private room then went on her way. His pulse spiked when he noted Rae, sitting on the edge of the bed looking small and ashen and, dammit, vulnerable.

She met Luke's gaze then broke into tears.

Gut knotted, he moved forward and pulled her into his arms. He held her close, stroking her back, making stupid hushing noises. He didn't know what to say.

Clutching his shirt, she wept against his chest. "I . . . I can't believe it."

Luke's stomach dropped to his toes and his heart lodged in his throat. He hugged her tighter, closing his eyes when they started to burn. "I'm sorry, Rae."

"What? No," she blurted between sobs. "I'm fine. Baby's fine."

Luke blinked. "What?"

"Baby's fine. I'm . . . I'm fine. They gave me some fluids to . . . combat dehydration, but . . . everything, the baby . . . she's okay."

Luke's pulse had gone from a dead stop to a full-out gallop. He eased Rae back and framed her tear-streaked face. "Then why are you crying?"

"I'm happy." She dragged her sleeved arm under her nose, sniffed, then looked at him with her heart in her eyes. "Are you?"

"Yes," Luke said honestly. He couldn't get a grip on all

the emotions swirling inside him, but relief was in there alongside happy.

"They did an ultrasound. Do you want to see?"

"Okay." Luke dragged a hand through his hair as she reached behind her then showed him a picture that sort of looked like an X-ray. He squinted, looking for the shape of a mini-person. "I don't see—"

"She's only the size of a bean right now." Rae pointed. "That's her. See?"

"Oh, yeah."

"You can't tell, but at six weeks her eyes, ears, and nose are starting to form and her organs are developing."

Luke rubbed his chest, cursed his burning eyes as he stared, and imagined a developing baby. "What if it's a boy?" he asked. "Will you mind?"

"No," she said, wiping away fresh tears. "Will you be disappointed if it's a girl?"

"No." Luke swallowed as Rae gently tucked the scan inside her purse. He had no fricking idea what he was getting into or how he was going to handle it, but he was going to be a dad. That meant forging some sort of relationship with Rae. It didn't hurt that he was physically, *enormously* attracted to her.

Their eyes met and Luke's heart jerked. They moved in at the same time and he lost himself in a kiss like no other he'd experienced. It was troubling. *Thrilling*. He'd never been into clingy, but there was something heady about the intensity of Rae's embrace. Just like that first time they'd kissed. Something that made him want to cling, too.

When they came up for air, Luke dropped his forehead to Rae's. Even though this hospital visit had had a happy ending, so many others in his life hadn't. The memory of Sam breaking down when Paula died filled Luke with sadness and remorse. He'd encouraged Sam's pursuit of Rae and then he'd sabotaged his cousin's efforts. Not on purpose. Still. Amazing that he could feel happy and like the world's biggest ass at the same time. "We have to talk to Sam."

"I know. I'll do it."

"No. It has to be me. He's not just family, he's a good man and I . . ." *screwed him over,* "handled this badly."

Looking miserable again, Rae rested her head on Luke's shoulder. "What are you going to tell him?"

"That we're involved."

Beyond that, Luke was clueless.

SIXTEEN

Rae had never felt as close to anyone as she had with Luke during those few moments in the examining room. It made her feel wonderful and sad and sort of pathetic at the same time. She was twenty-five. She'd never had a serious relationship with a man nor did she have any close friends. Not the kind you stayed in touch with no matter where you lived or how much time went by. The only friends she'd ever had, outside of the Cupcake Lovers, had been false or transient friends. People who sucked up because of her celebrity ties or money. Friendly acquaintances who faded from her life once they no longer crossed paths on a daily basis.

Weary of being taken advantage of, she'd erected a wall years ago. She didn't let people into her head or heart, which negated intimate relationships. She was tired of playing it safe. Tired of guarding her every thought and word. Tired of playing the martyr. She wanted to live and laugh and love. To be surrounded by good people and positive endeavors. To experience full out what she'd had a taste of that year she'd lived in Sugar Creek. She realized suddenly just how important it was to her that Luke accepted and welcomed their baby. Even though she knew she was capable of raising her child anywhere. *This* is where she wanted to be.

So what now? Shop for a house? An apartment? The prospect was daunting considering her determination to resurrect Sugar Tots and to influence the Cupcake Lovers book deal. Maybe it would be best to cool her heels at the Pine and Periwinkle until she'd tackled some of her goals. Until she and Luke had reached a formal understanding. Why rush forward when so much was unsettled?

Luke had kept to himself on the drive back to her hotel. Then again, so had Rae. She assumed he was contemplating the future, much like her. That kiss had sealed an emotional bond. She was sure of it. Knowing Luke's romantic history, this was probably a first for him. It was definitely new territory for Rae. Her thoughts and feelings were tangled. She couldn't process the true nature of their relationship. Couldn't envision their next step. So she focused on now and the simple facts.

Her baby was fine.

She was fine.

Luke was happy.

They were involved.

Even though Rae was dead on her feet, her senses tingled as he walked her to her suite. Lightheaded, lighthearted, she smiled up at him when her key card snicked. "Thank you, Luke. For everything."

"If that's my cue to go, forget it. I'm not leaving you alone tonight." He nudged her through the door then shut out the rest of the world.

Rae turned and bumped into his hard chest. "You don't have to—"

"I want to."

"I'm feeling much better."

"Good. Still staying."

"Overnight?"

"All night."

Luke never slept over with his girlfriends. One of his rules. Although they weren't dating. They were *involved*.

Whatever that meant.

"Sure you won't regret this in the morning?" she asked.

"How about we take one day at a time?"

"At the moment that's all I'm capable of," she said as he helped her out of her coat. "Between the food poisoning and subsequent drama, I'm wiped. All I want is a hot bath and a long nap."

"And food," Luke added. "You have to eat something. Even if it's just broth." He plucked his cell from his pocket. "I'll order in from the Shack."

"They offer room service here."

"I'm not trusting your stomach to anyone but Anna," Luke said. "Not until you're fully recovered."

He was being overprotective, which was sweet. Rae cursed her fluttering heart. He was ordering chicken soup, not an engagement ring. For all she knew, as soon as she felt 100 percent, he'd do a one-eighty.

"What's wrong?"

Rae shrugged as Luke pocketed his phone. "Nothing. I just . . . Are you sure about this sleeping over thing? There's only one bed."

"I can sleep on the love seat."

"Not comfortably."

Luke crossed his arms and angled his head. "Is that an invitation to sleep with you?"

His tone was casual but her cheeks flushed all the same. She thought back on their mad shag in Bel Air, the way she'd practically ripped off his pants. "I won't attack you, if that's what you're worried about."

"Why would you, when the sex wasn't all that great?"

Rae winced in memory of her crude brush-off. "You seriously took my jab to heart?"

"You sounded damned convincing."

"I lashed out because . . ."

"Go on."

Rae's heart hammered, knowing she was standing at a crossroad. He was asking her to speak honestly, to bear her heart, which meant setting herself up for disappointment.

"I don't know where this, us, is going Rae. But I can't move forward if you keep me in the dark."

"It was the best sex of my life," she blurted, "and you ruined it. Your regret was crystal clear. You were disgusted and angry."

"With myself," Luke cut in. "You'd been drinking. I took advantage."

"I wanted it. Wanted you. Sex with you."

"To get me out of your system."

She'd had no idea her words had inflicted such hurt. Words spoken in anger in order to salvage her own pride. "If I wanted you out of my system, I wouldn't have come back to Sugar Creek. I wouldn't be standing here. I certainly wouldn't be sharing my feelings."

Luke held her gaze, nodded. "I'm sorry I didn't handle things better. After."

"Me, too. I mean—"

"I know what you mean." He smiled a little, striking a death blow to her already weak knees. "You okay if I leave for a while?" he asked.

"Did I scare you off?"

"No." He reached out and caressed her cheek. "But there's something I need to do."

Rae's stomach clenched. "Sam."

"Sam."

* * *

Luke dialed his cousin as he walked toward his wheels.

"I'm in a meeting, Luke."

"I need to talk to you. It's important."

"I'll step outside."

"Needs to be in person."

"Can it wait?"

"No." Luke revved his car and tempered his pulse. "Where are you?"

"Moose-a-lotta."

Luke flashed on an earlier phone call from Rocky. "The emergency CL meeting?"

"Yup."

Damn. The only thing worse than confronting Sam with his news, was confronting Sam in front of the ladies who'd been rooting for Sam and Rae as a couple for months. "I'll meet you outside of the café in ten."

Rolling through the slushy streets of Sugar Creek, Luke considered three different openings to this conversation. None of them felt right. By the time he parked in front of Moose-a-lotta he'd resigned himself to a black eye or bruised jaw. If Sam struck out like he'd done once before, Luke wouldn't fight back. Unless Sam went batshit crazy on him. Luke couldn't see that happening. Then again his judgment had been dicey of late.

Luke zipped his coat and stepped onto the road, bracing for the frigid winds and Sam's wrath. Spying several familiar faces, including his sister and Gram, peeking through the closed blinds of Moose-a-lotta, Luke groaned. Great. They had an audience. If things got ugly between the two cousins, the Cupcake Lovers would have a front-row seat. He wondered if Daisy had told Sam and everyone about running into Luke and Rae at the hospital. He could almost hear the conjecture and gossip buzzing in his ears. He could feel Rocky's boot kicking his ass to the curb and out of the club for multiple reasons, but mostly for screwing over their poor widowed cousin.

Damn.

"I'm guessing this has to do with Rae," Sam said, making the first play.

"I haven't been entirely forthright," Luke said while stuffing his gloved hands in his pockets. "All I can say is, it wasn't intentional. I didn't pursue Rae. I didn't charm or seduce her. Hell, I didn't even flirt. That first kiss, it went down like I said. Purely innocent. Then, because I was worried about her, I hired Jayce to track her."

"You flew to Bel Air," Sam surmised.

"I saw red when I found out who she was and how she'd betrayed us. There was a confrontation and an incident. I didn't think I'd see her again. I sure as hell didn't think there was anything between us."

"But there is."

"There is." Luke rocked back on his heels, hunched his shoulders against the biting wind, and wondered if hell was going to freeze over before Sam reacted to the news.

The man just stared.

Most people crumbled under Sam's famous death glare. But Luke was too primed. Too pissed. It wasn't his fault that Rae had fallen for him and not Sam. He wasn't a homewrecker. They'd never been a goddamned couple. "Are you gonna slug me?" Because Luke was suddenly itching to slug back.

"No. I'll just wait."

"For what?"

"For you to screw up."

A haymaker would have hurt less. Luke had always looked up to Sam and before this thing with Rae, he'd been as tight with the man as any of his other cousins. And that was damned tight. The censure stung, but it also torqued Luke's pride. "What if I don't screw up,

Sam? What if I make a commitment to Rae and follow through?"

"You don't know jack shit about commitment, Luke."

"What? Because I've never been engaged or married?"

"Hell, you've never even been monogamous."

"You weren't exactly a Boy Scout before you met Paula."

"Are you saying you feel for Rae what I felt for my wife?"

"I'm saying we're involved. Back off, Sam."

The man warded him off with raised palms as if to say, *done.*

Luke didn't believe that for one minute.

"You coming in for the rest of the meeting?" Sam asked. "We're discussing key issues regarding the future of the club."

"Pass." The sooner he got back to Rae with that fortifying soup, the better.

"Yeah, well, some of us are actually invested in the cause." Sam turned toward the café.

Luke frowned. "When did you turn into such a dick?"

"Around the same day as you."

SEVENTEEN

"Here he comes!" Rocky tagged Daisy on the shoulder and motioned everyone else away from the window.

"Do you think he knows we were watching?" Ethel asked.

"We weren't exactly discreet," Chloe said.

"Luke looked right at me," Monica said.

"I wish we could have heard what they were saying," Judy said.

Daisy snorted. "I told you to let me crack the door, but *nooooh*."

Chloe shushed everyone as the bell above the door tinkled. They all flopped into chairs as Sam strode inside.

Rocky peered around her cousin, thinking her brother might follow. Even though he was a crappy baker he was still a Cupcake Lover until he resigned or they voted him out. Very few had ever been voted out. But Luke didn't follow and Rocky worried that the rift between her brother and Sam was drifting toward alienation. That was all kinds of trouble and all kinds of wrong.

"Let's get this out of the way so we can get on with

business," Sam said as he eased into a seat. "Luke and Rae are involved."

"As in *dating*?" Helen asked.

"Something like that."

Rocky didn't gasp like the others. She'd had a heads-up from Rae. But she *did* tense. Poor Sam. She'd had a similar snafu. At one time she'd been sexually involved with Luke's best friend Adam Brody. Then Jayce had reentered the picture. *Triangles*. Not pretty. One of the three usually ended up hurt. In her case Adam. In this case Sam.

"I knew it!" Daisy exclaimed. "I ran into them at the hospital. That is, I ran into Luke. He drove Rae to Pixley General. Apparently she got slammed with food poisoning."

"Luke didn't mention that part," Sam said.

"I assume she's okay," Daisy said.

"*Assume?*" Rocky and Sam chimed as one then both thumbed in a text.

"So Rae and Luke are going steady?" Judy asked.

"I don't think that phrase applies anymore," Chloe said kindly. "More like they're exclusive. I guess. I don't really know."

"It won't last," Monica said with a sympathetic glance at Sam.

"How can it?" Judy asked. "We're talking about Luke." She glanced at Daisy. "No offense."

"I know my grandson," Daisy said. "Big heart, wandering . . . you know."

The women nodded. Sam nodded. Everyone knew about Luke and his wandering you-know-what.

"Can we get on with the meeting?" Sam glanced at his smart phone. "Rae's all right by the way."

"On the mend," Rocky seconded as she read her own texted response from Rae.

"That's a relief," Daisy said.

The club broke out in assumptions and conjectures regarding Sugar Creek's most unlikely couple. Rocky scrambled to take control. Usually she wasn't so easily rattled, but this was family. "Granted this thing, whatever it is, between my brother and Rae is juicy stuff, but can we focus on business?"

"The publishing deal," Chloe said. "I agree. Let's wrap this up. Not to be rude, but it's been a long day."

"In other words, she wants to get home to my grandson," Daisy said. "The responsible one. Ah, true love."

Rocky didn't doubt Chloe wanted to get home to Dev, but mostly she thought her kind-hearted future sister-in-law was desperate to end things so Sam could make his escape. That made two of them. "As I said before, Rae volunteered to use her socialite status and her mother's fame to attract attention for the Cupcake Lovers."

"If we do this," Monica said, "we'll be pulling the celebrity card. Which doesn't make sense considering our small-town apple-pie identity."

"It makes sense if we want attention," Judy said.

"The goal is to raise awareness for soldiers in need of moral support," Helen said.

"And to generate money for our various other charities," Daisy said. "Why look a gift horse in the mouth?"

"Rae's the gimmick we're looking for," Ethel added.

Leave it to the senior CLs to cut through the crap.

Meanwhile Sam said nothing, although he did catch Rocky's eye. He thumbed something into his phone and then her phone pinged.

WE NEED TO TALK

Rocky frowned. *About Rae and Luke? Rae and Sam? Rae and the Cupcake Lovers?*

OK, she thumbed then garnered everyone's attention. "So we're going to fly with Rae's offer. All I needed to know. I'll touch base with her and the publisher tomorrow. Stay tuned." Rocky glanced at Chloe, silently begging her help.

Hand on her pregnant belly, Chloe pushed to her feet with a smile. "Great. Good. Thanks for coming everyone. Not that I'm rushing you out, but I'm rushing you out. See you Thursday for our regular meeting!"

Within minutes everyone was in their cars except Sam and Rocky, who lingered curbside. "I don't know what's up with my brother," she started.

"This isn't about Luke," Sam said. "It's about Harper."

"What about her?"

"I can't work with her."

"Why not?"

"I don't like her."

"I know she's a little self-involved."

"A little?"

"And obsessed with work."

"Shallow work."

Rocky gripped her cousin's arm. "I'm desperate, Sam. I didn't mention before, but Harper's obsessed with that house. She wants it to be perfect, her ideal, except she's doesn't know what that is and everything I suggest falls flat."

"Except for her bedroom."

"Except for that." Rocky shook off a chill that had nothing to do with the sub-zero temp. "For what it's worth she dictated the look of that room, not me. The colors, the style. You recognized the era, right?"

"1940s. The Rothwell decade."

"Kind of creepy, right?"

"A little."

Rocky hadn't said anything to anyone aside from Jayce. Even though Harper was eccentric, Rocky liked her. Plus she was a client. Gossiping about the woman's longtime fascination with the Rothwell Farm seemed cheesy not to mention unethical. She said as much to Sam, following with, "I don't think she's nuts or anything. Just sensitive."

"As in attuned to spirits?"

"As in a kind soul moved by another kind soul's plight."

"Kindred spirits," Sam said.

"Harper's known about the legend of the Rothwell Farm for a long time, Sam. I think she feels some sort of personal connection with Mary Rothwell. Not that she talks about it. I think she, Harper, is troubled, as in haunted by . . . something. I don't know. She won't talk about it. And that's fine. I don't mind dealing with her eccentricities, but I can't deal now. Not a week before my wedding. Don't bail on me, dammit. I know I owe you. Whatever. In spades and triple."

Sam looked away and worked his jaw.

"Something tells me there's more at play here than a strong dislike of Harper."

"I'm attracted to her."

"But you said—"

"As in I want to jump her frickin' bones."

"Oh." *Wow*. Sam didn't talk about stuff like this. Rocky sometimes wondered if he ever even thought about stuff like this. For all his alpha qualities, Sam McCloud was the ultimate gentleman. What she didn't get exactly, was why he looked so miserable. Noting oncoming pedestrians, Rocky tugged her cousin into the alley, away from prying eyes and the blustery wind. "You're not the first man to lust after a beautiful woman."

"I can't go there."

"Why? I mean she's unattached. You're unattached."

"Ben and Mina."

Rocky pulled her sock cap down lower over her freezing ears. Considering all Sam's male cousins, she wasn't sure she was the best confidant, but she was here and Sam was spilling. "The kids don't have to know about your sex life."

"I have to think about the future. I can't introduce a woman into their lives when there's no hope of . . . something more."

"That's sweet and thoughtful, but—"

"Old-fashioned?"

"I think you're too hard on yourself, Sam. You're a great dad, but you're also a man with needs. Pining for Rae just because you think she'd make a wonderful mom for Ben and Mina—"

"It's not just that. I like Rae."

"Are you in love with her? Or the *idea* of her?"

Sam jammed a hand through his hair.

Rocky pushed. "Do you want to jump her frickin' bones?"

The man's silence spoke volumes.

"Do you want my advice?" she asked.

"I can't believe we're having this discussion."

"If the physical attraction between you and Harper is mutual, strike an agreement and have a fling." She couldn't believe she was steering her cousin down this path, except she thought Sam was in serious need of female companionship—even if only in bed. "A friends with benefits kind of thing," she prodded. "No strings."

"Except we're not friends," Sam said. "Harper irritates the hell out of me."

"Maybe she'll grow on you."

Sam rolled his eyes.

"And maybe Rae will have a turn of heart when she's no longer the object of your desire. If you stop chasing her, maybe she'll chase you. That's if you still want to pursue a relationship with her even though she doesn't light you fire, so to speak."

"I don't know what I want any more." He blew out a breath. "Luke's going to break Rae's heart."

"Maybe. Maybe not." The fact that Luke had told Sam to "back off" (yeah, she'd made out that part loud and clear) told Rocky that this was new territory for her brother. "In the meantime, cuz, don't close yourself off to unexpected opportunities and please find a way to make peace with Luke. He's family and this town, as you know, is flipping small. Life is short."

Sam nodded and Rocky knew she'd hit a nerve. He cupped her elbow and guided her toward her jeep. "I'll do the work on the Rothwell Farm. Keep Harper out of your hair."

"And pursue the attraction?"

He cast her one of his famous death glares.

She smiled. "And make peace with Luke?"

"Let's just say I won't aggravate the situation."

EIGHTEEN

Rae didn't remember falling asleep.

She remembered taking a hot shower and changing into fresh sweats and a tee.

She remembered receiving texts from Sam and Rocky asking if she was okay.

She remembered Luke returning with an overnight bag, bottled water, and food especially prepared by his chef at the Shack and him assuring her that the food was safe and that Sam was aware Luke and Rae were "involved."

Too exhausted to maintain a conversation, Rae had picked at her soup and freshly baked bread while Luke had kicked back on the bed, utilizing the remote to surf channels. She'd received two texts from her mom and a call from Geoffrey, both of which she ignored. Turning off her cell, she'd taken comfort in Luke's companionable silence, crawling in next to him to watch a movie, only she couldn't recall the ending. She must've drifted off.

One thing was certain. She'd slept like the dead through the night. She'd awoken to muted sunshine peeking through the curtains and the feel of someone spooned in behind her. She knew without turning that it was Luke and the knowledge rattled her senses. At some point he'd joined her under the covers and at some point they'd snuggled up. What she didn't know is if he'd shed his sweats and tee. Did he sleep in boxers or in the buff? Or maybe he'd slept fully clothed. Her heart pounded as she imagined Luke naked. Even though they'd had sex, they'd merely jostled their clothing to make that happen.

"What are you thinking about?" Luke asked close to her ear.

You. Naked, you. Naked you doing things to naked me. Her pulse skipped. "You're awake."

"*Mmm.*"

He tightened his hold and she was suddenly, keenly aware of two things. His palm pressed protectively over her belly, and his erection pressed hard against her backside. Both sent her heart and mind into overdrive. "I have to pee." Flustered, she slid out of bed and hurried into the bathroom.

Luke was hard. For *her.* Or maybe it was just a case of morning wood. Guys just sometimes woke up hard, right? "Right."

Rae went about her business then washed her hands and splashed cool water on her puffy eyes. Not wanting to face Luke with morning breath, she hurriedly brushed her teeth. Two seconds later, she ventured back into the room, unsure of what to do or say.

"You okay?" Luke asked.

He'd propped up on one elbow. His hair was mussed and his jaw was shadowed. He was gorgeous. And shirtless. She wanted to jump his bones. "I'm fine. Great. It's just . . . Don't you need to be somewhere?"

"It's Sunday. Other than the traditional dinner with family, no obligations. And you?"

"Rocky texted saying my plan is a "go" for the Cupcake Lovers, but I can't do anything about that until Monday. Same for my next step with Sugar Tots."

"Then you're free." He smiled. "Come back to bed. I want to talk to you about something."

She realized suddenly that she was wringing her hands, which ticked her off. She'd committed to controlling her life, yet here she stood riddled with anxiety.

Show some backbone, Deveraux. Face your desires, make them known and take some flipping action.

Just as she eased onto the mattress, Luke eased off. "Be right back."

Rae noted the blue sweats hanging low on his narrow hips. Admired his muscular back as he disappeared into the bathroom. She tempered several racy thoughts. She wanted to fool around and he wanted to talk. What about? The baby? Their relationship? She heard the toilet flush then the water run. She fluffed two pillows and leaned back against the headboard trying to look casual. Maybe she should order room service. Coffee. Eggs and toast.

Luke returned and this time she got a prime frontal of his incredible torso. Did he work out every day? He wasn't overly bulked but every muscle was toned. And his abs . . . There were *ridges*. He slid back into bed smelling of soap and toothpaste.

Rae wished she were wearing skimpy undies or better yet, nothing at all. Could she be any less alluring in her baggy loungewear? "What did you want to talk about?" she blurted.

"You. Us. Something's bothering me."

"Okay."

"What you said about what happened in Bel Air. About it being the best sex you ever had."

Shoot me now.

"Were you serious?"

"Is that your pride asking?"

"It's me asking."

Rae bunched the sheet in her hand and focused on the thread count, not Luke's eyes. Not Luke's chest. Not . . . "Let's just say that my liaisons to date, not that there have been many, believe it or not, have been less than thrilling. You," she said with a quick glance, "were thrilling."

"I can do better. You deserve better." He rolled into her and smoothed her hair from her face. "I know we're on shaky ground, new ground, but when you're ready—"

Rae angled and initiated a kiss—bold, brazen. She was more than ready. She was hot for this man and growing hotter by the second. Last night and this morning he'd exhibited all the qualities she'd initially fallen for. Kind, caring, thoughtful, protective . . .

Luke Monroe set her soul on fire. Not to mention what he did to her libido.

Their tongues dueled and her heart swelled. Their hands groped and her senses tingled. She tugged at his waistband. She was ready for fast and furious. Hot and wild.

Luke finessed her beneath him, pinned her hands above her head. He gazed into her eyes and swear to God she melted. *Mel-ted*.

"This time we're taking it slow." He nipped her earlobe. "Relax, Reagan. Enjoy."

The sound of her full name stroked her intimate parts as surely as his hands. Not *hon*. Not *baby*. Not even *Rae*. Her brain glitched. "Okay."

He smiled against her check. Rained intoxicating kisses across her jaw and down her neck. His hands worked under her tee, skimmed her stomach, her rib cage.

He peeled off her clothes with practiced finesse, seduced her with hot looks and sexy remarks. He worshipped her body—his hands, his mouth, his eyes.

Impossible to relax, but Rae did enjoy. Every kiss. Every lick. Every nip. Every touch.

She groaned as he parted her thighs, gasped when he licked her *there*. Overwhelmed with sensations, she climaxed in a heartbeat. She was shuddering with the aftereffects when Luke rolled away.

"Where are you going?" she rasped.

"Condom."

Why did they need protection when she was already pregnant?

Maybe it was habit. She didn't ask. Could barely think. Luke had tongued her into some sort of euphoric daze.

Then suddenly he was looking down at her, a wicked grin on his sinfully handsome face. His buff body poised for action.

Her lungs seized.

The tip of his shaft grazed and teased.

Desperate for more, Rae gripped Luke's butt, anxious for him to slide home. The longer he stalled the more she ached, the more she begged. He took his time, damn him, inch by inch and then . . . "*Yes!*"

Luke plunged and rocked.

Rae bucked and soared.

The ride was slow and hard and achingly wonderful. He kissed her and she came, again and again, swept away by a tidal wave of mind-blowing ecstasy.

A second later Luke followed, stunning her with the intensity of his release.

She held silent as he shifted onto his back and pulled her into his arms.

"It's been a while," he said as if reading her mind.

"Since when?" she rasped.

He caught her gaze, his expression unreadable. "Since you."

* * *

Luke had always been fond of Sundays. His free day. His
play day. The one day he always took off from the Shack.
He'd spent countless Sundays with the Brody brothers—
fishing, skiing, bowling—and occasional Sundays with
one of his several girlfriends—picnics, festivals, hot air
ballooning via his piloting cousin, Nash. Once in a great
while he attended church, but not often, and usually only
as a favor to his parents or Daisy. They worried about his
soul. Not that he was a bad sort, just unfocused. Sure he
ran the Sugar Shack, but he was only half owner and his
attention to finances was half-hearted. If someone, typically a young woman, was desperate for a job, he'd take
her on even if he already had too many employees on the
payroll. Dev was constantly harping on Luke for allowing his soft heart to override good business. And Luke
was forever telling his big brother to take the stick out of
his ass.

Dev was a control freak, a workaholic, and too
grounded for his own good. Although he had loosened up
since meeting Chloe—a blessing for everyone.

Luke had always been one of those people who acted
on instinct. He didn't worry overly much about the conse-
quences of his actions since his actions were usually
rooted in good intentions. He didn't worry overly much
about the future. Didn't think twice about the fact that
he'd never committed to one woman. He was only thirty-
two for crissake. His happy-go-lucky lifestyle suited him
just fine—up until twenty-four hours ago.

The only thing typical about this Sunday was that
Luke planned on joining his family for their traditional
Sunday dinner. This morning he'd woken up in bed with
the mother of his child. Yeah, boy, *that* was a first. He'd
ached to make love to her, to brand her body with his
touch, to seduce her heart.

Another first.

He wasn't in love with Rae. He'd been in love a hundred times. That rush you get at the onset of an infatuation. This wasn't like anything he'd felt before. He didn't know what it was, but he knew he wanted to push on. Sam had accused Luke of not knowing how to commit. Pure and simple, Luke had never had the inclination. Seeing that ultrasound of his unborn child had sparked a proprietorial urge that extended to Rae. He was immensely attracted to her vulnerability, her seeming innocence, her quiet strength, and her rabid love of the baby in her womb. As of this morning, Luke no longer saw her as Rachel Lacey, the mousy teaching assistant, or Reagan Deveraux, the hot socialite with a master's degree and a freaking fortune. She was someone in between. Someone he wanted to know better. Someone who inspired him to be a better man. Or at least more focused.

After making love, Rae had excused herself to take a shower. Sensitive to her quiet mood, instead of joining her, Luke had exercised restraint. He got it. They'd gone from zero to a hundred overnight. They barely knew each other and he'd proclaimed them "involved." He knew from the voice mails that had accumulated on his phone that the news was already spreading throughout town. Once they left the sanctity of this room, they'd be viewed as a "couple" in everyone's eyes. Except Luke and Rae hadn't discussed specifics. For the first time in his life, Luke was contemplating the dynamics of an exclusive relationship.

His heart hammered when she emerged from the bathroom wearing a cinched robe and a determined expression. "I've been thinking," she said.

"Me, too."

"We need to talk."

"Agreed. Can we do it over breakfast?" he asked. "Or

at least coffee? I don't know about you, but my brain doesn't fully engage until I've downed at least one cup of beanjuice."

Her mouth curved. "We have one thing in common at least." She glanced longingly at the carafe on the table as well as the two plates brimming with eggs, bacon, and toast. "Unfortunately, I need to avoid caffeine. I'll have some of that orange juice though."

"Got you a glass of milk, too. Two glasses. One whole. One skim. Wasn't sure."

"I have to confess, I'm starving."

"Not surprised, given you haven't had much beyond broth and water since before yesterday." He pulled out her chair, waited until she was seated, then took a place across from her. "I ordered pancakes and oatmeal, too. I wasn't sure what you'd feel like or for that matter *what* you like. Take your pick."

"That's sweet. Thank you." She blew out a breath, shook her head. "It's also a reminder of how little we know each other and yet—"

"I declared us involved." A verbal, public commitment. Spoken from the heart with little to no deep thought.

"What does that mean exactly?" Her brow crinkled in confusion, and though her tone was calm, her vibe was intense. "I don't mean to push," she said, "but I need some sort of guidelines. I need to know how to plan. How to . . . act. What to say when someone asks about us— and you know they will."

Luke nodded toward his cell and said, "It's already started," then poured their coffee. "I checked my messages late last night after you'd fallen asleep. So far I've heard from Gram, Dev, Rocky, Nash, and Adam. All wanting to know what's up with the rumor. Either Sam spilled the beans or someone from the Cupcake Lovers overheard our conversation."

"Or maybe the CLs pushed Sam to spill," Rae said. "You did say that they were watching you two argue through the window."

"Either way, the word's out." Luke watched as Rae chose the skim milk and committed that to memory just as he'd noted her preference for sleeping on the left side of the bed. "I don't know about long term, Rae," he said honestly. "I can't think that far ahead. I can't predict. . . ."

"Either we're compatible or we're not. Something like that?" she asked while forking a generous helping of scrambled eggs.

"Something like." *She likes eggs,* he thought, *and wheat toast over white—no butter.* "I don't want you to see other men. Not the way I feel right now. Don't ask me to explain. I can't. Yet."

She eyed him over the brim of her glass.

"I wouldn't ask you to be faithful if I wasn't willing to do the same." The words sounded foreign to his ears and incited a short burst of panic. As Sam had pointed out, Luke had never been in a monogamous relationship for more than three days. What if he slipped? What if the Kelly twins tempted him with a ménage or what if he grew bored with Rae after a short couple of weeks?

"I'd feel flattered if you didn't look so miserable," Rae said with a soft smile.

"Unchartered territory, is all."

"Same here. What I mean," she elaborated after a sip, "is that I've never been in a serious relationship, a committed relationship. Especially of a romantic nature."

"Never?"

She shook her head then reached for the pancakes.

Hearty appetite, Luke noted then scrunched his brow. "Not to be shallow," he said plainly, "but you're rich, beautiful, and smart. How is it you haven't had men dogging after you since you were, I don't know, fourteen?"

"Plenty of dogs," Rae said, looking uncomfortable now.

"But no suitable contenders? No pledges of love? No marriage proposals?"

"None that I took seriously."

He weighed her words, starting to feel uncomfortable himself. "Are you saying you haven't met a man who met your standards?"

"I'm saying I haven't met a man who loved me for me." She set aside her fork, the pancakes untouched. "Can we get back to us, please?"

He felt a little blindsided. "Sure." He chugged his coffee and poured more. This was a three-cup morning, at least. "Except . . . hell. I feel awkward asking now, because—"

"You don't love me."

"I don't *know* you."

"Ask your question, Luke."

He dragged his hands though his hair, centered his thoughts then met her gaze. "I want to see you, Rae. Exclusively. I want to date you. I want to sleep with you. I want to learn what makes you tick, what makes you smile. I want to be with you the next time you visit a doctor. I want to talk about our baby's future and explore the possibility of a future for us. You can't deny there's a connection."

"What if the connection is the baby? Period?"

Luke didn't answer. It was possible. Sure. But he'd wager not something Rae wanted to hear. He reached across the table and gently grasped her hand. "Will you be my girl, Rae?" The question was so freaking old-fashioned, he half expected her to laugh.

Instead, she brushed her thumb over the back of his hand. "One stipulation."

The first time he'd ever offered a woman an exclusive commitment and she had a *stipulation*? "Shoot."

"If it's not working, if we're not compatible, we call it off. Before we start resenting one another, before it gets ugly. If nothing else, I want us to be friends for the sake of our daughter."

"Or son."

"I'm serious, Luke. If even one of us is unhappy in this exclusive relationship . . . It only takes one to end it."

"Not sure I like the sound of that."

"It's the only thing I feel comfortable with."

Huh. He should've been dancing on air. She'd just offered him the perfect out. It bugged the hell out of him. He squeezed her hand. "Okay."

"Okay." She smiled a little even though he sensed the tension in her body. "You're not going to ask me to wear your class ring, are you?" she teased in light of his adolescent proposal. "Proof to the men of Sugar Creek that I'm off-limits?"

"Lucky for you, I lost that ring years ago. But no worries," he teased back. "I'll make it clear you're my girl."

She narrowed her beautiful albeit suspicious eyes. "Should I be worried?"

Luke's brain buzzed with everything he'd learned about Rae so far, which wasn't much, but enough to know she hadn't been treated well by the men in her life, that she had a shitty relationship with her family, few friends, and few, if any, brushes with genuine affection. The mother of his child deserved better. Any woman deserved better. "Let's just say you've been warned."

NINETEEN

"In addition to toddler and preschool programs, I'm toying with the idea of enrichment programs for ages five through ten," Rae said. "Supplemental educational opportunities that complement the elementary school's core curriculum. Most classrooms are overcrowded these days and some children need extra help. I could—"

"You could what?"

Rae looked away from the locked doors of Sugar Tots to the man sitting next to her. On their way to J. T. Monroe's Department Store, Luke had pulled into the small parking lot of Sugar Tots. He'd invited her to share her plans for reopening the day care center. He'd been the first to ask and apparently she was dying to voice her aspirations because, she realized now, she'd been rambling nonstop for several minutes. "I could help." A flush crept up her neck to her cheeks. "I don't mean to sound arrogant, but I have a gift with children and head for education. Special techniques to make learning fun. I have all these ideas—"

"What kind of ideas?"

Rae fussed with her seat belt, angled away the heating

vent, and checked her watch. They'd been idling in Luke's car, in front of Sugar Tots for twenty minutes. It felt like a blip and a lifetime rolled into one.

"Why are you so shy about sharing your vision?" Luke asked.

"I'm not shy. I could talk about my vision for Sugar Tots for hours."

"So?"

"I've been rambling. You're probably bored to tears and too polite to say."

"If I was bored I wouldn't prod you to share more." He cocked his head. "How did you do it?"

"Do what?"

"Bottle up all that passion and knowledge when you were working here under Gretchen?"

Rae shrugged. "It leaked out sometimes, but she didn't want to hear it. She was set in her ways."

"And not half as committed to the children of this town as you are. She threw in the towel and you're not only picking up the pieces, but raising the bar." He narrowed his eyes. "How is it you're not already established as a teacher somewhere else?"

"Jobs are hard to come by."

"Surely not for someone as smart and influential—"

"You mean rich. I wasn't rich before. Not personally."

"But now you are."

"The thing about being smart and influential is that there's always someone smarter and more influential than you. And if that person wants to derail your life well then you're sort of screwed." Rae cursed the words as soon as they left her mouth. What was wrong with her? She'd never been so forthright. When she was younger, yes, but not for a long time. Not after learning how people twisted her words. Not after enduring disappointment, humiliation, and betrayal on multiple counts.

"Who wants to derail your life, Rae?"

"No one. Forget I said anything."

"Your mom? Geoffrey?"

Rae blinked.

"I'd have to be an idiot not to notice the tension between you and those two when I was at your house—"

"Their house."

"Factor in your unwillingness to raise your child anywhere near them? I'm sensing bad blood."

"We don't get along, that's for sure. Can we go now?" She wasn't ready for this conversation. She didn't want to think about her mom or Geoffrey, let alone talk about the misery they'd inflicted. But even as she pushed away the memories, anger and panic tripped her pulse.

Luke shifted into reverse. "Whatever it is—"

"It isn't anything." Rae massaged her aching chest. Could a person's heart burst through their rib cage?

Luke cast her an enigmatic glance then focused on the road. "Okay."

She nodded, swallowed. Told herself to chill. Her mother had dashed any hope of ever forming a genuine, caring bond. She'd chosen that bastard Geoffrey over her only daughter, and Geoffrey. . . . Even though Rae hadn't divulged details regarding his betrayal, the man had retaliated against Rae nonetheless. Retaliated and refreshed his threat. In turn, Rae had chosen a new life. This life. If only they'd leave her alone. She glanced at her cell, noting another text from the woman who'd given her life and little else.

JUST LET ME KNOW U R OK

As if Olivia really cared. What she cared about was the money Rae had promised her—an emergency fund should she ever find herself unwed for longer than two years. Unwed and broke. Like that would ever happen. If Geoffrey ever cut Olivia loose, she'd just latch onto another tycoon. Money and men—her drug of choice. Along with attention. Still . . . the aging pseudocelebrity was probably just logical enough to want a back-up plan— namely access to her daughter's inheritance.

Chest tight, Rae thumbed a response.

DON'T WORRY. WON'T CUT U OFF.

Not financially. But *emotionally* . . .

Severing that tie was crucial, otherwise Rae would forever mourn their wretched relationship.

She stared at the screen, dreading a reply. None came. Apparently she'd calmed Olivia's concern and that was that. For now. Disgusted, Rae tossed her cell in her purse.

"Everything okay?" Luke asked.

Rae forced a smile. "It will be." She scrambled to divert the conversation.

Luke beat her to it. "Join me tonight," he said as he pulled into a private side lot of J.T.'s.

"For what?"

"Dinner," he said as he pocketed his keys. "Rocky's house, formerly Daisy's house. Our traditional weekly dinner. Although Chloe will be cooking. New tradition."

Thud. Thud. "Thank you, but no."

"Why not?"

"It's a family dinner."

"Family and friends. Different guests every week, depending on who can make it. Monica and Leo will be there, if it makes you feel any better."

It didn't. A family and friends—close friends—dinner with the Monroes? It was too much, too soon. Too intimate.

"Daisy will be there, too," Luke added. "Chloe. Rocky. Aside from my sister you haven't met up with any of the Cupcake Lovers since you returned, right?"

"Just Sam."

"Right. Anyway it might make things easier, more

comfortable, if you reconnected on a personal level with some of the members instead of stepping in cold at Thursday's meeting."

It made sense, but she still wasn't convinced. "Speaking of Sam, will he be there?"

"I'm not sure. Even if he is . . ." Luke shrugged. "Maybe it would help to have the family as a buffer. Plus, I've never brought a girl to Sunday dinner, Rae. If I bring you along, Sam will know I'm serious. About you. Us. Everyone will know."

"Are you sure you're ready for that?"

"Hell, no."

She laughed at that. At his casual honesty. For some reason it made her feel better to know Luke was still wary of their new liaison. Otherwise she'd question the wisdom of this whirlwind commitment even more than she already did. "Okay. I'll come. In for a penny, in for a pound." As nervous as she was about this family dinner, Luke had made some good points.

His mouth twitched. "You sure?"

"Hell, no."

He smiled full out then cupped the back of her neck and pulled her in for a kiss.

It was slow and deep and sweet, causing Rae's body to hum with memories of their lovemaking a few hours before. Aside from the sheer physical pleasure, Luke had intensified the moment by admitting that he hadn't been with another woman since their tumble in Bel Air.

"*Since you.*"

Since December.

She didn't want to read into that, but it weighed on her mind.

He'd flown all the way across the country on Christmas Eve to confront her and he'd come home affected. The fact that he'd been celibate since spoke volumes.

That he'd asked her to be his girl, that he'd suggested an exclusive relationship, had intimated even more.

Rae had no illusions. This wouldn't be easy. But maybe, just maybe, she and Luke were meant to be. Maybe the happily ever after she'd always dreamed of—a kind and caring husband, children of her own, and a down-to-earth existence—was within her grasp.

Framing Luke's handsome face, Rae deepened the kiss while mentally stripping away one layer of her massively shielded heart.

Yes, she was opening herself up for hurt, but she was a warrior and her dream was worth fighting for.

Luke was buzzed.

On a kiss.

He practically floated through the side entrance of J.T.'s.

Yeah, boy, *this* was bad.

He'd told himself he was going to take this thing with Rae slow, that he was acting in a logical and responsible way. Considering he didn't want her seeing any other guy, he owed her an exclusive. Considering he wanted to take an active role in his child's life, it made sense to explore their physical attraction. If they were compatible, if it evolved into a matter of the heart, then he'd cross that bridge when he came to it.

He kept reminding himself of the complications—her fortune, her secrets, her inability to trust, and her penchant to run from her problems. That damned stipulation of hers ate at him.

"If even one of us is unhappy in this exclusive relationship . . . It only takes one to end it."

What about talking through the problem, sorting things out? If every couple split up just because one or the other had an issue, marriage would be obsolete. His parents had

had their fair share of problems over the years, his grand-parents, too, both sets. When the going got tough they toughed it out, worked it out. Granted, Luke had been in and out of a hundred relationships, but every one of those relationships had been casual. No strings attached. No expectations. Great sex and good times. Companionship. *Period.*

Now that he'd committed to Rae, Luke was inspired to give it his best shot and beyond. It was in his blood. As was wanting what was best for his child. If that meant making some sacrifices or going the extra mile then, dammit, he'd do whatever it took.

He knew just where to start.

"You know your way around the store," he said to Rae as they neared the old-fashioned candy counter. "Mind if I swing off for a few minutes? I need a word with Dev."

His big brother had been the acting COO of the family department store ever since their dad had "retired" to Florida. As a workaholic, Dev used to practically live here. Things were different now that Chloe was in his life, but Luke knew Dev was here this morning because of the voice mail Dev had left on Luke's cell the night before.

"You're not going to tell him about the . . . you know," Rae whispered. "Are you?"

"That's not my intention, no. This is about something else. Business," Luke clarified to ease her mind. "Although we can't keep *you know* secret forever."

"Just until I'm further along."

Luke remembered what she'd said about the potential for miscarrying in the first trimester and made a mental note to bone up on pregnancy. He wanted to know what Rae was experiencing and what to expect. He wondered if they had audiobooks on the subject at the library. He'd just tell Monica or the other librarians that he was curious because of Chloe. Nothing suspicious about expressing interest in what his brother and future sister-in-law were going through, right?

He smoothed Rae's shaggy bangs from her eyes and smiled. "Be warned. I'm going to spoil *you know* rotten."

"Genuine affection would be preferable over toys," Rae said in an odd tone.

As if he wouldn't naturally love his own child? How the hell had her concept on family gotten so mangled? Chest tight, Luke pulled Rae into his arms, right in the middle of the aisle, in between the assorted "moose" souvenirs and the table stacked high with assorted Valentine's chocolates. Well aware that he'd attracted the attention of a couple of patrons plus scattered employees, all of whom he knew, Luke lowered his head and spoke soft and close to Rae's ear. "No one's going to love this baby more than me. Except maybe you."

Feeling the tension in her body, he met her gaze, troubled by the tears shimmering in her eyes.

"The store's only open until noon," she said as if Luke wasn't well aware. "I should get my shopping done. And your brother, he'll be wanting to leave soon so you should go. I'll be around," she said, flailing her hand left then right. "Somewhere. Find me when you're done."

He watched her disappear into the women's section. "Well, hell." Instead of lingering and wondering what he'd said wrong, Luke hightailed it upstairs. His brother worked out of the same office as every other senior Monroe who'd once been at the helm of J. T. Monroe's Department Store—family owned and operated for six generations.

With every step, Luke thought about all Dev had accomplished in his thirty-five years. In addition to running the department store, the man had multiple business interests. Most recently he'd established his own investment firm, specializing in strategic financial planning. Which sort of put him in to the "making people's dreams come true" biz. Hard to top that.

Their sister Rocky, the youngest of the Monroe siblings, had purchased a bed-and-breakfast in her early twenties, and though it had been a money pit, she'd run it on her own until it had burned to the ground. Now she'd launched a budding interior-decorating boutique.

Luke hit the second floor thinking about how his siblings and most all of his adult cousins owned and operated their own businesses. Luke was the face and heart of the Sugar Shack, but he wasn't the brains. It hadn't bothered him before, now it did.

"Why is it that no one knocks anymore?" Dev asked as Luke slipped inside the office that brimmed with gleaming wood and childhood memories.

Luke shrugged. "Door wasn't closed all the way."

"A courtesy knock would be nice."

"I'll remember that next time."

"No you won't."

"Probably not." Luke flopped into the chair across from Dev's desk. "What would it cost to buy you out?"

Dev turned away from his computer, brow raised. "Come again."

"I want sole ownership of the Shack."

"Why?"

"Don't you have your fingers in enough pies?" Luke asked.

"Are you pissed at me because I gave you the riot act regarding last month's budget?"

"No, I'm pissed at myself for exceeding last month's budget. I need to pay better attention to the financial aspect. Need to exercise better judgment. I've spent too many years focused on the hospitality angle when I should've have been crunching numbers. Or at least learning to crunch numbers."

Dev grunted. "You hate numbers."

"I'm done with taking the easy way out, Dev."

"Who are you and what have you done with my brother?"

"I know I scoffed when you first offered to teach me the accounting aspect of the Shack, but I'd like to take you up on that," Luke said. "Maybe I can hire you as an outside accountant until I've got a handle on everything. You've been promising Chloe you'd lighten your workload. Here's an opportunity. Sell me your half of the Sugar Shack."

Dev leaned back in the same high-back chair once occupied by their dad, and before him, Daisy's husband—Grandpa Jessup. All dominant forces, all respected, all successful.

Luke had never aspired to any of that. He just wanted to make a decent living doing what he liked. Tending bar, jawing with customers, hanging with friends, chasing babes. In the past forty-eight hours his priorities had shifted significantly.

"What's going on with you?" Dev asked point-blank. "You haven't been yourself since Christmas. You know, the Christmas you almost missed with your family because you flew off to California to help some past girlfriend out of a jam. Or so you said. That's where Rae flew in from, right? L.A.? Rae who we once knew as Rachel. The woman who worked at the Shack for, what, a week before she skipped town for wherever. I'm thinking California."

If Luke didn't know better, he'd think Jayce had confided in Dev regarding the investigation into Rachel Lacey's whereabouts. They were lifelong best friends after all. Except Jayce was a noble sort who was deadly serious about things like client confidentiality. Nope. Dev was fishing.

"I assume, because she's only been back for a couple of days and you're an item now," Dev plowed on, "there was something between you before. Sam learned about it and that's why you two have been at odds these past few months. Am I close?"

"Pretty close." Why lie?

"Is she pregnant?"

Luke didn't flinch. Not outwardly anyway. "Why would you ask that?"

"Why else would you commit to a girl you hardly know? Alienating your own cousin in the process?"

"I didn't screw Sam over. Not intentionally. They were never a couple in the first place. Rae had no interest in Sam. Not romantically. Not ever. Why doesn't anyone get that?" Luke pushed out of his chair and turned his back on his brother. "Jesus. I'm trying to do the right thing here and I'm on everyone's shit list."

"Not everyone." Dev moved past him, to the sidebar installed by their grandfather more than fifty years ago. "Drink?"

Luke eyed the bottle of scotch then his watch. Eleven thirty. "What the hell."

Dev poured. "How far along is she?"

"About seven weeks."

"Not far."

"Rae asked me not to tell anyone. Not yet. She said the first trimester is iffy." Luke took one of the glasses from his brother. "I need you to keep this to yourself, Dev."

"Understood."

They both drank then Dev said, "At the risk of pissing you off, let me ask you the same question you asked me when I faced this situation all those years ago with Janna. Are you sure the baby's yours?"

Janna. Dev's high school obsession. A girl who'd played loose with his heart and slept around. A girl who'd run to him when her parents tossed her out because she was pregnant. The girl he'd married, accepting the child as his own even though there was a chance it wasn't. A child he'd mourned when his wife, now ex-wife, had miscarried five months into the pregnancy. If anyone could commiserate with Luke, it was his big brother.

"Timing's right and I wasn't protected. Don't ask." Luke slammed back the rest of his shot. "Rae said the baby's mine and I believe her."

"You're taking the word of a woman who pretended to be someone else, who lived a lie for an entire year?"

"Yeah." Luke jammed a hand through his hair. "Listen, Dev. There's a lot I don't know about Rae. What I sense is that she's a good person. Even though she led a privileged life, I think it was a shitty one. I met her mom and her stepfather. If they're any indication . . ." He shook his head. He hadn't like Geoffrey Stein. He had a feeling he'd like him even less when he learned the source of tension between that arrogant bastard and Rae. Luke would bet money Stein was the one angling to derail her life. But why? "She's as good as alone in the world. I know she can take care of herself, but there's the baby to think of, too."

"This is a pattern with you, you know," Dev said. "You rescue desperate women like Jayce rescues unfortunate animals."

"This is different," Luke said.

"Yes and no."

"I invited Rae to dinner tonight."

"Should be interesting."

Luke set aside his glass. "I'd appreciate it if you'd make her feel welcome."

"When have I not been welcoming?"

"Oh, let's see. The first time Gram invited Vince to Sunday dinner?" There'd been a huge blow out between Daisy and Dev because Dev had been prickly and wary of the two seniors hooking up. "You're kind of intimidating when you're in protector mode. Let me assure you Rae's not looking to take advantage of me. She's smart. She's rich. She could live anywhere. Work anywhere. She came back to Sugar Creek with good intentions. To help the Cupcake Lovers. To reestablish Sugar Tots. And to offer me a chance to know my kid."

Dev raised his palms in surrender. "I promise to be nice."

"And to keep our secret?"

"Your secret's safe."

Luke blew out a breath, his shoulders feeling lighter by the second. Dev's support meant a lot. "The Shack?"

"I'll have the papers drawn up. We'll work it out. You'll be sole owner by the end of the month, maybe sooner."

"Great. Good." Luke offered his hand. "Thanks, Dev."

His brother clasped his palm, "Sure," then raised a brow. "Anything else?"

Bothered by a wisp of doubt, Luke shrugged. "About the numbers. The bookkeeping. It might take me awhile."

"You'll get it." Dev squeezed his shoulder. "I'll make sure of it."

TWENTY

It had taken Rae a while to get a hold on her mini melt-down. Deep down, she knew Luke meant well when he'd assured her he would love their baby. It was the *"more than me. Except maybe you"* that had thrown her into a panic.

She didn't doubt Luke would love his child. He was all about family. Except for that brief period in Bel Air when he'd been a total jerk, he was one of the kindest people Rae had ever known. Salt of the earth. What spooked her was the uncertainty of their relationship. Once she contacted that New York publisher, once she flaunted her socialite status and made her whereabouts known, the paparazzi would start trickling into Sugar Creek. Even if it was only one rabid cameraman, it wouldn't be pretty.

The question beyond *Could Luke handle the invasion of privacy for a while?* would be *Could he handle the gossip-hungry media for life?* Rae could lay low, absolutely. But there would always be a reporter looking for that one sensational story—*Had her mother really had a secret affair with that uber famous and uber married actor?* And a photographer always hoping for that one compromising shot. Even royalty had been caught with their pants down or tops off. Those super-telescopic lenses could capture the most intimate or careless moments. What if they snapped a shot of Rae breast-feeding? Or Luke going down on her? Of the two of them making love?

What if Luke couldn't handle the constant threat? What if he considered it detrimental to their child? Would he cut himself off from Rae and fight for sole custody? Growing up surrounded by Hollywood drama, she could name dozens of domestic disasters. Bitter divorces. Custody wars.

Those were the fears that stormed through her mind in what should have been a sweet moment—Luke pledging his love and support to their child.

"I can turn back."

Luke's soft, deep voice jolted Rae out of her obsessive mania. "What?"

"The closer I get to Gram's, strike that, Rocky's house, the more panicked you look. I was wrong to push." He plucked his cell from his jacket. "I'll cancel."

Rae stayed his hand. The last thing she wanted was to be perceived as a coward. A hindrance. She'd always been a hindrance to Olivia. "No," she said. "Let's do this." She refrained from elaborating. Luke had stated why he thought it was advantageous for her to mingle with key Cupcake Lovers before the official Thursday meeting and she agreed.

"Are you sure?"

"Positive."

Next thing she knew, Luke was hanging in the living room with his grandma and great-aunt and the attending male contingent, and Rae was standing in a state-of-the-art kitchen surrounded with women she'd considered "friends" throughout her "lost year." Considering she'd lied about who she was, it should have been awkward. It wasn't. It was as if she'd never left.

She didn't trust it.

Instead of greeting her with questions—*Why did you pretend to be someone else? Were you and Luke attracted to each other before or did he fall head over heels for your new, polished look? What's a celebrity heiress like you doing in a low-profile town like Sugar Creek?*— they'd drawn her into conversations about sending Valentine's cupcakes to lonely heart soldiers and a joint club venture to bake and decorate Rocky and Jayce's wedding cake.

"I know I didn't send you an official invitation," Rocky said as Rae helped her to prepare the salad. "But I would love it if you'd attend my wedding. I assume Luke will bring you as his guest, but I wanted you to know I'm hoping you'll come."

Rae swallowed, feeling humbled and flustered. "I wouldn't miss it. Saturday, right?"

Rocky nodded. "Jayce suggested Valentine's Day. But how sappy is that, right?"

"Jayce said that was *your* idea," Chloe teased as she tended to several pots on the stove.

"To be honest," Rocky said as she moved toward the fridge, "I can't remember who brought it up first, but we decided against it. Valentine's Day is for all lovers. We want our day to be special."

Monica snorted. "Like *that* isn't sappy."

Rocky glanced over her shoulder at Rae. "Ignore her. I am. I'm also having a beer. Want one? Or maybe a glass of wine?" She nodded toward the other women. "These two are teetotalers these days."

"I'm good. Thanks." Rae hoped her cheeks didn't look as flushed as they felt. She didn't realize she'd feel this uncomfortable keeping her pregnancy secret, most especially from these women. She wasn't lying outright, but she wasn't being forthright either. When they did find out, would they feel betrayed? Again? Would they judge her, thinking she'd used the baby to rope the biggest hound in Sugar Creek? She shouldn't care, but she did.

"I've found that if I already have a drink in hand," Rocky said, "it's easier to avoid partaking in Daisy's Cocktail of the Week. I swear she picks the most disgusting recipes."

"Far be it from Daisy to be unadventurous," Chloe said with a smile.

"Even Luke gagged on last week's creation," Rocky said.

"I missed that one," Monica said as she sliced lemons for the iced tea. "Most disgusting ingredient?"

"It wasn't the taste so much as the texture. Something called a Cement Mixer. Bailey's Irish Cream and lime juice," Rocky said. "The combination made the Bailey's curdle in your mouth."

"*Eww,*" Monica said.

Chloe shuddered.

"Hence my beer," Rocky said.

"I can't take it," Rae said.

"Just say you're still recovering from that bout of food poisoning," Chloe said. "That'll get you a free pass from Daisy."

"I'm not talking about the cocktail," Rae said. "I'm talking about you guys. You're acting as if I never left. As if I'm Rachel. But I'm not. I mean we have the same personality pretty much, but . . . Don't you want to know why I did it? Why I lived under an assumed identity for a year?"

"Of course we want to know," Monica blurted.

Chloe elbowed her best friend. "We figured you'd tell us when you were ready."

"Or not," Rocky said. "Maybe it's none of our business. What we know is that you came back to Sugar Creek to help the club and to revive Sugar Tots for the children and parents of this community."

"We know you inherited a fortune on your birthday," Chloe said. "Most twenty-five-year-olds would've gone on a trip around the world."

"Or opted to spend the winter in Tahiti or some other tropical isle," Monica said.

"Instead you're here," Rocky said. "In this frozen, freaking cold tundra."

"We're giving you the benefit of the doubt because you're here for selfless reasons," Chloe said.

"Not entirely selfless." Rae clasped her hands so as not to wring them. "Some of my happiest days were the days I spent working with the children at Sugar Tots, the nights I spent baking cupcakes with the Cupcake Lovers. I may have kept to myself, but I absorbed every word, every action. I got a dose of how it should be between friends and family. Of good people with the best of intentions. Of the simple life. I can't have that life in L.A. and certainly not within my mother's circle—the only circle I know aside from this one."

Rae blew out a breath and went out on an emotional limb. "I hid out in Sugar Creek to escape certain pressures having to do with my upcoming inheritance. I didn't want to deal with my mom or my influential stepfather and their intrusive advice. I wanted to prove that I could make it on my own—with or without fame or fortune. In the process I learned a lot about myself. You know that saying, *home is where the heart is*?"

"Your heart's here," Chloe said.

"With Luke," Monica ventured.

"Luke's certainly a draw," Rae said. "I developed a crush the first time I laid eyes on him. It snowballed and there was this kiss and then . . ." She glanced away. "There's this connection. I can't explain, but we're going for it and . . . we'll see."

The women traded a look then focused back on Rae. "Just remember," Rocky said. "Anything, anyone, worth having is worth the fight."

"How to say this," Chloe ventured. "Luke has a lot of female admirers."

"He's notorious for playing the field," Monica said.

"A natural born charmer," Rocky said.

"A huge flirt," Chloe said. "Half the time I don't even think he means anything by it."

"But if you're the jealous sort," Monica said.

"Or the shy sort." Rocky picked the label on her bottle. "Not that I'm trying to scare you off, Rae, but Luke loves people. Loves to socialize. I'm not sure he'll ever be a homebody."

Monica nodded. "If you're looking for a homebody—"

"I'd be better off with Sam?" Rae stared back at the women, sensing they had her best interest at heart and probably Luke's as well. Still, she was pretty fed up with being pushed toward the man everyone considered her perfect match. "To be perfectly clear," she said in a calm but firm voice. "I don't love Sam."

"Do you love Luke?" Monica winced when Chloe gave her another jab. "What? Like I'm the only one who wants to know?"

"Yes. Yes, I do," Rae said. She glanced toward the closed kitchen door, envisioned Luke enduring one of Daisy's nasty cocktails just because she was his grandma, his senior, and it was the nice thing to do. "I think I've always loved him, which probably sounds crazy."

"Not so crazy," Rocky said.

"I haven't told him," Rae said, feeling a little panicked now. She didn't want to scare Luke off. She was already scaring herself. Everything was moving so fast and she couldn't shake the feeling that it was all too good to be true.

"Well, he should definitely hear from you first," Chloe said with a smile.

"Don't worry, hon. One thing about this family—blood and associated," Rocky said with a nod toward Chloe and Monica. "We know how to keep a secret."

"Interesting dinner."

"I'll say."

Jayce placed a pile of dirty plates on the counter.

Rocky started rinsing while he dropped a soap disk in the dishwasher.

Brewster trotted in behind them and sniffed the floor for crumbs.

"The canine vacuum," Rocky said.

"I've got to break him of that," Jayce said.

"You say that every night."

After a couple of licks, Brewster curled up on a braided rug and Rocky and Jayce settled into their routine. Since Chloe did the majority of cooking on Sundays, Rocky had insisted she handle the cleanup after everyone left. Jayce had insisted on helping, making it a couple thing, which made it kind of nice. They had some of their best discussions while putting their dining room and kitchen back to rights.

"I think Rae might be pregnant," Rocky blurted.

"What? Why?"

"There were signs."

"What signs?"

Rocky passed Jayce the first rinsed of several food-caked dishes. "For one, she's not drinking alcohol. She declined my offer when she stopped over the other night, then again earlier in the kitchen. At dinner, Dev poured wine for everyone at the table except for Chloe and Monica. Only Rae never touched hers. At one point, Luke discreetly swapped his empty glass for her full one."

"Maybe she doesn't drink."

"I've seen her drink. Not a lot, but typically, when offered, she at least sips at wine or beer. Another thing," Rocky said. "Did you notice how often she excused herself to go to the bathroom? Chloe mentioned that as one of her first symptoms. Having to pee a lot more."

"Crossing into the too-much-information zone, Dash."

"Did you notice how attentive Luke was?"

"He's always affectionate with women."

"In a playful way. This was different. The way he kept touching her and holding her hand. The way he looked at her. It was almost . . . protective." She passed Jayce another plate then two cups. "You're a PI. Half of your job is observing. How could you not notice?"

"I noticed."

"Lastly—"

"Why would a dog like Luke commit to an exclusive relationship with a woman he barely knows?"

She raised a brow. "What are you, a mind reader?"

"A PI. I deduced your train of thought."

She grinned. "Smart-ass."

Jayce moved in behind her, wrapping his arms around her middle. "I think you're jumping to conclusions, babe. Rae's a knockout. Her face, her body."

"Thanks for pointing that out."

He spun her around and tugged on her braid. "Can't compare to you in my book. But you have to admit, physically, she's Luke's type. Plus she's sweet and motivated. Hard not to get swept up in her enthusiasm about kids and education."

"Her plans for Sugar Tots are pretty impressive," Rocky said.

"Considering her background and the fact that she's worth a fortune, you also have to admit she's down-to-earth."

"Amazingly down-to-earth."

"Maybe Luke's serious about Rae because he's seriously in love."

"Luke's been in love a million times. Ask him. He'll tell you."

"Maybe this is the real thing."

"Or maybe he screwed up and got her pregnant and now he's trying to do the right thing."

"I guess we'll find out. That's not something you can hide forever."

"True." Just then Rocky's cell rang. She glanced over to where she'd left it on the counter. "It's Mom."

"Calling to talk about the wedding, no doubt." Jayce kissed her forehead. "Take it. I'll finish loading the dishwasher."

Rocky slid out of Jayce's arms, giddy at the thought of chatting with her mom about girly bridal stuff. Totally out of character given Rocky had always been a bit of a tomboy, but she'd been in love with Jayce since she was a kid. And considering their rough road, this wedding was more than a dream come true. It was a miracle. "Hey, Mom. What's up?"

"Is Jayce with you?"

Rocky scrunched her brow. "Standing right next to me. Why?"

"I have some troubling news sweetie. It's about your daddy."

TWENTY-ONE

Luke hadn't realized how uptight he'd been about subjecting Rae to the Sunday family dinner until he was driving her back to the Pine and Periwinkle. "I'm almost afraid to ask," he said. "But did you enjoy yourself?"

"I did. Your family's lovely, Luke. I thought so before and now . . ." She rubbed her chest. "I don't remember the last time I felt that happy. Great food, great company. Everyone went out of their way to make me feel welcome. Even Dev, who can be pretty intimidating."

"Yeah, well . . ."

"Jayce is on the quiet side, but he's sweet."

Luke grunted. "Not sure he'd appreciate that description."

"I've always been crazy about Daisy. She's a hoot."

"That's one way of describing her."

"Vince is so reserved in comparison. Yet they seem like the perfect couple. Very happy."

"It's a mystery. Vince is the exact opposite of my Grandpa Jessup, who I thought Daisy adored, but maybe not."

"My mom adored all four of her husbands and they

were all very different—personalitywise anyway. They were all as rich as God."

"So she married for money."

"Absolutely."

"That's one thing you'll never have to do," Luke said. "You're set for life."

"I wouldn't marry for money even if I was dirt poor."

Luke winced at her sharp tone. "I didn't mean it like that."

"Sorry. It's just . . ."

She angled then and, even though the moonlight was muted by snow clouds, Luke got a pretty clear view of her troubled expression. "It's just what?"

"When you first learned that I was an heiress, when you saw me over Christmas at Olivia and Geoffrey's mansion, you assumed the worst. That I was a spoiled, conniving rich bitch."

"I'll cop to that and I apologize. I jumped to conclusions."

"We haven't talked about it, but is my bank account an issue with you?"

"I haven't given that a lot of thought." Or rather he tried not to think about it.

"Well, you should because, unless I give all or most of it away, *I'm* almost as rich as God."

"That rich, *huh*?"

"Do you know how many relationships have fallen apart because the man resents the fact the woman makes more money than him?'

"You plan on flaunting your fortune in my face on a daily or weekly basis?

"Of course not."

"I didn't think so." Driving into a snow flurry now, he flicked on the windshield wipers. "Anything else?"

"The media. Reporters. Photographers. I'm planning

to use my association with Olivia—the Hollywood
connection—along with my heiress status to create buzz
around the Cupcake Lovers and their cause."

"As a way of pushing the book deal forward. I know."

"They can be a little intrusive," she said. "The media,
that is."

"Are you preparing me for an invasion of paparazzi?"

"I'm not sure what to expect. Precisely. But it's possible. I'm not keen on unwanted attention, but I can handle it. Can you?"

Was she testing him? Luke flexed his fingers on the
wheel. "I guess we'll find out."

"It's just . . . I'm thinking about the way you reacted
when that college kid grabbed me. Punching a member of
the paparazzi wouldn't exactly advance my cause for the
Cupcake Lovers."

"If you think I'm going to stand by while someone,
anyone, disrespects or God forbid threatens you, forget it."

She surprised him with a smile. "Just promise me
you'll exercise some restraint."

"I promise I'll try."

Her smile widened and Luke's heart did a funny jerk.
She was looking at him with something akin to hero wor-
ship. It made him feel good and wary at the same time.
He kicked up the wipers as the snowfall intensified. Adjusted the defroster then blurted his mind. "Why are you
attracted to me, Rae?" He'd never asked that question of
any other woman. He'd never wondered. But this was Rae.
Reagan Deveraux. Rich. Smart.

"There's a shallow answer and a deep answer," she
said. "Which do you want?"

Luke flexed his hands on the wheel as he pulled into
the parking lot of the inn. "Both."

Rae shifted in her seat. "Shallow answer: You're hot.

Your body. Your face. Although I'm sure you've heard that a thousand times."

"First time I've heard it from you." First time he'd taken the compliment to heart. "What's the deep answer?"

"You're the kindest man I've ever known."

He was afraid of that. Chest tight, Luke keyed off the ignition. "Now that's troubling."

"Why?"

"Because it means you mostly have been exposed to a lot of dickheads. Excuse my language."

She didn't elaborate or counter. She dodged. "Why are you attracted to me?"

"Shallow answer or deep?"

"Both."

"You're hot. Your face, your body."

"I've heard that before. I don't care. What else?"

He reached over and palmed her cheek. "You move me."

She blinked.

"You touch my heart like no woman I've ever known. As Rachel. As Rae. You inspire me to be a better man."

"I'm not sure that's possible."

"Trust me, it is." Her faith in him stoked his already burning lust. He'd been hot for Rae all night. Most especially from the moment she'd challenged Nash on the importance of a college education. Not that Luke fully agreed with her viewpoint, but it was impossible not to respect her opinion. Every time she got hopped up on kids and education, he got a freaking hard-on.

He cupped the back of her neck and pulled her in for a kiss. His pulse went into overdrive the moment their lips met. She tasted like the lemon cake they'd had for dessert. He'd loved that she'd had two slices. He wasn't sure if it was because she was eating for two or because she enjoyed sweets as much as him. He didn't care. He liked her curves. The feel of her, the look of her. Sexy. Classy. He suckled her tongue, feasted on her lush lips. Slow. Deep. He couldn't remember when he'd been so keen on kissing.

His Android went off and he ignored it. The damn thing started ringing again almost as soon as it had gone to voice mail.

Rae eased away, her eyes glazed, her lips puffy. "Must be important," she rasped.

He wanted to take her—here, now—in the front seat of his car. *Classy, Monroe.* Groaning, Luke glanced at the profile pic of the caller. "It's Jayce." Since Rae had already retreated to her side, he took the damn call. "This better be good."

"Rocky got a call from your mom. Your dad's had a setback. He needs to go in for important testing but he refused because it interferes with our wedding date. I sent Rocky up to pack. The only way to reason with your dad is one-on-one. We're flying down to Florida tomorrow. I told Dev. I'm telling you."

"I'll book a flight."

"That's what Dev said."

Luke disconnected then looked across the moonlit car at Rae. "Something's up with my dad. I need to fly to Florida tomorrow. Dev and Rocky are going, too."

"How bad is it?"

"I don't know. Jayce called it a setback. The thing is my dad was going to postpone a crucial test because it clashed with Rocky's wedding date."

"Sweet, but foolish."

"I swear Dad thinks he's Superman. Who messes with frickin' cancer?"

Rae reached over and grasped his hand. "Is there anything I can do?"

"Come with me."

"Why?"

Luke faltered. He couldn't think of anything beyond not wanting to leave her behind. Which in essence meant he didn't trust her to take care of herself. Instinctively he knew she wouldn't appreciate that stance.

"You need to focus on your dad and mom, Luke. I'd just be in the way. Fly south, be with your family. Meanwhile I'll wage some battles of my own."

"Such as?"

"Tomorrow, I've set up a call with our editor at Highlife Publishing regarding the CL book deal. Later, I have a meeting at the bank regarding ownership of Sugar Tots. Also I thought, well, maybe I should look for a long-term rental. I've only been in this suite for three days and I'm already longing for my own kitchen. Tonight made me realize how much I miss cooking, and especially baking."

Luke had a vivid vision of Rae, barefoot, pregnant, and baking cupcakes in *his* kitchen. A week ago the thought of any woman in that condition going all domestic in his home would have sent Luke running for the hills. He kissed the back of Rae's hand. "I'll walk you to your room.

"You don't have to."

"I want to."

Rae's brain churned like mad during the walk from the icy parking lot to her fourth-floor suite. Today had been close to perfect.

Luke had made sweet love to her, he'd asked her to be his girl, he'd included her in his family's traditional weekly dinner. Her random anxiety attacks aside, she'd started to believe they were a real couple with a real future. Especially when he held her hand or when they kissed. He'd kissed her a lot today. He'd kissed her in front of his family. A sweet brush to her cheek. Still.

She'd practically floated through the latter half of dinner. There'd been thirteen of them in all, fourteen if you counted the furry guy, Brewster. Daisy and Vince, Dev and Chloe, Jayce and Rocky, Monica and Leo, Daisy's sister Rose and her husband Spike, Luke and Rae, and Nash, who didn't seem to care a whit about being the only loner.

Rae had found herself sucked into animated discussions and debates and a bit of town gossip. She'd smiled more in that hour at the lively dining room table than she'd smiled in ages. She'd laughed, too. She couldn't believe Luke had actually asked her if she'd had a good time. Did he think she'd faked it to be polite? At one point she'd pinched herself. Somewhere around when dessert had been served, a split second where she'd felt so comfortable, she felt like one of them. The family she'd always dreamed of. The kind of family featured in Hallmark movies.

Not one dinner *ever* with her own "family" could compare. Conversation hadn't revolved around one person—Olivia. It had involved everyone, including Rae. It was the exact atmosphere she wanted for her child and now, more than ever, she wanted things to work out between her and Luke. Rae wanted it so bad, surely something would spoil it.

That phone call about Luke's dad had reminded her that life has a way of kicking you around. There was never one challenge in a day, but many. Tomorrow Luke would be miles away dealing with a family crisis. He'd have to leave the Shack in someone else's care. He'd probably worry about his staff and patrons and general business the entire time he was away. One thing she admired about Luke was how hard he worked and how much time and care he put into making the Sugar Shack one of Sugar Creek's hot spots.

While Luke was juggling balls and hashing things out with his dad, Rae would be tackling important business matters and pushing herself past deeply ingrained personal issues—like her intense dislike of superficial attention. Tomorrow marked the return to reality. In her mind, she heard the first rip of her and Luke being torn apart. It made her ache all the more to prolong the illusion of this day.

Heart racing, Rae slid her key card into the locking mechanism. *Click.* "I suppose you need to get home to pack."

"I can throw a few things into a duffle tomorrow."

"You'll need to talk to Anna or someone about maintaining the Shack."

"I can call later tonight."

With the door partially cracked opened, Rae turned. "Would you like to come inside?" She yanked him in by his jacket collar before he had a chance to answer. They kissed with the same intensity of the kiss that had launched the fated shag against the wall, peeling off their coats, their scarves, without breaking contact.

Rae came up for air. "I thought about this, you, all day."

"Same here."

"Why are we wearing so many layers?" she asked as they continued to peel away clothing.

"Ten below out there with the windchill factor."

"Hot as hell in here with the horny factor."

Luke smiled at that. "Come here." He swept her off her feet, whisked her across the room, and gently tossed her on the bed.

"I'm going to miss you," she said as he unlaced her boots.

"I'll have to give you something to look forward to for when I get back. A sampling of things to come."

"Like what?"

"Like this." After peeling off her jeans, he flipped her over on her stomach.

She expected an erotic entry from behind, she was primed, but instead she felt the dizzying assault of feather-light fingertips trailing down her bare back. Tickling. Teasing. He skimmed lower, to the small of her back. Circling. Soothing. Then she felt a tug on her thong, felt the fabric sliding over her skin, down her legs, past her ankles.

Naked. She was naked.

Luke was naked, too. Straddling her now, tracing his fingertips over her shoulders, down her arms.

"Want to see you," she said.

"Not yet."

He repeated his initial path down her back, over her butt. Goose bumps prickled every inch of her skin as she shivered with erotic delight. Blissful torture.

Then it got worse.

He shifted down, parted her legs, trailed his fingers over the back of her thighs then—*oh, God*—over her inner thighs. Skimming up and down. So close to the part of her that ached most to be touched. But he didn't touch her there. Not for the next ten minutes. Or maybe it was only ten seconds. She had no concept of time, let alone rational thought. Her vocabulary had trickled down to four words.

Touch me. Take me.

Wait. That was only three words.

Then she felt him flick her nub. Once. Twice.

Rae exploded. She actually screamed into the thick comforter as Luke fingered her to a blinding orgasm.

"Ah, Reagan," he said in a husky voice as he rolled her onto her back and rained kisses over her belly. "That was too easy."

"Easy?" She was supposed to hold out longer? Was he mad? She was still catching her breath when she felt him push off the bed. She knew his mind. "No condom. I want to feel you. The real you."

"I thought you'd be concerned."

"About what?"

"I've been with a lot of women."

"Oh, that." She forced herself up on her elbows and drank her fill of his stark naked body. She ached to explore every plane, every ridge. "Are you clean?" she asked bluntly. She didn't know how else to handle this and she wanted to move the conversation along. Actually, she didn't want to talk at all. Especially not about the other women in his life. She knew they existed, but she didn't want them in their bed.

"I'm clean."

"Come here." She reached out and grabbed Luke's arm, yanked him down on the bed. She pushed him onto his back. "I'll have to give you a sampling of something to look forward to for when you get back."

"Like what?"

"Like this." She kissed her way down his magnificent torso—every plane, every ridge. She teased him with feather-light brushes of her lips and an occasional hot flick of her tongue. She wondered if the ritual was working magic on him the way it was on her. The more she savored and dominated the greater her desire to be taken.

He groaned when she took his hard shaft in her hand, tensed as she stroked, gasped when she took him in her mouth. She didn't have a lot of experience, but that didn't mean she was inexperienced. She knew what to do and by Luke's reactions she knew she was doing it right. The crazier she made him, the greater her excitement.

Then he shifted, and in a heartbeat, he had her on her

back. "Keep that up," he said, "and we'll be done too soon. I need to be inside you, Reagan."

She parted her legs and crooked what she hoped was a teasing smile. "Who's stopping you?"

The tip of his shaft grazed her slick folds as he gazed into her eyes. "I think I need to spend the night."

The man was mesmerizing, but she somehow found her voice. "Have some other things to share, samplings to hold me over until you get back?"

"Got a dozen or so tricks in my repertoire. You?"

"Not so many. But I could make some up."

He arched one brow. "I'm definitely spending the night."

And with that he plunged deep—the first stroke of heaven.

TWENTY-TWO

"Daddy, I'm f-f-freezing!"

Sam's eyes flew open. Not that he saw too much. It wasn't pitch-black in his bedroom, but it was pretty damn dark.

He instantly knew three things. His daughter was standing beside his bed, the sun was on the verge of rising, and, holy hell, it was cold.

"Da-deeee!"

"Hold on, honey." He grabbed his Blackberry from the nightstand. Six fifty a.m. Eleven degrees. Outside anyway. *Inside?* Not that cold, but fricking cold. "Must be a problem with the heater, Mina. Let Daddy check."

"But—"

"Go wake Ben. We'll get a head start getting ready for school. I'll make pancakes."

She hugged her favorite teddy bear tight to her chest and frowned. "Don't wanna go to school."

"Mina—"

"Too cold."

"Okay." Sam had already thrown off the covers. He slept in boxers and a tee. He used to sleep in the buff, but that didn't seem right now. Not when the kids could walk in unannounced at any hour. The privacy talk he'd given them had faded from their memories, since he didn't have the heart to enforce it. He squinted down at his daughter. "Why are you wearing a boa?"

"The feathers keep me warm—like a bird."

"And the sock monkey sock cap?"

"Wool keeps me warm—like a sheep."

"Ah." He plucked her off the floor—teddy bear and all—and onto his lap. "How about I hug you warm—like a daddy." He squeezed his daughter tight, his heart bouncing when she giggled.

"Can I sleep with you Daddy?"

"I need to check the furnace, sweetie. But go ahead and crawl in." He lifted the covers. "I warmed it up for you."

"Yaaaaay!"

"Dad."

Sam flicked on his bedside light while pulling on sweats and a hoodie. He glanced toward the skinny silhouette hovering on his threshold. "Yes, son?"

"I think the furnace is on the fritz."

"I think you're right. Want to help me check it out?"

Ben shrugged. "Sure."

Sam didn't miss the reluctance in Ben's tone, but he didn't take offense either. "Be right back," he said to Mina then guided his son down the hall and the steps, flicking light switches along the way. Ben followed in sullen silence. Ben wasn't intrigued with mechanics or carpentry. Instead of building stuff or fixing stuff, he liked to make stuff up. He was more of an intellectual, a dreamer. He preferred brain-buster electronic games as opposed to outdoor sports. A bit of an artistic nerd, Ben spent his spare time reading fantasy books or doodling anime characters in one of his many sketchbooks. Sam didn't mind, but he knew Ben took some heat at school from some of the other boys. Going on nine, he was short for his age and on the puny side. And Ben was quiet. Painfully quiet. Unlike his chatty, effervescent sister.

For over a year now, Sam had been pushing Ben to try new things. Even if he didn't like tinkering with engines, it would help to know how they worked. No interest in playing football? Fine. But if he understood the concept and rules at least he could offer an educated opinion when cornered by his sports-minded classmates.

As they hit the first floor and headed toward the basement, Sam reflected on an incident a few months back. He'd been stoked when his son had contributed several ideas for a jungle gym Sam had started building for a local playground. But when Sam had invited his son to help with the actual construction, Ben had looked at a hammer like it was an object from Mars. Still, Sam felt compelled to teach Ben a handful of basic survival skills. Every man should know how to change a flat tire or how to swap out a fuse. Or in this case, how to reignite an extinguished pilot light, which is what Sam assumed was the problem with the fritzed furnace—and it was.

"Luckily," he said to Ben, "this should be a quick fix. See here? We lost the pilot light. Must've been a draft. First thing we're going to do is turn this gas valve to *off*. See?"

"Yes, sir."

"Now we wait three or so minutes then switch the valve to pilot setting. See here? Three positions. On, off, and pilot setting."

Hands thrust in his hoodie pockets, Ben nodded.

"Next step. Hold a lighted match to the pilot opening while pushing the reset button on the pilot control panel." Sam pointed. "This button here. Hold that button in until the pilot flame burns real bright, then set the valve to the *on* position." He glanced over his shoulder, swallowing a sigh because of the bored look in Ben's eyes. "If you ever forget," Sam said, "there's a list of directions right here. Most manufacturers provide an instruction sheet."

Ben leaned forward and squinted at the posted directions. "Has it been three minutes?"

Sam smiled a little, moved by his son's feigned interest. He then went through every step just as he'd described.

"It's not working," Ben said after Sam's third attempt.

"No, it's not. Valve must be clogged." Sam didn't bother explaining this part. Ben was shivering and Sam was suddenly anxious to check on Mina. He nabbed a roll of wire from his workstation and got down to business. Unfortunately, nothing he tried worked. Which meant they had a faulty thermocouple or worse.

"Now what?" Ben asked as he pulled his hood up over his ears.

Sam rose and guided the boy upstairs. "Now we dig out the space heater and call a professional."

"Want me to start breakfast while you do that stuff so we're not late for school?"

"I promised Mina pancakes."

"I'll get out the Bisquick. Can we add blueberries?"

Sam's heart ached as he squeezed his sensitive son's shoulder. A boy who preferred libraries and kitchens to garages and work sheds. "Sure."

Two hours later, Sam was on his way to the Rothwell Farm. He'd dropped Ben at school. He'd tried to drop Mina at school but that didn't go so well. For the first time this year, he'd totally buckled and given in to her desperate sobs. He just didn't have it in him today to deal with the guilt and misery of deserting her in a place she didn't want to be. No sitters were available and Mina was being especially clingy anyway. He could take her home, but that would mean huddling in front of the space heater until the repairman showed and that wouldn't be until late afternoon. Besides, Sam had promised Harper he'd come over early to work on her kitchen. It was the one room, aside from her bedroom, that she used a lot and there were some safety issues.

"Remember what I told you," Sam told Mina as they rolled into the driveway. "Daddy's here to work."

"Okay."

"Miss Day is a busy lady, so leave her be."

"Okay."

"I stocked your backpack with a mess of movies and cartoons, three books, and your Miss Kitty color set, so you have plenty to keep you busy." He pointed to the ratty teddy bear Mina had dolled up in a pink dress and tiara. "And Princess Pinky to keep you company."

"We'll be good, Daddy, don't worry."

Sam smiled across the seat at his daughter. He'd bundled her up against the cold—coat, scarf, gloves, thick leggings, and insulated boots. She'd accessorized by topping her sock cap with a tiara and augmenting her pink wool scarf with a purple-feathered boa. She was cute as a button, but she was also a handful. Deep down Sam acknowledged that maybe part of the reason he'd buckled and brought Mina on the job was because she'd work as a buffer between him and Harper. He'd put in a few hours yesterday, working on her stairway. They'd pretty much kept to themselves—him sanding and varnishing wood, her yakking on the phone and flipping through entertainment channels like a celebrity news junkie. But whether they were inches apart or in entirely different sections of the house the sexual tension between them raged. Sam figured the presence of his daughter would diffuse that tension—one way or another.

Harper answered the door dressed in clingy activewear

and her phone pressed to her ear. "Yeah. I got it. I know. On it. Have to go. What?" She held one finger up to Sam, holding him off for a minute. He was used to her doing that, not that he liked it. "I'm supposed to be on a short holiday, Martin. Okay. Fine."

Sam took in her appearance as she ended the call. Her thick hair was pulled in a high ponytail and an iPod was visible in a sports armband. She wasn't sweaty or flushed so Sam assumed she was preparing for a workout and not just finishing up. He struggled not to admire the way her formfitting attire accentuated her curves—although he was beginning to think she'd turn him on even if she was draped in a gunnysack. He held her gaze, acknowledged the mutual sparks, then the glitch when Mina moved out from behind Sam and into Harper's view.

"Hi," Mina said.

Harper tucked her phone into her waistband and raised a lone brow. "Hi."

"This is my daughter, Mina. Mina, this is Miss Day."

"Don't worry," Mina said. "I won't bug you. I have movies and Princess Pinky to keep me busy."

"It's been an unusual morning," Sam said.

"Our furnace is on the futz."

"Fritz, honey."

Mina sighed, shrugged. "Fritz. Futz."

Harper's other brow rose. "Nice tiara."

"Daddy bought it for me." Mina leaned a hard right, peeking past Harper. "This place is haunted, you know."

"So I've heard."

"Seen any ghosts?"

"Not a one." Harper moved aside and waved them in. "Let me know if you do."

"You betcha!" Mina rushed forward, dragging along her bear and backpack.

Harper stared at Sam, pressing her hand to his chest. "Cute kid, Rambo."

"Thanks."

"Shouldn't she be in school?"

"Yup." He looked down to where her palm burned through his jacket.

She snatched it back. "I'm not sure this place is kid safe."

"I'll keep an eye on her."

"You sure don't have much furniture," Mina said while spinning in the center of the living room.

"Not yet," Harper said. "You can sit in that red chair if you want. It's pretty comfy."

"Okay." Mina set her bear on the chair and her pack on the floor then peeled off her scarf, gloves and coat. They landed in messy puddle.

Normally Sam would have told her to pick them up, but he was waiting for a snarky comment from Harper, a roll of the eyes, a disgusted groan. Something. Anything detrimental regarding his daughter. That would sure as hell snuff his attraction to the shallow publicist.

Harper shifted and crossed her arms as Mina dragged the portable mini-DVD player from her Miss Kitty back-pack. "Would you like something to drink?" she asked Mina.

"Do you have hot cocoa?"

"No, but I have herbal tea."

"Chocolate milk?"

"Skim milk."

Mina wrinkled her nose. "No, thank you."

Sam suppressed a smile while shrugging out of his jacket.

"Wanna watch a movie with me?" Mina asked.

"I have business upstairs," Harper said. "A workout and some fancy footwork."

"Dancing?"

"Something like that." She eyed the staircase, checked her phone. The woman was itching to make her escape. "Do you like cupcakes?"

"Do I ever!" Mina's eyes lit.

Sam's ears perked. "Thought you were a health nut."

"Health conscious," Harper corrected. "I used all-natural and low-fat ingredients."

"You bake?"

"Don't look so shocked, Rambo."

"Who's Rambo?" Mina asked.

"Never mind, honey." Sam followed Harper into the kitchen, his gaze drawn to the old cookstove she'd used for baking cupcakes. The same cookstove used by Mary Rothwell. An original appliance that had never been replaced. He shook off a weird feeling, eyeing the cupcakes Harper produced from the fridge. "Mina's allergic to peanuts."

"No nuts," Harper said as she took one from the plastic cupcake holder and placed it on a paper plate. "Apple-cinnamon with low-fat buttercream icing. Want to try one?"

"No thanks."

"Suit yourself." She whizzed out of the kitchen with the cupcake and an attitude.

Sam dragged a hand through his hair, tempering a raging hard-on. "Shit." By the time he peeked back into the living room, Harper was gone and Mina was immersed in a movie and her cupcake. He stepped back into the kitchen and nabbed the toolbox he'd left there the day before. He had a list of things Harper had asked him to look into and he had a list of his own. He'd always considered the kitchen the heart of the house and this heart needed mending. He wasn't surprised when Harper had asked him about restoring the cabinets and counters to a vintage 1940s look. What surprised him was that he instantly visualized a scheme and that they'd easily agreed on style and colors. It was one of the only amicable moments of their short acquaintance.

Considering Sam needed to be home when Frank showed up to service his furnace and considering Mina would be hungry for lunch in a few hours, Sam figured he had three hours ahead of him at most.

Out of nowhere, Rae crossed his thoughts. It bothered him that he was suddenly unclear regarding his feelings for her. And the more he thought about his verbal clash with Luke, the greater his unease. Sam had reacted and spoken in the heat of the moment. He didn't like being at odds with family and he especially didn't care for the feeling that he might be in the wrong and that Luke's feelings for Rae were sincere. He was pretty clear on the fact that Rae was hung up on Luke. He could see it now.

"Hell."

The moment Sam pushed Rae from his thoughts, Harper was waiting in his mind's eye. He could name a dozen reasons not to pursue the attraction. Unfortunately none of them snuffed his desire. Anxious to divert his thoughts, Sam immersed himself in basic repairs. The actual carpentry and painting would come later.

Time flew.

He checked on Mina twice, and both times she was lost in a movie. Once she peeked in to ask him for a glass of water and notified him that she still hadn't seen a ghost ("*Drat!*"). Other than that she was true to her word. She didn't bug Harper. She didn't bug him. She kept herself entertained, which surprised him a little. She'd been so clingy earlier in the day.

Before he knew it ninety minutes had passed and Sam had a question regarding the lighting. He'd probably have to interrupt some phone call or Skype session or whatever

Hollywood gossip show Harper was immersed in, but he didn't want to assume and all he needed was a quick answer.

He smiled at Mina as he passed but she was focused on her DVD player. He scaled the stairs and moved down the hall and into Harper's room—just as she dropped the bath towel she'd had clutched to her body. A body still glistening with water droplets. She was reaching for the underwear laid out on her bed. A lacy black bra and thong. Oh, yeah. Sam was close enough to make out details. Close enough to smell the remnants of her shampoo. It was a blip of a moment—maybe two seconds max—but the image of Harper's lush naked body was burned on Sam's retinas forever.

She sensed him, turned, and gasped. "Don't you knock?" she asked, clutching her undies over her sexy assets, not that they covered much.

"The door was open."

"No it wasn't."

It wasn't?

She grappled for the towel and Sam raked his memory. Had he really waltzed into this room like he owned the place?

"How come Miss Day gets to walk around in her birthday suit and I don't?"

For the love of . . . Sam turned and ushered his daughter out of the room. "We'll talk about it later." He imagined Harper throwing a shoe at his head. He couldn't remember ever feeling this flustered. Flustered was not in his vocab. At least not until this moment. He couldn't even remember why he'd come up here in the first place. His brain was scrambling. How was he going to explain to Mina why he was in the bedroom with a naked lady?

While he urged his daughter to pack up her gear, Sam gathered his coat then paused and plucked his Blackberry from his pocket. Knowing Harper's phone was always nearby, he thumbed an apology.

SORRY ABT THAT.

The response was immediate. NOT AS SORRY AS ME.

LEAVING NOW.

GOOD. WAIT. CUPCAKES IN FRIDGE. TAKE 4 KIDS.

Sam blinked at the message. What the . . . B BACK L8R 2 CLEAN MESS IN KITCHEN. He waited a heart-pounding three seconds before she texted . . .

BRING WINE.

TWENTY-THREE

Rae spent the majority of Monday morning and a good part of the afternoon trying not to think about Luke. He'd spent the night with her twice now and she was hooked. The sex was amazing, but it was more than that. She liked falling asleep and waking up in his arms. She liked his company. The conversation—although so far they'd kept it relatively light.

She knew he was itching to know more about her past, specifically regarding her relationship with her mom and Geoffrey. So far Rae had managed to dodge that conversation. It was too personal, too painful, and she was trying very hard to establish her happy place here in Sugar Creek. With Luke. If she didn't feed the drama, maybe it would fade away. She wasn't running from it exactly, or maybe she was. All she knew was that she'd given it her best and last shot with her mom. As for Geoffrey, clearly the best course was to heed his threats and to stay silent regarding his transgression. Another reason not to share certain aspects of her life with Luke. She was pretty sure he'd be hot to confront Geoffrey.

In which case Geoffrey Stein, of Stein & Beecham

Industries, would use his wealth, power and influence to squash Rae like a bug. Or worse, to ruin the lives of the people she cared about most. Those people, starting with Luke, were right here in Sugar Creek.

"Okay," Chloe said. "Everyone's out. Locking the door."

"Closing the blinds," Daisy said.

Rae sat tight as the women hurried their daily ritual of closing up their café. She couldn't help smiling as she noted the eclectic décor. The mismatched antique furniture was charming. Even the salt and paper shakers and napkin holders were mismatched. What tied everything together were the scattered accessories featuring the glory of Vermont's wildlife—the moose. Embroidered pillows, various clocks and paintings, and assorted chatkas—all featuring a moose in some form or fashion. They'd also created a cartoon logo that was painted on the window and featured on coffee mugs. Rae easily saw why Moose-a-lotta was such a huge draw for locals and tourists alike. Cozy atmosphere, great food, gourmet java, and—something you didn't find a lot of in these parts—free Wi-Fi access.

Rae sipped her decaf cappuccino, while Chloe and Daisy slipped off their aprons and joined her at her cozy table.

"Spill," Daisy said.

"Your news, not your coffee," Chloe said.

"Don't leave anything out," Daisy said

"Feels strange talking about a CL project without the rest of the CLs being here," Rae said. "Especially Rocky."

"We'll catch everyone up," Daisy said. "As for Rocky, she's busy giving my crazy son what for."

"That's if she can get a word in over Dev," Chloe said. "He was fit be tied when he left this morning."

"Luke was worked up, too," Rae said. He'd called her when he'd landed in Miami, to let her know he'd arrived safely and to make sure she was okay, but she hadn't heard from him since.

"Between the three of them and Jayce, they'll make Jerome see reason," Daisy said.

"I feel awful for Rocky," Chloe said. "She's waited so long for her happy ending with Jayce."

"They'll get their happy ending," Daisy said. "Just like you'll get your happy ending with Dev as soon as you set a date," Daisy said.

"Can we not go there?" Chloe asked. "I don't want to take away from Rocky's wedding day. As soon as she's married to Jayce, I'll settle on a date with Devlin."

"Chicken shit," Daisy said.

"I'm not . . ." Chloe nailed Rae with a desperate gaze. "Would you please share what you learned about the book deal?"

"Sure." Honestly she'd been dying to tell someone all day, but she'd had a crammed schedule and everyone had been busy with work. But then she'd stopped by Moose-a-lotta for a late-afternoon snack and Chloe and Daisy had begged her to hang out until they'd closed the café.

"I'm sure I'll know more by the time the club meets on Thursday, but I can at least fill you in on the preliminary discussion."

"Did he believe you right off when you told him who you are?" Daisy asked. "Or did he ask for some sort of proof?"

"I'm pretty sure he was fact-checking on his computer while we chatted," Rae said. "You have to admit it's kind of a tall tale. Why would a socialite, the daughter of a Hollywood celebrity, hide out in Sugar Creek for a year under an assumed identity?"

"How much did you tell him?" Chloe asked.

"Only as much as I had to." Rae flushed thinking about the way she'd manipulated the conversation. She'd never been one for playing games, but in this case she'd definitely danced around the truth. "I told him that I'd elected to live a year incognito and by my wits in order to test myself. I wanted to know what it felt like to live a more normal life, without the benefits of a hefty allowance, my stepfather's influence, and my mother's fame. That's why I refused to participate in the photo session and video shoot arranged by the publishing company. I didn't want to risk blowing my cover. I told him things had changed now and my experiment was over." All of which was true.

"Juicy stuff," Daisy said.

Not as juicy as the deeper details Rae thought, but no way was she sharing those with the world. "Brett was definitely intrigued. Even more so when I told him about my newly acquired inheritance. I could live anywhere and do anything, I told him, but what I wanted most was to be part of this caring community. Most especially to run the local day care center and to devote my efforts to raising awareness for the charitable causes of the Cupcake Lovers. I told him," and Rae still couldn't believe she'd gone this far, "that if his house didn't publish our recipe/memoir book, and soon, I would."

Chloe's mouth fell open.

Daisy blinked.

"I know it was presumptuous of me," Rae hurried on. "I didn't ask the club first. Honestly the thought came to me out of the blue, in the midst of my discussion with Brett. I don't know much about it, but I know the publishing industry is in flux. You don't need a publishing house in order to get your project out there. You, we, can self-publish *Cupcake Lover's Delectable Delights*. We'd need to hire someone to show us the ropes, handle certain aspects, but we'd be in full control and make more money besides. More money for the charities of our choice. I'm more than willing to finance the effort. It's such a great cause and . . . I'm rambling."

Chloe traded a look with Daisy. "It's definitely something to consider."

"Maybe we'd be better off," Daisy said.

"Devlin negotiated the contracts," Chloe said. "When he gets back—"

"Maybe it's as simple as returning that advance," Daisy said.

"I really don't know," Rae said.

"Devlin will." Chloe met Rae's gaze. "Are you sure about backing us?"

"I can't think of anything I'd rather do with my money. Other than buying Sugar Tots and developing a top-notch day care and after-school facility."

"We'll have to discuss this self-publishing venture with the other Cupcake Lovers," Daisy said.

"Thursday's meeting," Chloe said. "Meanwhile I'll do some research on the Internet."

"Me, too," Rae said.

"If we do this," Daisy said, "we'll need someone to help spread the news. Get our name and book out there. You know. One of those publicity people. Like that woman Rocky's been working for."

"Harper Day," Chloe said. "She's a publicist for a big firm out in Hollywood. Recognize her name?"

Rae shook her head. "I typically steer clear of publicists. I'm betting Olivia would know her though. My mother's pretty up on anyone who can get her face and name in the media."

"Harper bought a second home here in Sugar Creek," Chloe said.

"The Rothwell Farm," Daisy said. "We'll see how long that lasts."

"Because that house is haunted?" Rae asked. Living in Sugar Creek a year, she'd heard plenty of stories about the Rothwell place. Especially since it was supposedly haunted by one of the original Cupcake Lovers.

"No one's ever lived in that house for more than a two-year stretch, Daisy said. "There's the legend—the longer you live there, the sadder you get—but it's also a money pit. Every time you fix something, something else breaks."

"Harper's not living there full-time though," Chloe said. "She just pops in for a random few days each month or so. Since she spends so little time there, maybe the legendary 'funk' won't affect her. As to the money pit aspect, Rocky pulled Sam in to set that house to rights. I'm betting his repairs stick. That man's amazing."

Rae's stomach rolled with guilt. She hadn't heard from Sam since Luke had told him to back off. She felt bad that she'd caused friction between the two cousins. She felt worse thinking she'd hurt Sam's feelings. They'd formed a friendship of sorts and she'd pretty much botched it. She needed to mend that bridge, but she wasn't sure how. One thing was certain, she couldn't avoid Sam forever. He'd be at the CL meeting on Thursday for sure.

"When Rocky gets back," Chloe said, "maybe she can pick Harper's brain."

"Why wait?' Daisy asked. "Sam bailed on dinner last night because he's set on putting that house to rights as quickly as possible. Means he's spending a lot of time there. I'll ask him to pick Harper's brain. That way we can have even more specifics for Thursday."

"Couldn't hurt," Chloe said.

"I guess not," Rae said.

"I'll text him right now," Daisy said while whipping out her phone.

"Why not just call?" Rae asked.

Daisy rolled her eyes. "That's so yesterday."

Chloe grinned then reached over and squeezed Rae's hand. "So what about the rest of your day? How did it go with the bank?"

Rae smiled back, anxious to share her good news and knowing Chloe would encourage her to share every detail. "Sugar Tots is as good as mine."

TWENTY-FOUR

Sam was in the liquor store when his phone pinged for the twentieth time in the last hour. He'd been trading texts, sexy texts with Harper. If he didn't know better, he'd think he'd been possessed by a twenty-year-old. Sam was almost forty. He texted out of necessity, not on the norm. He sure as hell didn't thumb racy thoughts into his phone and hit Send.

Except for tonight.

She'd started it. He'd just gotten Ben and Mina settled with a bucket of fried chicken when Harper had sent him her first note.

GET OVER HERE SOON OR I'LL COME W/O U

He'd had to read it twice. Did she mean what he thought she meant? Would she be so brazen?

Yeah. She would.

Balls tight, Sam had walked out of the kitchen and thumbed a response. DO THAT AND I'LL HAVE TO PUNISH YOU

THREAT?

PROMISE

IN2 KINK?

IN2 U

There'd been a pause and he'd thought he'd blown it. But then she'd responded . . .

NOT IF U DON'T GET HERE SOON

To which Sam texted: RED OR WHITE?

For the next half hour he'd been in a bit of a blue-ball haze. He'd dropped the kids at their grandparents' on the pretense that a friend had a plumbing problem and he'd promised to lend a hand. He wasn't sure how long he'd be. An hour? Two? He'd be in touch.

Looking his mother-in-law in the eye hadn't come easy. His pocket had pinged with another incoming message and Sue had raised a brow.

"Impatient friend," she said.

Did she suspect Sam had a date? She knew he'd gone out that one time with Rae and both she and Charlie had approved. They knew he'd loved their daughter. Time to move on. So they and everyone else in Sugar Creek kept telling him. Only this wasn't a date. And it wasn't Rae. This was Harper and an hour or two of hot sex. Maybe kinky sex. It had been a long time, long before his wife, but Sam could do kink.

He'd driven to the liquor store conjuring different scenarios. He'd been ready to describe one when he'd received that ping in the Merlot aisle, only the text wasn't from Harper, it was from Daisy and it was freaking long. Sam didn't know many texting acronyms, but he used the few he did know and tried to be succinct. Daisy was a text-a-holic and never, ever abbreviated. She had a lot to say about Rae and the book deal and Harper getting them some "buzz." The note rambled on and was killing his own "buzz" so he texted back "WILL DO" and made a mental note to reread in depth . . . L8R.

Sam reached the Rothwell Farm just before six. It was already dark. The temp—five below. The night air stung his cheeks and his boots crunched on icy snow as he made his way to the dimly lit porch. He was too hot to be cold. Too randy to be nervous. Harper had worked him up good and hard with her sexting. And the visual of her naked body, that beautifully sculpted body with its lush assets, was a constant in his mind's eye. Harper was everything he'd imagined that first day when she'd landed in his arms—*Sports Illustrated*–bathing-suit-model-perfection—and Sam was going to nail her.

In spite of the freezing temperature, she answered the door in that black lace thong and bra and—thank you Jesus—stiletto heels. He was pretty sure he he'd died and gone to heaven or maybe hell depending on whether he'd gotten in over his head. She could be into some serious S&M for all he knew. Not his thing. Regardless, he moved inside.

"Brought the wine," he said.

"Brought something else, too," she said, palming the bulge in his jeans. "The wine can wait. I can't. But first, I've got some rules."

Sam shut the door and set aside the wine while Harper launched into a laundry list of do's and don'ts and within the first five seconds he knew her kink didn't extend to S&M, although she wasn't opposed to D&S or B&D. She added a couple acronyms he didn't recognize, but he wasn't really listening at this point so much as thinking about that lush mouth wrapped around his—

"No sleeping over. And when we're done, we're done. We won't discuss it after or ever. I—"

"We doing this?" Sam asked as tossed his jacket. "Or are you going to talk it to death?"

Blue eyes sparking, Harper grabbed the wine bottle then launched herself at Sam, wrapping her legs around his middle and using her mouth for something other than yakking. Holy hell, this woman could kiss. Counting his lucky stars and cradling her beautiful ass, Sam opted to move this party upstairs, pronto.

"Bad time to talk?"

"Great time to talk." Rae lowered the volume on the television via remote, repositioned her laptop, and rested back against her pillows. She was beginning to think she wasn't going to hear from Luke again today, so she'd immersed herself in work, rather than dwelling on his absence. "How'd it go with your dad?"

"Believe it or not the old man put up a fight even with the four of us and mom facing him down."

"Who gave Jerome more grief? You or Dev?"

"That would be Rocky."

"Really?"

"She lost it, Rae. I mean big-time. She was all up in his face, accusing him of being a selfish SOB. What if he took a turn for the worse by not addressing this present glitch? What if he died? Then she'd forever associate her wedding day with the day that killed him."

"*Wow.*"

"Then the zinger. How dare he potentially ruin what should be the happiest day of her life."

Rae cringed. "That's—"

"Harsh? You should've been there. It was worse in person. I mean, yeah, I'm pissed at Dad for the way he's handled a lot of this," Luke said, "but it's hard to take a tough stance when he looks like a shadow of his former self."

"Not hard for Rocky apparently."

"I don't know. I think she went bonkers for a few seconds. Right after she gave him hell, she burst into tears and threw herself into his arms. That's when the old man broke."

Rae's eyes burned as she imagined the scene, the

emotions. She thought about the intense love between the Monroe siblings and their parents and acknowledged a gaping hole in her heart. She'd never had that kind of connection with her mother. She couldn't remember her birth father. She'd never had a chance to bond with her second and third stepfathers because Olivia kept sending her away. As for Geoffrey . . . there would be no bonding there. Ever.

"Rae."

"What?"

"I asked if you were okay."

"Yes. Yes, of course." She palmed her forehead, gathered her wits. "I was just thinking about how your father's illness has impacted everyone. I thought he was beating this thing."

"He was. And there's still a strong chance he will."

"So where do things stand?"

"Dad buckled regarding the test. Dev called the specialist and I don't know who did what, but they were able to move the CT scan up to tomorrow. Whether Rocky and Jayce postpone the wedding hinges on the results."

"Awfully close to the wire," Rae said.

"Things are a little tense," Luke said. "So how was your day? How'd it go with the publisher? How's it looking with Sugar Tots?"

Rae snuggled back against her pillows, smiling and jazzed to share her day with Luke. Hoping she could brighten his mood with uplifting news. "Everything went great. Just as I'd hoped Brett, our editor, was intrigued with the concept of exploiting my name, or rather my fortune and my mother's name, to give our cupcake book an edge over every other cupcake book saturating the market right now."

"I would think that the history of the Cupcake Lovers,

the military angle and charitable aspect, would be edge enough," Luke said.

"A celebrity tie-in is a guaranteed sales boost. Not to mention it ensures free publicity. Brett's taking this new angle—Daisy calls it our gimmick—to a marketing meeting tomorrow. Except, my wheels started turning while we were talking and, I have to say, Luke, I'm not sure it's in our best interest to go for forward with Highlife."

"What do you mean?"

"I just don't sense they believe in our cause the way we do. I don't trust Highlife will do right by the CLs. Which got me to thinking . . . what if we self-published the book instead of going through a conventional publisher? Cut out the middle man allowing us more profit for the charities?"

"The Cupcake Lovers signed a contract."

"There might be a way around that. Especially since they've fudged on their end. Chloe said she'd have Dev look into it."

"You spoke to Chloe about this?"

"And Daisy. The opportunity was there and I was dying to run the idea by someone. Chloe and I are researching self-publishing so we'll be able to present a strong and educated case to the club on Thursday." Rae got all tingly just thinking about it. The prospect of taking control, in playing a vital role in furthering such a great cause.

"If you cut out the middle man," Luke said, "someone else will have to take on that work."

"It would mean hiring some freelance help."

"The club's nonprofit, Rae. They, we, can't afford that kind of upfront investment."

"I can."

Luke fell silent for a moment and Rae frowned.

"I sense apprehension," she said.

"Seems like you're taking on an awful lot. Financing and overseeing the publishing of a book plus purchasing and reorganizing, hell, *running* the day care center. We're talking about a lot of money."

"I have a lot of money."

"And time and energy."

"I have that, too."

"What about as you get further along in your pregnancy? What about after you have the baby?"

"Did you think I was going to be a stay-at-home mom?"

"You can afford to be."

She didn't know why that statement bothered her. It was true. And there'd been no sarcasm in Luke's tone. He'd just stated a fact. "By the time the baby comes, the Cupcake Lovers' book will already be out—one way or another. As for Sugar Tots . . ." Her mind whirled with all her plans—the renovations and expansion. The programs and staff. She didn't want to skimp on one single aspect and yet she knew it would be a lot of work. Frustrated now, she blew out a breath. "I'll figure it out. Lots of women juggle motherhood and a career."

"Don't get angry."

"I'm not—"

"You are. I hear it in your voice. I'm not telling you what to do, Rae. I'm just pointing out that you have some pretty aggressive and time-consuming plans. I know you'll do right by the baby. I guess I'm wondering how you'll make time for us?"

Rae blinked.

"You know what? Forget I asked. That was . . . never mind. I'm not myself tonight. This thing with Dad. I should go."

"Luke."

"Did you scope out any rental properties today?"

Off balance now, Rae palmed her forehead. "Although that had been my plan, no. The day got away from me."

"Good. Hold off."

"Why?"

"I hope to be back by Wednesday. Just hold off."

"Okay."

"I love it when you say that."

And just like that Rae sensed a change in Luke's mood. She smiled a little, arched a brow. "You love it when I say 'okay'? Why?"

"Mostly when you say it to me, it means you're putting your faith in me. Trusting my judgment. My abilities."

She frowned now. "Why would I doubt—"

"I know you know about my reading problem."

Rae pushed off of the pillows, shocked and primed by the turn in conversation.

"Are you going to pretend otherwise?"

"No. That is, I suspected." Rae licked her lips, choosing her words carefully. "I have a stepbrother who struggled with dyslexia. Plus part of my studies involved the complexities of learning disabilities," she said straight on. "I picked up on signs most people wouldn't. You cope well."

"If by cope you mean I hide it well, then yes. I do. It's always been enough for me. But now . . . now I worry it won't be enough for you. Or our child."

"Luke—"

"Regardless of my . . . challenge, I can take care of you, Rae, and our baby. When I said you could afford to be a stay-at-home mom, I wasn't thinking about your fortune. I'm a hard worker and more than capable of being a good provider."

Her heart swelled and ached knowing his pride was taking a monumental hit. "You're not telling me anything I don't already know."

"I just wanted to get it out there."

"Okay."

He laughed a little. "Did you say that on purpose?"

"Yes." She hugged a pillow to her aching chest, wishing she could hug Luke instead. "I can help you. If you want. I just need to know what type—"

"Visual."

Her shoulders sagged with relief. Not *trauma* or *primary*. "I can definitely help."

"I appreciate that, but . . . I have to tell you that would be hell on the ego."

"Not me then. Someone else. You can tackle this, Luke." His silence quickened her pulse. She knew enough not to push. Not now. That he'd admitted the problem at all was huge. "How about we leave off for now and discuss this more in person?"

"That won't come easy for me."

"Whenever you're ready."

After a moment, Luke said, "I should let you get some sleep."

"It's been a full day, that's for sure." She scraped her teeth over her lower lip, praying she was handling this right. She knew his disability didn't necessarily factor into business sense, but did he? Generally those who suffered dyslexia were highly intuitive. Uber street-smart. "Luke?"

"Yeah."

"When you get back, I was hoping I could get your two cents on Sugar Tots. My meeting went well at the bank and if everything goes smoothly the day care center will be mine—lock, stock, and barrel—by month's end. I've never owned a business. You run one of the most successful establishments in town. I'd appreciate your input."

"You don't have to patronize—"

"I'm not."

"All right. First thought? Change the name. You mentioned launching after-school programs for older kids. I can tell you right now, if I were a ten-year-old boy, I wouldn't be keen on spending my afternoons at a place called Sugar Tots."

"Good point." Truly it was. "Any suggestions?"

"Not off the top of my head. Maybe we can brainstorm when I get home."

"Sounds good." She tamped down a whirlwind of emotions, thinking this would be a good place to stop for the night. "I'll say a prayer for your dad."

"I appreciate that. Goodnight, Reagan."

"Goodnight, Luke."

TWENTY-FIVE

Rae spotted the first photographer around noon. He didn't get in her face. In fact he was pretty far away and for all she knew he could've been taking a picture of the white-steepled church or quaint storefronts. Sugar Creek, with its old-fashioned brick facades and Americana charm was beautiful in any season. Mid-February and the roof of every building as well as the branches of the trees were blanketed in snow. Frosty windowpanes were framed with twinkling white lights. A good many of the antiques shops, art galleries, and specialty boutiques offered displays featuring hearts and flowers, chubby cupids, sleek statues of kissing couples, and assorted romantic images. It was the month of love, after all.

Yes, indeed. It was possible that the photographer was an amateur, a tourist snapping shots of the town he'd chosen for his holiday getaway. She just happened to walk into the frame.

But Rae's prickling hair follicles told her different.

She told herself not to panic. Not to avoid and not to engage. This is what she'd wanted, right? Free publicity for the Cupcake Lovers. A way and means to build buzz around their recipe book? It's just that she hadn't expected action so soon. Especially since she'd yet to broadcast her whereabouts. Although maybe Brett had tipped off the media. Except that meeting with the Highlife marketing department wasn't taking place until later today. He wouldn't jump the gun, would he?

Get a grip, Deveraux.

Seriously, if she couldn't withstand one innocuous guy with a camera, what would she do when the paparazzi flocked. *If* they flocked. Maybe she had a skewed vision of her potential popularity. Maybe the media wouldn't give two hoots about the daughter of a B-movie actress who intended to use her fortune to promote cupcakes and early education. Now that she thought about it her goodwill mission wasn't nearly as titillating as the wild antics and illegal shenanigans of any number of infamous celebrity kids.

Hunching her shoulders against the blustery winds, Rae shoved that photographer from her mind and hurried toward Romancing the Stone, an artisan shop featuring handcrafted jewelry by Casey Monahan. Casey had been one of the first people Rae had met last year when she'd first settled in Sugar Creek. Although Rae had pretended to be someone else, she *had* been honest about certain aspects of her life. Like having a brother (albeit stepbrother) stationed in the Middle East. Something she had in common with Casey and one of the reasons Casey had invited Rae to check out the Cupcake Lovers. Rae had been hooked after one visit. Casey had been as good of a friend as *Rachel* had allowed, and Rae hadn't seen the quirky artisan since she'd returned to Sugar Creek. Up until late last night, Casey had been out of town.

The bell above the door tinkled and a warm blanket of air enveloped Rae as soon as she stepped inside. The shop was just as she remembered. Small, tidy, and creative.

Beautiful jewelry displayed in imaginative ways. As always, the room smelled of evergreen.

Casey popped into view, straightening from a stooped position behind her front-of-house workstation. She took in Rae's makeover and smiled. "*Wow*. Just *wow*."

Rae took off her big, dark sunglasses then brushed snowflakes from her wind-tousled hair. "Short and really red. I know." She'd lost count of how many times she'd said that in the last few days.

"You look fabulous. Hang your coat on the tree and stay awhile. We have some catching up to do."

Rae raised the logoed bag she'd been carrying. "Brought coffee from Moose-a-lotta."

"The best in town." Casey pulled a cushioned stool next to hers. "Mind if we talk here instead of my office? Fran was supposed to be here today but she called out sick."

"Just happy for the chat." They'd caught up a little over the phone this morning. Casey now knew about as much as everyone else regarding Rae's reason for living a one-year ruse and her reasons for coming back. Rae sat next to the bohemian-dressed woman and passed her a cup of hazelnut coffee.

"So tell me about Luke."

Rae rolled her eyes. "I knew you were going to ask that."

"Well, come on. It's the talk of the town. You bagged Sugar Creek's biggest playboy."

"I didn't bag him."

"He's gotta be head over heels in love with you, girl. Why else would he go exclusive?"

Why indeed? Rae didn't doubt Luke felt something for her. They had a physical and emotional connection. But he'd never mentioned love and she was sure a good part of his feelings were wrapped up in the baby and the prospect of being a dad. Something she understood. The moment she'd learned she was pregnant Rae's world and her priorities shifted.

She tried to relax and enjoy reconnecting with Casey, but the longer Rae dodged mention of her pregnancy, the more uncomfortable she felt. Her reason for keeping the baby secret no longer outweighed her need to be forthright with all the people she'd once deceived. As soon as Luke got back, they'd have to talk.

Just then her phone rang. "I'm sorry, Casey. Just let me see . . . It's my lawyer in L.A."

"Go on and take it."

"I'll just see what he wants . . . Al?"

"A heads-up would have been nice, Reagan."

He didn't sound happy. "What do you mean?"

"I've had six calls in the last forty minutes from various organizations, all vying for your money."

"What?"

"When you announce to the world you're devoting your inheritance to philanthropic needs—"

"I didn't announce anything. Hold on," she said when her phone blipped with another incoming call. "Sorry," she said to Casey then, "Yes?"

"Miss Devereaux? This is Shawna Frost of *Vermont Today*. I understand you're backing several local charitable organizations. We'd like to interview you—"

Beep.

"I'm sorry. Could you hold please?" She thumbed call incoming. "Al?"

"It's Chloe. I'm worried Daisy unleashed a monster."

Rae's pulse tripped. "What do you mean?"

"I'm not a Hollywood gossip monger, I swear. But I confess to the guilty pleasure of checking in now on omg! or TMZ."

"What's on the Net, Chloe?"

"You."

Rae blinked, swallowed. "Thanks. I'll be in touch." She looked at the screen, saw one "on hold" and it wasn't Al. "Miss Frost? Yes. Thank you for your interest. Crazy morning. I'll be in touch." She disconnected then redialed Al. "I lost you before. Sorry. About the news blast . . . I can explain. That's a lie. I'll try to explain. Once I'm clear on what's happening. Stay tuned. And don't give my money to anyone without my consent. Not that you would. Sorry. I'm . . . discombobulated."

"Advise ASAP, Reagan."

"Will do." She turned to Casey. "Apparently I'm in the news. Got a laptop handy?"

Ten seconds later a screen was up and singing the praises of one Reagan Devereaux.

omg!

TMZ

E! Online

"Holy cow," Casey said.

Rae stared in shock as they tripped upon a few more sites, including a string of mentions on Twitter. The headlines read: TRUST FUND BABY TURNS PHILAN-THROPIST!

The articles were short blips. Her father was mentioned. Her mother was mentioned—although not in the most flattering way. Rae's educational background was applauded and the fact that she was so low-key that she'd been off the media's radar until now was commended. There was mention of her newly inherited fortune and how she's devoting her time, money, and effort to worthy causes such as a Vermont-based day care center and a cupcake club that supports troops via cupcakes.

"Talk about coming off as the Mother Theresa of the Me Generation," Casey said. "Who's your publicist?"

"I don't have a publicist. Oh, crap. Maybe I do. May I use your office for a sec?"

"Sure."

"Be right back."

Rae moved to the back of the store and instead of calling Daisy direct, opted for a more direct answer from Sam. It would be the first time they'd spoken since he'd learned about her and Luke, but Rae was too focused on this media glitch to worry about the potential awkwardness.

He answered on the first ring.

"Sorry to bother you, Sam."

"No, bother. What's up?"

"Daisy sent you a text yesterday, right?"

"About you and your offer to throw your money behind the CL recipe book project. Generous."

"My pleasure. Except, we're still under contract with Highlife and it hasn't been discussed or voted on either way by the club. Nothing is settled, yet word is out."

"You know the Sugar Creek grapevine."

"No, I mean, word is *out,* Sam. In a big way. On major entertainment venues on the Internet. Daisy said she was going to ask you to pick Harper Day's brain regarding potential publicity opportunities. What did Daisy say exactly and did you share it with Harper? What did she do? Who did she contact? This morning I received a call from a reporter at *Vermont Today.* Should I brace for *Good Morning America*? I need to know what to prepare for."

"Give me time to sort this out. Are you okay?"

"I'm fine."

"You don't sound fine."

"Just caught off guard. Speaking of." She ignored her unease, needing to get this out of the way. Wanting to smooth things over with Sam. "I'm sorry I haven't called before now. I know you were blindsided when Luke told you we were involved and—"

"Do you love him?"

"Yes."

"Enough said."

Rae collapsed on the one cushy chair in Casey's office. Why did she keep blurting that? Before long, Luke would be the only one in town who didn't know the extent of her feelings. "I haven't told him yet. I haven't said the words. I don't know why I told you, except you asked and I . . . I don't want there to be hard feelings between us."

"No hard feelings," he said in his ever calm tone. "We can't choose who we love, Rae. Let me talk to Harper. I'll get back to you when I have answers."

"Thank you, Sam."

Rae disconnected, her mind spinning in a dozen directions when Casey cried out, "Oh my God! Someone wrote about you on *Huffington Post*!"

TWENTY-SIX

Sam reread Daisy's text from the day before, slowly, word for word.

Just as he'd feared, he'd screwed up.

The text had been so damn lengthy and convoluted and Sam had been distracted. By Harper. Sex with Harper. Kinky sex with Harper.

The roll in the sheets (and a few other places) had been amazing. The moment after, not so much. Harper and her damned rules. He wasn't supposed to linger. Conversation pertaining to their sex-a-pade, including the sexting, was off-limits. Considering they had nothing in common, aside from an animal attraction and an appreciation for the Rothwell Farm, Sam had been at a loss for words. In fact he couldn't seem to grasp one cohesive thought. Celibate for two years, Sam had overdosed on Harper's uninhibited approach to sex.

Sensory overload.

He knew now that he'd definitely experienced some sort of brain freeze because he sure as hell hadn't been thinking straight when he'd forwarded Daisy's text to Harper.

He'd felt awkward leaving her bed without a word and as he'd dressed he'd been keenly aware of his surroundings. The room in which an original Cupcake Lover had pined away for her love. Which made him flash on the club and the recipe book and Daisy's text.

After he'd climbed into his cab, he zipped off a text to Harper, their only comfortable means of communication.

NEED A FAVOR

INTRIGUED

He'd then forwarded Daisy's text following up with his own message, telling Harper that the Cupcake Lovers would be grateful for any help. He hadn't expanded beyond that. He hadn't expected her to act without checking with him first. Honestly he hadn't thought she'd give the CLs the time of day. It's not like they were Hollywood celebrities.

She'd texted back: WILL DO. And Sam had pulled away from the farm feeling as though they'd at least had some sort closure on the night and that it wasn't just some twisted rendezvous. It helped to put him in a better place as he drove to pick up his kids. He'd put the liaison out of his head as best he could, including the bit about Daisy's text, as he segued back to real life. His life as a single father. He'd managed through the night and morning by focusing on the kids. Not to mention being in his own house, a house filled with memories of his sweet wife had pretty much snuffed erotic thoughts about Harper.

Rae's phone call had put an end to that.

Sam texted Harper. YOU HOME?

ON A CONFERENCE CALL

COMING OVER

BAD TIME

MAKE TIME

Sam was learning that the only way he got anywhere with Harper was by bulldozing his way in and over. She was always busy, always headstrong, and always taking control. Yes, sir, he'd gotten a good dose of her domineering ways last night. Sam had allowed so much of it because, hell, it was stimulating, before he reversed roles—even more stimulating.

Five minutes into his drive and he had an erection. What would she be wearing? Skintight jeans or clingy workout clothes? Red lipstick? Pink? Hair loose and wild or swept off that beautiful face? Now that he was out of his house and away from his kids, one erotic thought after another slithered through his brain.

The first thing he noticed when he pulled up to the house was that Leo had repaired and returned her car, which, turns out, she'd rented from the local mechanic and garage owner to begin with. The second was that whoever had shoveled her walk after last night's late snow had done a poor job. Surely not Leo. Maybe Harper herself. Sam could imagine her hurriedly scraping a path just wide enough to navigate while she yakked on that damn phone. He made a mental note to clear a better path, throw down some salt. He didn't want her, or anyone else, to slip and fall.

He knocked on the door. Wasn't surprised she greeted him with a phone pressed to her ear, or when she held up a finger to bid him silent. She waved him inside, engrossed in conversation with someone named Gabby. From what Sam could make out, the woman, girl, whatever, had spent a wild, drunken night in Vegas and someone had snapped compromising shots that showed up on Twitter. Sam wasn't into the social networking scene but he knew a lot of people who were and he knew that once something was on the Internet it was there forever. If something went viral it was either a blessing or, in this Gabby girl's instance, a curse.

"Where was your bodyguard when this wild bunch

talked you into playing strip pool in their suite?" Harper asked. A beat later she rolled her eyes. "I was afraid you were going to say that. First thing you need to do is to fire that irresponsible reprobate. His job is to keep you out of trouble, not to incite it or, in this case, play along. I don't care if you begged him to. I don't care if you'd been dying to see him naked. Yes, I know. Most bodyguards *are* built. Listen to me Gabby. *Gabby!* We need to concentrate on damage control. I'll handle the bulk of it, but here's what you're going to do."

Sam slipped off his coat and sat on the edge of the same red chair Mina had settled into yesterday. Rather than lose patience, he listened while Harper took calm control of a disastrous situation. Apparently Gabby was an up-and-coming star, a featured actress on a show being touted as the next *Glee*. She played a bubbly cheerleader type, a good girl, and that's how her fans perceived her to be in real life. Salvaging her now-tarnished reputation struck Sam as a PR nightmare. Yet Harper was on fire, looking as though she were eating up every second of the challenge.

He didn't get her. At. All.

When she finally signed off, her cheeks were pink, her eyes bright. "What's up, Rambo? I've got a crisis to spin."

Sam rose, not quite towering over her, but making his presence known. Holding Harper's attention was a challenge in itself. "That text I sent you last night."

"You don't have to thank me. It was nothing. Seriously. I sent a couple of e-mails and texts, pitched the story with an heiress-turned-philanthropist angle. Cake. Caught on like wildfire. Did you see the flurry on TMZ?"

"What the hell is TMZ?" Every time she mentioned it his brain went to DMZ (demilitarized zone). He was pretty sure they weren't connected.

She scrunched her brow. "What world do you live in?"

"The real world?"

She snorted then took off toward the kitchen. "Did the kids enjoy my cupcakes?"

"Yes. Thank you."

"Did you try one?"

"No."

She tossed a narrow-eyed glance over her shoulder. "Why not?"

"About this media hype revolving around Rae. I need you to snuff it."

"What? Why?"

"Because the Cupcake Lovers are contracted to release that recipe book with a New York publisher."

"The text specified self-publishing."

"I know. This isn't your fault, precisely. It's mine."

She whirled then, hands on hips. "What do you mean *precisely*?"

"Why didn't you check with me before you took action?"

"Why would I? You said you needed a favor. The text you forwarded me was pretty clear."

"It was?"

"Clear on wanting to promote buzz regarding Reagan Devereux's goodwill projects—the school, the recipe book—capitalizing on her mother's name and her father's fortune. Drawing attention to Sugar Creek in order to increase tourism. Drawing attention to the Cupcake Lovers to increase sales of their book and inspire additional contributions to their charitable work."

"You got all that from Daisy's text?"

"Didn't you? Look," Harper said as she turned toward her coffee maker. "Is Rae relocating to Sugar Creek?"

"Looks like."

"Is she purchasing the local day care center and launching additional educational programs for the local kids?"

"The plan as I know it."

"Are the Cupcake Lovers in the process of publishing—one way or another—a recipe book that will benefit various charities as well as our troops?"

"Yes."

"Then I don't see a problem." She turned and handed Sam a mug of coffee. "If the club decides to go with the publishing company then I'll shift the spin. Let me know when you know."

Sam watched her stir raw unrefined sugar into the mug, watched as she sipped, and tried not to obsess on where those lush lips had been last night. His cock twitched in memory. "How much is this PR *spin* going to cost us?"

"Nothing." She glanced at the ceiling and beyond. "I think Mary's smiling down on me and the fact that I did something in support of the Cupcake Lovers. That's enough for me."

"What is it with you and your fascination with Mary Rothwell?"

"Why didn't you taste my cupcakes?"

Sam was still focused on her mouth and distracted by the sexual tension pulsing between them. When she met his gaze, Sam felt a full-body *zap*. "About last night—"

"Uh-uh." She took that as her cue to leave. "Off to save Gabby's ass," she said as she pushed away from the counter, mug in hand. "Love the designs you left on the table for the vintage-looking cabinets, by the way. Can you really build those from scratch?"

"Yeah."

"Impressive."

"Harper," Sam said, causing her to pause on the threshold. "I thought you bought this place as a getaway. A place to unwind."

She cast him an enigmatic look before sliding out of the room. "What do you think last night was?"

TWENTY-SEVEN

Luke was reminded yet again of how much he hated hospitals when he accompanied his dad to the medical center. It didn't matter that the sun was shining or that it was a balmy seventy-nine degrees. His mood was sour and his blood ice cold. Had his dad taken a turn for the worse? Had the cancer spread? Would he need to undergo surgery? Or had there been a glitch in the previous assessment? Would he be cleared to go home?

Needless to say they were all praying for the latter.

"I hate waiting rooms," Rocky said as she paced back and forth.

"Join the club," Luke said. This one, in particular, rattled his composure. The few other people awaiting news about loved ones looked stone-cold miserable. The place was a chaotic mess. Magazines scattered all over. Crushed beverage cups abandoned willy-nilly instead of properly discarded. The ugly blue carpet was sun-spotted and worn from countless visitors, countless worried souls who paced incessantly like his sister.

Luke turned his focus from Rocky and the disheveled room to his composed and ever-tidy mom. Her chin-length hair, curly and blonde like her daughter's, was pulled back in a neat ponytail. Like Rocky, she wore no makeup. She didn't need it. She was fifty-seven and looked maybe forty-five. She'd married young, had her kids young, and had often boasted about her good fortune. About how her golden years would be her best.

Only they'd turned out to be the worst.

Luke's heart ached as he tried to read his mom's mind. She was sitting two chairs down reading a paperback book. Kaye Monroe had been a pillar of strength throughout Jerome's diagnosis and treatment. She never doubted her husband's ability to persevere. Never fell apart. Yet Luke knew she was shaken to her kind-hearted core. What kind of strength did it take to keep that kind of intense fear bottled? How the hell did she do it? "You look so calm, Mom."

"Not calm," she said. "Patient and optimistic. This has pretty much been my life for the last several months. I've learned to cope."

Luke and Dev traded a look. They were of the same mind. Pissed that their dad had kept his condition a secret for so long. Pissed that their mom had had to "cope" on her own.

Jayce strolled into the waiting room carrying a tray with four steaming cups. "I sampled mine," he said. "Swill compared to Moose-a-lotta's coffee, but loaded with caffeine."

"Come to papa," Luke said. He'd barely slept last night and considering the bedraggled look of his brother and sister and Jayce, he knew they'd suffered the same restlessness.

Rocky paced by and grabbed her cup without missing a step. When riled or upset, Rocky became a frenzied blur. That was *her* coping mechanism. "Why is it taking so long?"

"It's been less than an hour, dear," Kaye said.

"The scan should be over soon," Dev said. "I was told the images would be stored electronically on a computer and that after reviewing, the radiologist would inform Dad's doctor, who promised to expedite the entire process. We should have a report shortly."

"Pacing won't help, dear."

"Cool your heels, Dash." Jayce moved in and took his soon-to-be-wife in hand. "You're messing with your mom's zen," he said with a soft smile.

Luke sipped his coffee and tried to relax. Any other time he would have enjoyed being in Florida. Especially in February. A respite from the harsh Vermont winter. Not that he typically minded the cold. But who wouldn't enjoy flying south for a few days? A few days of warmth. A few days of sand and surf.

Out of nowhere, Luke imagined Rae and her kickass curves. He pictured her in a tiny bikini. Imagined them walking along the beach, hand in hand with a little girl or boy, splashing up the frothy waves, kicking up sand. He'd have to make that happen someday. In a heartbeat, Luke imagined a few other happy scenarios—all involving Rae and their kid. Tension eased from his shoulders, his head throbbed a little less. Apparently fantasizing was Luke's coping mechanism.

He'd spoken to Rae a few hours earlier. A brief call. He'd promised to call her when he knew the results. *Her* trip to the hospital had turned out well. Maybe Luke was on a roll. Maybe this visit would also end with tears of relief.

Because the scan wasn't invasive, his dad would come walking into the waiting room any minute now and then, like Dev said, they'd know something conclusive not long after. *Come on, good news!*

Luke glanced at the television hanging on the opposing

wall, seeking mindless distraction. Some gossip show—
Hollywood Insider? Hollywood something. The sound was
down. The featured reporter babe was gossiping about
whatever. Several candid photos scrolled by—Paris Hilton, Lindsay Lohan, Miley Cyrus . . .

"What the . . . Is that Rae?" Luke bolted out of his
seat. Coffee sloshed on his pants. "Damn." He ignored the
burn and moved closer to the screen. Rocky and Jayce
moved closer, too.

"It is," Rocky said.

"That second shot," Jayce said. "That's Main Street."

"Paparazzi in Sugar Creek?" Kaye asked.

Luke stared at the headline at the bottom of the screen,
scrambled to get the letters straight in his head. "Trust
Fund Baby—"

"—Turns Philanthropist," Rocky finished.

And just like that the show jumped to the next story.

"What's going on?" Kaye asked.

Luke had a clue, he just hadn't expected the news to
break so soon and not while he was away. He turned and
saw Dev, Rocky, and Jayce scrolling through their smart
phones.

"It's all over the Net," Dev said.

"Mostly entertainment venues," Jayce said.

"This has Harper written all over it," Rocky said.

Still focused on his phone, Dev asked, "See that bit
about the Cupcake Lovers self-publishing a recipe book?
What's that about?"

Rocky shook her head. "I don't know."

"You have a signed contract with Highlife."

"I know."

Luke thumbed his own phone. "I'll call Rae."

"I'll call Chloe," Dev said.

"Calling Harper," Rocky said.

"I'll do my thing," Jayce said, which meant some sleuthing.

"I'll be reading," Kaye said, sounding irritated now. "Someone let me know something when someone knows anything. Wait. I'll call Daisy. She knows everything about the Cupcake Lovers."

Luke crossed the room, searching for a quiet corner as everyone connected with someone in Sugar Creek.

Rae answered on the first ring. "What's going on with your dad?"

"Still waiting for news. What's going on with you?"

"I guess you saw one of the reports."

Luke jammed a hand through his hair, torn between worry and frustration. "Why didn't you wait until I was back to unleash this media blitz?"

"I wasn't me. It was Harper Day."

"The publicist Rocky's been working with."

"That's right," Rae said, sounding a little out of breath. "It was a mix-up. A miscommunication. Daisy sent a text to Sam asking for Harper's advice. Sam forwarded the text and . . . Harper's a real go-getter who jumped the gun. She thought she was acting on Sam and the club's wishes and a couple of leaked leads later. . . . It's mushroomed throughout the day."

"Are you being hounded?" Luke asked. "Reporters? Photographers?"

"I've gotten more phone calls than anything. Nearly as many as my lawyer. There are a lot of organizations desperate for a hefty donation."

"Why did Gram tell Harper you wanted to give away your money like that?"

"I don't think she did. I think that's the angle Harper used to get the most publicity bang based on my buying the day care center and offering to fund the publishing of the Cupcake Lovers book. Speaking of," she rushed on, "I heard back from Brett late this afternoon. Highlife does want to push on with the release. Except, the rest of the CLs heard about my offer through the news and, according to Daisy, everyone wants to bail on Highlife and go our independent way. I don't know what to tell Brett. I don't know the legal ramifications and my lawyer, Al, isn't familiar with the contract. I don't—"

"Reagan. Calm down." Head down, voice low, Luke spoke in a soothing tone. "Getting worked up about this isn't good for you or the baby. Listen, if all goes well, I'll be home tomorrow. Hell, maybe I can catch a red-eye. I don't know. Whatever the case, just lay low until I get there. Stop taking those calls and stay out of sight. I'll give you Adam's number. If you need to go somewhere, call him. Or hell, Sam or Leo. I'd rather they handle some obnoxious photographer than you."

"I don't think it's that bad, Luke."

"Humor me."

She blew out a breath.

"Say 'okay.'"

"Okay," she said on a wobbly laugh. Then, "I'm sorry, Luke. Not knowing your dad's condition I didn't want to trouble you about any of this. Not until later. I know Chloe and Daisy felt the same about Rocky and Dev. I should've known one or another of you would've caught wind of the news via some outlet."

"We'll sort it out when I get home."

"I know. I'm not worried."

"You sound worried."

"It's the contract thing. What if I caused a legal mess for the club? What if—"

Her voice hitched and Luke frowned. "I'll talk to Dev about it. He'll know what to do. He always does. He's a wiz at that stuff."

"I know."

Luke heard his family signing off their own calls. "I should go. I'll call you again later."

"Luke, I . . ."

The emotion in her voice, set him on edge. "What?"

"I . . . I'm thinking good thoughts for your dad."

"Thank you for that." Luke disconnected, his own emotions jumbled. If Rae hadn't been so jazzed about so many projects, if she'd exercised a little restraint . . .

"I'm guessing you got the same scoop as us," Rocky said. "What a mess. Although Harper swears she can spin things either way regarding the book deal."

"I went over that contract with my lawyer with a fine-tooth comb," Dev said. "There's a way out if the club wants it."

"From what Daisy said," Kaye said. "They do."

"From what little Chloe shared about self-publishing," Dev said, "sounds to me like a sound financial risk."

"How's Rae holding up?" Rocky asked.

Luke crossed his arms, shook his head. "Not great. She's caught me off guard more than once this week. Moments of supreme confidence and enthusiasm and then—*wham*—she's fragile and vulnerable. It just hit me but, sometimes she's like two different people."

"Hormones," Dev said. "Chloe was like that when . . ." He trailed off but not soon enough.

"I knew it," Rocky said. "Rae's pregnant." She elbowed Jayce. "I told you . . ." She trailed off, too, suddenly conscious, as was Luke, of their mother hovering, eyes narrowed.

"Lucas Monroe," she said in a tone every kid dreaded. "What have you done?"

And just because the situation wasn't awkward enough, Luke's dad ambled in, took one look at his family, and glowered. "What's going on?"

TWENTY-EIGHT

Rae chose to spend the rest of the night in her suite. Shutting out the world until Luke returned to Sugar Creek seemed like a fine idea. Not that she wasn't capable of handling things on her own—for the most part she'd been navigating life solo for a long while—but in this instance, she didn't have to. In this instance she had a friend and partner in Luke. Somewhere along the way he'd garnered her trust, so she trusted his advice regarding her immediate crisis.

She shut off the television and monitored all calls, most of which tapered off after six, although she had jumped on the call that had come in from Luke just past five. The relief in his voice had been evident, filling Rae with instant joy. Her heart had pounded as Luke shared the results from the scan.

The cancer had not spread. His dad's condition had not worsened. Treatment and monitoring would remain status quo.

The Monroes—including Jerome and Kaye—were flying home to Sugar Creek tomorrow.

Rocky and Jayce would be married on schedule Saturday afternoon.

Rae had been so thrilled for everyone concerned that she hadn't taken offense when Luke had rushed her off the phone. She knew he was overwhelmed and that he was heading to dinner with his family to celebrate their good fortune. It wasn't until after that she realized he'd sounded a little awkward when they'd said their good-byes. When he'd added they had a lot to discuss when he got back, she assumed it was the media frenzy coupled with her house-hunting mission. But maybe it was something more. Or maybe her imagination was running amok. Her emotions certainly were. She'd been on a roller coaster all day.

Desperate to strike an even keel, Rae ordered in a healthy dinner and focused on everything positive. In addition to reporting the good news on his dad, Luke had assured her that Dev was on top of the contract issue and that neither she nor the club had anything to worry about. In anticipation of moving forward with self-publishing the CL recipe book, Rae turned her energy to researching the subject. She wanted to be adequately educated when the group met on Thursday.

After that, she created a file on her computer, listing every organization that had either reached out to her or Al regarding a donation. But of course she wanted to share her good fortune with those who needed it most. How she was going to narrow that down when there were so many noble and worthy causes, she didn't know.

Sipping water and pulling on the last of her energy, Rae looked over her notes regarding possible supplemental programs for Sugar Tots. She also jotted a list of new names for the school though nothing really appealed. Maybe Luke would have some catchy ideas. Thinking of Luke, Rae Googled *dyslexia,* reacquainting herself with techniques that would help with his visual processing.

She'd been yawning incessantly for the past hour. She finally shut down her computer around nine thirty, grabbed her Kindle Fire and, lying back in bed, opened the last digital book she'd purchased—*What to Expect When You're Expecting.*

She didn't remember falling asleep. Barely registered a knock on her door then the sound of Luke's voice. Although that couldn't be right. Luke was in Florida. She must be dreaming.

"Rae. Sweetheart."

He sounded so real, so close.

Rae forced her eyes open and blinked into her dimly lit room, gasping when she saw a figure hovering near her bed.

"Shh. It's okay. It's me."

"Luke? What are you doing here? What time is it?"

"A little after four."

"In the morning?" Her vision and thoughts had yet to clear. Foggy, she pushed to her elbows, noting her laptop on the bed. Her Kindle was still in her hand. The only light in the room came from a muted bedside lamp. "I must've fallen asleep while reading," she croaked.

"I can see that," Luke said while peeling off his outer wear. "I called you around ten to let you know I was catching a red-eye. When I didn't get you, I figured you'd switched off your phone. I knocked, but you didn't answer, so I used the key you gave me."

"That's fine." She set her Kindle on the nightstand and reached for her laptop.

"I got it," Luke said. "You crawl under the covers."

At least she'd changed into pajamas before crashing.

Luke moved her laptop to the desk then started shedding clothes. "I'm wiped."

"I can imagine. I thought you were flying in tomorrow. Did your entire family take the red eye?"

"Nope. Just me. Wanted to get back to you."

Even though she was groggy, her heart pounded at the sentiment. "That was sweet." Her dopey smile widened when he switched off the lamp, crawled under the covers, and pulled her into a spooning position.

"I'd take advantage of your sleepy state," he said, "if I weren't so tired myself."

"Rain check," Rae said, snuggling into his embrace.

"*Mmm*. Rae?"

"*Hmm?*"

"I didn't spot any paparazzi lurking outside or in the lobby, but I could be mistaken. Someone might've seen me let myself into your room. It could end up on fricking TMZ. *Bartender serves up a midnight special for heiress philanthropist.*"

Eyes closed, she smiled into the dark, comforted by Luke's presence. "I don't care."

He kissed the back of her head, draped one of his legs over hers, and palmed her tummy. "I'm glad."

Luke woke to the feel of Rae trailing kisses over his shoulders, his collarbone, his chest. His lips curled in a lazy smile. "Good morning to me."

She grinned up at him and Luke's heart jerked. He'd always wanted a woman to smile at him like that. The way Chloe smiled at Dev and Rocky smiled at Jayce. Hell, even his grandma had a secret smile for Vince. Like he was the center of her universe. Adoration mixed with admiration. Not superficial, fleeting love, but good and true love. Luke never thought he'd see the day. But there it was. That secret smile.

For him.

Was it possible? Did Rae love him? Good and true?

"Weren't you wearing pajamas when we fell asleep?" he teased.

"I'm feeling frisky," she said with a waggle of her brows.

"Yeah?" He smoothed her longish bangs out of her beautiful face. How had he ever thought her mousy?

"How about we move this show to the shower. Long day yesterday. Should have rinsed off last night but all I wanted to do was climb into bed with you."

She rolled onto him and surprised him with a full body hug. "I'm glad you're here, Luke."

"In your bed?"

"In my life."

Another heart jerk.

Clingy women usually scared him off, but Rae wasn't being clingy as much as affectionate and emotionally forthright. She was usually more guarded and he wondered what had shifted between them and when. Luke hugged her back, wondering about the tender feelings stirring inside him. He was certain he'd never felt this way before. And he was pretty sure this particular rush wasn't connected to the baby.

He flashed back on a discussion they'd had the other night. "Maybe the person you're attracted to is a reflection of where you are in your own life," he said mid-thought.

She pushed up a little and looked down at him with a scrunched brow. "Are you still wondering why I'm attracted to you? Or the other way around?"

"I'm wondering why our relationship is escalating so fast."

"Is it?"

He arched a brow. "You don't feel it?"

"I feel it."

"Something you want to tell me?"

Her cheeks flushed. "Not at the moment."

Yet her heart shone in her eyes. Luke tempered his pulse. Rae loved him. Good and true. He'd bet the Shack on it. He wasn't sure what to do with the knowledge. He wasn't sure how he felt beyond freaking good.

"So where are you?" she asked. "In your life that is."

"At a turning point."

"Obviously."

Luke skimmed his hands over her bare back, loving the feel of her skin and the way her body molded so perfectly to his. "I was on unsteady ground even before I knew about the baby. I first felt the shift when you started working for me last fall. Something about your quiet confidence, your intelligence and kindness. I started lusting after you even when you were sporting that mousy look and those shapeless clothes. Then that kiss, that first kiss. *Jesus.* I sensed something special, something just beyond my reach." He smoothed his knuckles over her cheek. "Only you're not. You're here. In my arms. In my life."

She burst into tears.

What the . . . Luke rolled her onto her back, smoothed tears from her cheeks. "Did I say something wrong?"

"You said everything right."

"Then why are you crying?"

"I don't know. I mean I'm incredibly touched by what you . . . you said. But this is crazy. The last few days, I can't seem to control my . . . my emotions."

"Hormones," Luke said. "Mood swings are natural at this stage of pregnancy. Dev said . . ." *Damn.*

She sniffed back tears, frowned. "You told Dev?"

"It's one of the things I wanted to talk to you about. Part of the reason I flew home early. I wanted to brace you . . . I just, I didn't mean to blurt it out like this."

"But you promised—"

"I didn't offer the information, I swear. I . . ." Luke dragged a hand down his face. "Could you pull on a robe or something? I can't look at you naked without thinking dirty thoughts. Trying to focus here."

She smiled a little and Luke took solace in knowing he might not be dead meat after all.

"Dev guessed," he said while she pulled on her pajama top. "A logical deduction in his mind because why else would someone who played the field like me suddenly turn monogamous for a girl he barely knows? Rocky suspected for the same reason only her suspicions were tweaked even more by you."

"*Me?* I didn't say anything. I'm sure I didn't slip—"

"And then my parents—"

"Your *parents* know?" She gave up on buttoning her top after buttoning it crooked twice. "How the . . . surely they didn't guess."

"No, that was definitely because of a slip. All I can say is that it happened under extraordinary circumstances. We were still in the waiting room, tense about Dad, then we saw you on the TV and, hell, I don't remember how it happened exactly." He blew out a breath. "I'm sorry, Rae."

She lowered her head, took a moment, then met his gaze. "What did they say? What do they think?"

At least she was still talking to him. Luke pushed up and leaned back against the pillows. "Mostly they wanted to know I'm doing right by the baby, followed by, are they going to get to know the baby? Essentially they wanted to know my, our, plans. I said we're feeling our way through."

Sitting on her knees now, Rae nodded. "That's a fair and accurate description." She dragged her hands through her messy hair, messing it up more. "Your parents moved to Florida not long after I first moved to Sugar Creek. I know *of* them, but I don't *know* them. And now they're coming up for Rocky's wedding. Should I be nervous?"

"Not at all. My folks are great. Mostly. Dad can be a pain in the ass, but he won't be with you." Luke tucked her hair behind her ear. "Are you mad?"

"I'm not mad."

"Seriously?"

"You took me by surprise and I wish we could have discussed it first—the how, when, and who—but, honestly I had planned to broach the subject with you anyway.

About letting people know. I've been feeling uncomfortable about keeping the baby a secret from the Cupcake Lovers, the people I betrayed before. I don't want everyone always wondering what else I have up my sleeve."

"I get that." Luke raised a brow. "So we're going share the news with close friends and family?"

"Just those here in Sugar Creek."

"Not your mom?"

"Not yet. She'd taint it somehow. I'm sure of it."

Now she sounded angry.

Luke waffled between pulling back and pushing. His curiosity got the best of him. "What is it with you two?"

Rae reached for her pajama bottoms and pulled those on, too.

Frisky mood shot, Luke thought. *Got it.*

"I don't know how to explain without sounding pathetic or weak or, I don't know, like I'm playing the poor little rich girl card."

Luke felt her warring with her pride. He got that, too. "Just spit it out."

She sat on the edge of the mattress, spine rigid. "Olivia never wanted me."

She paused and caught Luke's gaze. When he didn't comment or judge, the floodgates opened.

"I was a mistake. I cost her her precious figure. I cost her a movie role. I cost her the unadulterated, exclusive, and obsessive attention of her husband because he, unlike her, wanted and adored me. Or so my grandma, my dad's mom, told me before she passed away. I don't remember my dad. I wish I did. He died when I was two."

Luke listened as she described her life as the daughter of Olivia Deveraux. A woman who'd abandoned her daughter's care to nannies, allowing her to concentrate on herself and husband number two. The woman who'd shipped her daughter off to school the moment she married husband number three. The woman who always chose the spotlight over school awards ceremonies or family vacations or even holidays with her only child.

Luke pulled his best poker face because he knew Rae didn't want his sympathy, but by God she had it. Given his upbringing—his loving parents and tight-knit family—Rae's situation was beyond his imagining. And to think he'd mixed one of his best appletinis for her selfish witch of a mother.

"No matter how many times she pushed me into the background," Rae went on, "I held out hope that we'd bond someday. That she'd put me, our relationship, above her obsessive need to be the center of attention. All my efforts to establish a deeper relationship failed. It doesn't help that she's married to someone as egomaniacal as herself. It doesn't help that she ignores his indiscretions. I thought it was a money thing. Olivia couldn't afford the extravagant lifestyle she adores without Geoffrey's money. Once I gained full access to my inheritance, I offered to support her in the means she was accustomed to if she left Geoffrey. I told her we could move anywhere. New York, maybe. Or London. It wasn't the life I wanted for myself, but I saw it as her chance to break free from that bastard. I saw it as our chance to spend quality time together. To bond."

Rae shook her head, forecasting the outcome with a bitter laugh. "She pretended she knew nothing of Geoffrey's wandering eye. Accused me of trying to break them up because I'm jealous of what they have." Rae snorted. "What they *have* is a shallow, dysfunctional relationship. I can't support it. Can't be around it. Them. Him. Her." She nailed Luke with dry, bright eyes. "I didn't run away from my problems. I walked away from a life I don't want. Not for me. Not for my child."

It was all Luke could do not to pull her into his arms.

Yes, he wanted to comfort her, but right now, boosting her confidence seemed more important. "I don't blame you."

"You don't think I'm an awful person because I want to sever ties with my own mother?"

"From what you've told me, Rae, Olivia doesn't deserve the privilege of being part of your life."

"I'm not cutting her off completely," she said. "Not financially. I mean if she's ever desperate. If Geoffrey ever dumps her. I couldn't let her flounder."

"Something tells me she'd get by. There's always husband number five."

Rae's lip twitched with the semblance of a smile. "She's always admired Elizabeth Taylor. I thought it was for the icon's talent and beauty. But maybe it's more about her ability to collect husbands. I think Liz had seven or eight. Olivia has a way to go."

Feeling a break in the tension, Luke offered a gentle smile. "I know this thing with Olivia is a point of pride with you. I know you don't like to talk about, but I'm glad you did."

Rae swallowed then reached for Luke's hand. "Thank you for listening and understanding. I'm glad you pushed because, now that it's out, now that you know, maybe I can truly put Olivia behind me."

"Unfortunately that media blitz Harper incited plays up the fact that you're the daughter of a Hollywood celebrity," Luke reminded her. "Olivia's name and picture appeared in those gossip features almost as much as yours."

"Oh, yeah." Rae sighed. "No doubt Olivia's basking in the attention."

Luke raised a brow. "She was referred to as a "has-been" and there was mention of plastic surgery and botox."

"Doesn't matter what they're saying as long as they're talking about her. That's the way Olivia looks at it."

Luke shook his head. "God, I'm glad you're here and not there."

Rae swallowed. "Me, too."

He sensed lingering anxiety, traced his memories for any holes in their discussion. "Anything else you want to tell me?"

"No."

Brain still scrambling he flashed back on a discussion a few days prior. Something Rae had said and then tried to brush over.

"*The thing about being smart and influential is that there's always someone smarter and more influential than you. And if that person wants to derail your life, well, then you're sort of screwed.*"

Olivia didn't strike him as smart and she probably wasn't all that influential. No. That would be Geoffrey Stein. Of Stein & Beecham Industries.

Luke shifted closer to Rae. "Does Geoffrey know you encouraged Olivia to leave him? Is he threatening you in some way?"

She sidled to the edge of the bed, ready to flee, only Luke stayed her. She licked her lips, a nervous tell. "Geoffrey and I have been on bad terms for a couple of years now."

"Did you catch him with another woman?"

"No."

"Did you accuse him of having affairs? Of mistreating your mom?"

"No."

"Was he trying to manipulate you somehow? Coerce you into allowing him to manage your inheritance?" Luke's temper flared. Rae's silence on the matter only made it worse. "Dammit, Rae. Is Geoffrey threatening you?"

Her face was beet red now. "It doesn't concern you, Luke."

"What?" The anger he'd been feeling toward Geoffrey took a sharp turn toward Rae. He struggled to keep his calm as she wiggled out of his grasp. "We're a team now, Reagan. Every aspect of your life is of concern to me."

"That goes both ways."

Clueless, he spread his hands wide. "Am I stonewalling you on something?"

"Yes. Yes, you are." She shoved off the bed and scrambled back two steps, fists at her side. "Your dyslexia."

"I told you—"

"You told me and then you shut me down. You said you didn't want to talk about it. That you didn't want my help."

"I said it would be hell on the ego and you're changing the subject."

"No, I'm not. We're talking about levels of comfort. You'd rather handle your visual challenges on your own and I feel the same way about Geoffrey."

"So there *is* a problem."

"Not as long as I don't talk about it." With that she fled to the bathroom and closed the door.

Luke followed and knocked.

In response she turned on the shower.

It reminded him of their blowout in Bel Air. When she'd shut him out. When, in anger, he'd given up and left. Only this time he wasn't going anywhere. He'd order up breakfast for them both and wait her out. He'd cool off and mull over the best way to handle this new kink in their relationship. He'd always considered himself an expert on women. Always knowing what to say, what to do, how to manipulate the situation. Rae stumped him at every turn.

Maybe Sam was right, Luke thought as he pulled on his sweats then nabbed the menu. Maybe there was something to be said for patience.

TWENTY-NINE

Rae wasn't sure how long she'd been in the shower. Hands braced on the tiles, chin dipped, she allowed the pulsating water to pound the back of her head and shoulders. A small fanciful part of her willed the water to wash away her problems. Another small part of her beckoned the pounding water to jog her good senses.

Rationally she knew her judgment and emotions were all over the place. She knew for a fact she was a smart person. A grounded person. Yet lately she'd been making questionable choices and acting in irrational ways. Chances were most people didn't notice. It's not like she socialized all that much. But she noticed. And she was pretty sure Luke noticed.

He'd mentioned hormones. She'd read something about that. No doubt a contributor, but not the sole cause. She couldn't pinpoint her reasons for acting rashly or out of character. She didn't like media attention and yet she'd fully planned to monopolize on her new inheritance and famous mother in order promote the Cupcake Lovers cause. She'd told herself and Luke that she could handle it and then she'd bobbled her composure when the news had actually hit the fan.

She'd put the Cupcake Lovers at legal risk when she'd offered to back their publishing project without fully researching the matter first.

She'd dealt a low blow to Luke by bringing his dyslexia into their argument, but she'd felt backed into a corner and she'd lashed out.

For all her education, for all her confidence, Rae was intimidated by Geoffrey Stein. Olivia had been married to him for five years now. And although Rae hadn't lived in their home all that much, she'd been there enough to overhear several snatches of Geoffrey's business conversations, whether in person or over the phone. The man was ruthless. Ruthless and powerful.

And he hated Rae for rebuffing him.

She remembered the first time she caught him looking at her in an inappropriate way. And the second and the third. It made her uncomfortable. Then again, she'd caught him looking at other women as well, his appreciative gaze lingering a scant second too long. Since he was always highly attentive and even affectionate toward Olivia, Rae had chalked Geoffrey's wandering eye up to annoying, but harmless.

Lots of men ogled.

Lots of men flirted.

That didn't mean they cheated.

Since Rae so badly wanted to bond with her mother the few times she was home from college, she made a concerted effort to get along with Geoffrey. She'd considered their relationship platonic if not genuinely warm.

But then he'd cornered her last year, on the Christmas just after her twenty-fourth birthday. That year, Rae had joined Olivia and Geoffrey for a string of holiday parties. Olivia had been drinking heavily and enjoying the attention of a Hollywood producer. Rae had been exhausted and uncomfortable and ready to call a cab. Only Geoffrey had offered to drive her back to the mansion, saying he'd return later for Olivia.

Rae hadn't realized how inebriated Geoffrey had been until he'd followed her up the stairs and pinned her against the hall wall, just shy of her bedroom. She'd been stunned when he'd pressed in and kissed her. She'd been horrified. She'd turned her head, broken the kiss. She'd told him to back off but he'd leaned in harder, accusing her of playing games.

"*You know you want this.*"

But she didn't.

Her stomach turned, remembering how she'd frozen when his hand slid up her thigh. But then her instincts had kicked in and she'd shoved and kneed him, escaping into her bedroom and locking the door. She'd broken out in a sweat, heart pounding in fear. Would he try to break in?

He didn't.

But he did issue a threat through the door, his voice tight with anger and pain. He'd accused her of asking for it. He'd listed signs. He'd called her a prick-teaser and he'd promised if she breathed a word of this to Olivia or anyone else, he'd deny it. And if that didn't work he'd say Rae started it and he'd ended it. That she was trying to make trouble because he'd scorned her.

Rae had spent a sleepless night with those taunts ringing in her ears.

"*You asked for it.*"

She'd racked her brain, recalling the instances Geoffrey had mentioned. The *signs*. But she was certain in her heart of hearts that he'd misconstrued her intentions. She kept telling herself that he was drunk. Maybe he'd apologize in the morning. . . .

But it had only gotten worse.

A knock on the bathroom snapped Rae out of her tawdry reflections.

"Everything okay?" Luke called.

Rae turned off the shower, sluicing water from her face. "Be out in a minute."

Her fingers were pruney so Rae knew she'd lost track of time. She hadn't expected Luke to hang around. She'd expected him to leave in a huff, to go home, or to the Shack. She'd expected him to call her later. Her stomach fluttered and cramped at the same time. Her temper had cooled, but had his?

She combed her wet hair off her face, slathered on lotion, and pulled on the thick, complimentary robe provided by the hotel. She padded out of the bathroom in her bare feet, a lingering cloud of steam billowing behind her.

"You were in there an awfully long time," Luke said. "Must've felt good." He gestured behind her. "Mind if I—"

"Help yourself."

He nabbed his duffle then paused at her side, his free hand brushing hers. "Truce?"

She nodded, relieved that he didn't press more about Geoffrey. She was overwhelmed and desperately trying to sort out her feelings on several matters. Being at war with Luke wouldn't help.

"Breakfast on the table. Dig in." He squeezed her fingers then moved toward the bathroom. "I won't be long. When I get out, what do you say we go house hunting?"

She looked over her shoulder at him. "Don't you need to go to work?"

"Not until tonight."

"I have a real estate booklet that I picked up down in the lobby," she said. "I circled some contenders."

"Sounds good. I have a place in mind, too. Eat up and get dressed, Champ. Full day ahead."

He disappeared into the bathroom, leaving Rae alone and wondering. *Champ*? He'd never called her that before. An endearment of sorts and not one she'd ever heard him use on anyone else. Something unique to her. She smiled. The warm feeling blossomed as she followed her nose.

Scrambled eggs, wheat toast, and a side of pancakes. OJ and milk. He'd remembered the things she'd like most from the other morning. She massaged an ache in her chest, touched by Luke's thoughtfulness.

He cared.

Cared enough to remember what foods she liked. Cared enough to take off half a day to help her find a house. And because he cared, he'd pressed her about Geoffrey. Logically, she knew that and her mind whirled, unsure how to handle the subject if it came up again. Because Luke cared, if he learned Geoffrey had made a sexual advance, and then proceeded to use that against her. . . . If he knew how the man had continued to taunt Rae. . . . How he'd made her question her judgment. . . . How he'd tried to influence how she handled her inheritance. . . .

Luke would intercede on her behalf.

She couldn't allow that.

She couldn't risk Geoffrey using his power and influence to push back and push back hard. Who knew how far he'd go? What if he somehow compromised Luke's finances? His business? His reputation?

Although she couldn't prove it, Geoffrey had somehow cost Rae the two teaching positions she'd recently applied for within the Los Angeles school district.

"Maybe you'd have better luck in another part of the country," he'd taunted the last time Olivia had had Rae over for dinner, just days prior to Rae learning she was pregnant.

Clearly Geoffrey wanted Rae out of their lives and the farther away the better. It was the first time she'd seen eye to eye with the man. Considering Olivia had no intention of leaving her husband and especially after Rae had learned she was pregnant, leaving California—for good—had been an easy decision. The way Rae saw it, as long as she didn't rattle Geoffrey's chains, she was free and clear to live the life of her choosing.

The in-room phone rang and Rae abandoned her breakfast to answer. "Yes?"

"Ms. Deveraux? This is Len Jeffries, comanager of the Pine and Periwinkle. I thought you'd want to know that a couple of photographers and reporters are lingering in the lobby. I think they're hoping to get a picture or a word with you. One of them asked about you at the front desk. We didn't give out your room number or any personal information. But they seem tenacious. As they haven't done anything wrong, I can't ask them to leave. I just thought you should know."

"I appreciate that, Mr. Jeffries."

"If you're planning to leave at some point today and don't wish to interact with these gentlemen, I could come up and escort you out through a lesser known exit."

"That's very kind."

"We at the Pine and Periwinkle appreciate your business and strive to respect the privacy of all our guests. I'll give you my cell number. Call any time."

Rae jotted down the number and thanked the man. She hung up then contemplated switching on her laptop and the television. Was she in the news again today? What were they saying? Her curiosity almost got the best of her but then she decided she didn't want to know. Not this minute. She'd had a roller-coaster morning with Luke. She was eager find an even keel. To get her thoughts together. What did she want most to accomplish and how much could she reasonably take on while allowing time to settle into a new home as well as building a relationship with Luke? Problem was there was so much she wanted to do, so many people she wanted to help and now that she had the finances to work wonders, she was like a flipping kid in a candy store.

Anxious to get on with her day, Rae gobbled down two more forkfuls of eggs and bit off a hunk of toast before moving to the bureau. She rooted through her wardrobe, settling on dark blue jeans and a funky tunic sweater. She also pulled on a pair of flat-heeled sweater boots, a style she'd favored while posing as frumpy Rachel. Only these boots hugged her legs to the knees instead of scrunching to her ankles. She dragged some gel through her hair then, standing at the small vanity, used the blow dryer and her fingers to style her hair.

She'd just finished lining her eyes and swiping on red-tinted lip balm when Luke emerged from the bathroom.

"You look pretty," he said.

"You look sexy." He'd pulled on a pair of jeans and zipped, but had yet to fasten the button. The waistband parted enough to tease Rae with thoughts of the delectable package just below. She dragged her hungry gaze up his bare torso, amazed yet again at all the glorious ridges. "I think your muscles have muscles."

"Are you ogling my body, Ms. Deveraux?"

"I shudder to think what you have to do to look like that. How many hours do you spend at a gym?"

"Home gym and not all that much. I've always been athletic."

"Not me. I'm a klutz when it comes to sports."

"Do you like sports?"

She shrugged. "In school, I was one of those people who was always last to be picked on the team. So, no."

"What about something like pool? Or bowling?"

"Not something I've been exposed to."

"We'll have to do something about that." He held up an incredibly wrinkled brown tee. "Would you be embarrassed to be seen with me wearing this?"

"Would you like me to iron it for you?"

"I guess that's a yes. You iron?"

"Don't you?"

"I toss wrinkled stuff in the dryer."

"No dryer here as you can see." Rae moved to the closet and took out the ironing board.

"Let me help. The least I can do since you're ironing my shirt."

Rae grabbed the iron while Luke unfolded the board. "The comanager of the inn called while you were in the shower," she said.

"Len?"

"Yes. Len Jeffries. Do you know everyone in town?"

"Pretty much."

"Anyway he said there are reporters and photographers waiting for me. He said he can sneak me out the back if I want."

"How do you feel about that?" Luke asked as he poured a cup of coffee from the carafe.

"I don't know what they're going to ask me and I'm undecided on how I want to move forward with a couple of things." Rae said as she ironed. "I think I'd like to avoid the press until I know more details about what's happening with Sugar Tots and the CL recipe book. I also have to figure out how I'm going to handle all these requests for donations. Of course, I could always just answer their questions with "No comment.""

"I'm not sure that's the best tactic. Sounds like you're hiding something that will only make them snoop or hound you more."

"True." Rae glanced up. "Why are you smiling?"

"I like watching you iron."

Her stomach fluttered. "That's just weird."

Still smiling, he finished off his coffee.

Rae tossed him his shirt and unplugged the iron. "To be honest, I usually throw wrinkled stuff in the dryer, too. This suite is spacious and lovely, but I'm missing the conveniences of a house or apartment. The place you want to show me. Does it come with appliances?"

"It does," Luke said as he pulled on the tee and then a green and brown long-sleeved flannel.

"Where is it?" Rae asked as she stuffed her own real estate booklet into her purse.

"Opposite end of town, about five miles from city limits. Nothing fancy, but it has a great view of the mountains."

"I love the mountains," Rae said. She unplugged her phone from the charger and tossed it in her purse. No doubt there were several messages. From her lawyer. That anchorwoman at *Vermont Today.*

Just then Luke's phone rang. He glanced at the caller ID, then glanced at Rae with a raised brow while answering. "Hey, Sam."

Rae reached for her coat, hoping Sam had called to make peace.

"No," Luke said. "Flew back last night. Yeah. Me, too. Dad's had some tough knocks." He nodded, cleared his throat. "I appreciate that, Sam. Thanks. Rae? She's right here. Ah. That's because she turned off her phone last night and I'm guessing has yet to turn it back on. No. Why?"

Rae looked over and caught Luke's gaze as she slowly zipped her coat. He didn't look happy.

"*Huh.*" He looked away and snatched up his own jacket. "That's fucked. No. I . . . What's Harper's advice? Yeah. Okay. I'll let you know. Thanks, Sam." He signed off, brushed a kiss over Rae's mouth, then passed his phone. "Call Len and tell him we'd like to be escorted out the back."

THIRTY

Luke asked Len to wait with Rae while he jogged to the side parking lot and drove his car around to pick her up. He didn't want to risk walking her a good distance in plain view. Aside from the yahoos waiting in the lobby, who knew how many lurked outside? Luke didn't have any personal experience with the paparazzi, but he'd seen enough in the news to know they were aggressive and upon occasion dangerous.

He didn't want to risk an ambush and he sure as hell didn't want one of them asking for a response to her mother's attack before Luke had a chance to give her a heads-up. Maybe he should've told Rae in the hotel room, but his gut said to get her the hell out of Dodge and away from the media first.

Luke pulled up to the back door of the inn and Len hustled Rae into his car. Two seconds later, he peeled out and away from the Pine and Periwinkle like a thief in the night. "I guess this would be considered a standard getaway in Hollywood."

"Except we're not in Hollywood and I'm not a celebrity."

"You are, however, a person of interest."

"What did Sam say?"

Rae's tone was as fierce as her expression. In light of what he was about to tell her, Luke welcomed this side of the woman who torched his senses. The lion as opposed to the lamb. Her duality was perplexing and fascinating at the same time. Not just hormones, he thought. Rae was still finding herself. He thought back to when he was twenty-five. She was juggling a lot more responsibility than he had at that age. Not to mention her life was more complicated. Impending parenthood alone was a bitch.

"Harper called Sam because she got a tip from a colleague," Luke said. "Unfortunately the tip came five minutes before the story broke."

"What tip?"

Luke consciously split his mind. Half dealing with the icy road. Half dealing with Rae. It wasn't easy, but he focused on both dicey slopes. "Olivia released a statement basically pegging you as a troubled soul. A warped child of a Hollywood star. A needy, pathological liar desperate for attention."

When Rae didn't respond, Luke glanced over. She was sitting ramrod straight in her seat. Staring out at the oncoming salt-and-snow covered cars, no expression. "Go on," she said.

"Olivia focused on the fact that you told her you'd spent the last year struggling in a remote and repressed area in China, working with underprivileged children when in fact you'd been hiding in a quaint, thriving town in America."

"I can't argue that," she said. "I misled her. But in my defense I wanted to retreat to somewhere unreachable. I needed to get away. Far away. I only made it as far as Sugar Creek. But I didn't want to be accessible, so I lied. I said I was in a remote region of China. Olivia wouldn't go to the trouble of trying to contact me, especially since

I said there was little to no cell or Internet service. She wouldn't have any interest in visiting a place like that or any interest in what I was doing. I know it was extreme, but the situation warranted it."

"How so?" Luke said. "That's what those reporters will want to know. How are you going to defend such an extravagant lie, Rae?"

She pinched the bridge of her nose as if warding off a headache. "I wanted to disappear. I was tired of dealing with Olivia's BS. She looked down her nose at my career aspirations. Why would I want to waste my youth and beauty working long hours in what she perceived as a thankless job? Why did I want to work at all when I was financially set for life? I got tired of her trying to match me up with men I had nothing in common with. And I resented the way she and Geoffrey kept harping on my upcoming inheritance and trying to influence how I should manage those funds.

"I felt hounded and manipulated in every way possible," she went on. "The pressure mounted on my twenty-fourth birthday and I knew it wouldn't let up. Maybe I flipped a little, some sort of life crisis, but I suddenly wanted to be anyone other than me. One year clear of my name and ties. One year to prove that I could make it on my own, living by my wits and doing what I love—working with children. I don't understand why that's so horrible!"

"It's not." Luke flexed his fingers on the wheel, rolled tension from his shoulders. He couldn't remember ever disliking anyone as much as he disliked Olivia and Geoffrey. "Why did you stay in those circumstances for so long to begin with? Why subject yourself to Olivia's company at all? Hell, I would have flown the coop and severed the cord once I turned eighteen."

"I just kept hoping things would change. I don't have a

big family like you, Luke. I have, *had* Olivia. It's hard not to want to be adored or at least loved by your only parent. It took a long time, but I'm over it. I know now we'll never have the relationship I always craved. If she thinks I'm going to allow her to taint the life I'm working toward. . . ."

Luke looked over and saw Rae turning on her phone. "What are you doing?"

"Surfing the Net. I want to see what she put out there."

"I told you."

"I need to see it for myself."

Luke blew out a breath. He was no stranger to drama— between patron mishaps at the Shack, occasional flare-ups with former girlfriends, and assorted sagas within his only family—but this took the cake. Publicly trashing someone, a family member no less, via the media? "Why would Olivia want to hurt you like this?"

"I'm not sure. She's always been insensitive, but never spiteful. Nothing like this."

"What are you seeing?"

"Pretty much what you told me. Her tone . . . It suggests she feels sorry for me. But she spins it in a way that puts the spotlight on her. The suffering mother of the rich-kid-gone-wrong." Rae made a disgusted sound. "The attention. She did it for the attention."

"It can't be as simple as that," Luke said.

"There's mention of her potentially starring in a new reality show. I'm telling you, Luke. She took advantage of the media's interest in me, added fuel to the fire by introducing something scandalous, and then spun the attention on to her. I haven't commented on anything. I haven't given any interviews. *She* will!"

"Sam said Harper's advice was not to respond in anger, so whatever you're thinking—"

"I'm thinking I want to hire Harper."

"What?"

"Olivia will milk this for all it's worth. I'm out of my league. I can't sit by and let her ruin my reputation. It will reflect badly on the Cupcake Lovers and how will the parents of Sugar Creek feel about their children being taught by a pathological liar?"

"Good point."

"Sam gave me Harper's number," she said. "Just in case. I'm going to see if she can meet with me this evening. And I'm going to invite the Cupcake Lovers. I don't want anyone blindsided by anything. I'll call Rocky. See if she can arrange an emergency meeting. That way we can make sure we're all on the same page regarding the self-publishing issue. They might want to bail on that idea now that I've been outed as 'a troubled soul.'"

Luke didn't think that would be the case, but he held silent since he hadn't seen or heard Olivia's rant for himself. While Rae made her phone calls, Luke concentrated on the slow moving traffic as he neared the edge of town. Given the heavy snowfall of late, Sugar Creek was more congested than normal with an influx of tourists. The surrounding fields and mountains were a haven for any sports lover with a snowmobile, sled, or a pair of skis. Hell, if it weren't for Rae he'd be taking to the slopes himself with Adam and Kane.

"It's settled," Rae said. "Harper agreed to act on my behalf. She said this is nothing compared to what she's been handling lately and that she'd put a Band-Aid on it until we decided on a course of action. Rocky's calling all of the CL members, but since she won't be back in Sugar Creek until after four, and since some people need to close up shop, the meeting's at five thirty. Harper advised I lay low until then. I'm thinking we can still scope out some houses. If you're still game, that is."

"I'm game." Luke spared Rae a surprised glance.

"Considering how private you are, I thought you'd be more upset about being slammed in the media."

"(A) What's being said isn't true. (B) Instead of being upset, I'm taking control." She looked at him then, her heart in her eyes. "I just want this to be over, Luke. Olivia's a negative force, and I'm itching to do a lot of good."

In that moment, Luke put a name to the tender feelings he'd developed for Rae. It wasn't like any love he'd experienced before. It was the big one. The real deal.

Luke loved Rae good and true.

Rae couldn't believe how calm she felt in the face of Olivia's betrayal. Taking control of the situation had been key. She was actually looking forward to the meeting this evening with Harper and the Cupcake Lovers. She was especially keen on setting everyone's mind at ease regarding her mother's exaggerated accusations.

Daisy had texted Rae asking if she'd seen the news. Rae had texted back: YES. NOT TRUE. WILL EXPLAIN 2NITE

Chloe had called right after, also voicing concern. Rae had asked her to please spread the word to rest of the club that she could and would explain at the meeting. After that, Rae had lowered the volume on her ringer, determined to enjoy the rest of her morning with Luke.

The roadways were slushy and slick, but he was an excellent driver. Before long the quaint snow-covered businesses had given way to snow-covered trees and houses and then, after crossing over Sugar Creek—the river, not the town—glistening slopes and valleys. She recognized the area. "Don't you live out this way?"

"I do," Luke said.

Rae smiled. He'd located a rental not far from his own home, which meant he wanted her and the baby near. How wonderful to be wanted after so many years of being pushed away.

A few minutes later they turned off the main road onto a side road and then into the next long driveway.

Rae leaned forward, peering closer at the two-story house ahead. "It's bigger than I expected."

"Not all that big. Nothing close to Olivia's house in Bel Air."

"You mean her mausoleum?"

"One large master bedroom with a bathroom and walk-in closets. Two smaller bedrooms. Living room with a fireplace and vaulted ceilings, decent-sized kitchen, den, laundry room. Sits on ten acres of land," he said as he drove up to a two-car garage.

The rentals Rae had ticked off in her real estate booklet had been on the fringes of town, small saltbox houses on small lots of land. This house was lovely and the mountainous scenery breathtaking, but it seemed like a lot of living space and property for her and the baby. As Luke escorted her up a shoveled pathway, she noted his confidence and ease. He hadn't mentioned meeting a real estate agent here, and when he slipped a key into the front door, she instantly knew. "This is your house."

"Bought it a couple of years ago."

"I thought you had a place in mind for me."

"I do." Hand at the small of her back, he urged her over the threshold. "This is it."

Heart pounding, Rae slowly turned. Surely, he didn't mean . . . "You want me to live with you?"

Luke held her gaze while unzipping his jacket. "If we're going to do this, *us,* why not?"

"Because it's a huge commitment. What if we're not compatible? What if we drive each other crazy after a week or four?"

"Then we'll reevaluate and if need be, find you a place of your own."

Rae palmed her swimming head, trying to make sense of this unexpected turn. "Is this some sort of knee-jerk reaction to the media storm?"

"No."

"Did your parents suggest—"

"No." He gave her zipper a playful tug. "Take off your coat and stay awhile. I'll give you the grand tour. If you hate something, we can change it. Except for my fitness room. That's off-limits."

While Luke took her scarf and gloves, Rae slipped off her coat and peeked into the living room. "I don't know, Luke."

"I know it's rustic, but it's comfortable. Rocky insisted on helping me furnish the place, so I know it's not ugly. That said I'm not opposed to adding moderate frill. I'll even let you crowd up the couch with a bunch of those useless little pillows."

"Throw pillows," Rae said with a small smile. "I'm not questioning the décor, Luke. I'm wary of the timing. Don't you think we should let our relationship evolve more before moving in together?"

"Don't take this the wrong way," Luke said as he guided her into the heart of the living room, "but between all your impending projects and my work schedule, when will we have a chance to *evolve*? Sharing a living space makes sense. What better way to get to know every wonderful and irritating detail about one other?"

Rae laughed. "True. Still—"

"Here's the thing." Luke stopped as they entered the living room and turned her into his arms. "I like sleeping with you. I like being with you. The thought of coming home to you every night is appealing. Plus . . . as you get further along in the pregnancy, I want to be close in case you need me." He shrugged. "For anything."

His words were so kind they took her breath away. Rather than cry she made a joke. "Such as running out for pickles and ice cream when I have a mad craving in the middle of the night?"

"Couldn't you at least crave something good? Like *cookies* and ice cream? Then I could join you."

Rae hugged Luke tight, desperately wanting what he offered. "You make it sound so tempting, but we'd be jumping out of the frying pan into the fire."

"So? We may get singed, but we'll survive. One way or the other." He gave her a squeeze then took her by the hand. "Let me show you around."

Rae felt as though she were floating through a dream as Luke toured her around his home. She loved the vaulted ceilings, the rich woodwork, the stone fireplace. The living room was spacious and sparsely furnished with an overstuffed couch, recliner, club chair, and ottoman. She adored the cushioned window seat with its view of nearby evergreens and distant mountains. Now *there* was a space crying for brightly colored throw pillows! She could sit in that picturesque cubby and read for *hours*.

She fell in love with the kitchen. The den—not so much. The dining room was nice, but she could make it nicer. Luke's fitness room was what it was—a room crammed with weights, a treadmill, and various other torture devices.

He steered her upstairs and into the first room on the right. It was sparsely furnished—a futon and what looked to be one of Sam's handcrafted, hand-painted bureaus. "I thought we could turn this spare room into a nursery. As you see it has a great view of the mountains and plenty of sunlight. I could paint the walls yellow or green—something neutral since we don't know the sex of the baby and—"

"Okay."

"Okay to yellow? Or okay to green?"

"Okay to living with you." Her heart roared in her ears. Her blood sizzled with lust. Hearing Luke talking about their baby's nursery was an electrifying turn-on!

Zap!

She turned and kissed him and he must have felt the same jolt because Luke swept her off her feet and carried her . . . somewhere. Rae was too lost in the kiss to take note of his path. Too aware of the way he was holding her, too absorbed in the heady feel of his lips, his tongue. Too crazy in love to think beyond, "*Take me.*"

Luke laid her down gently. Someplace soft.

Bed, she thought.

He said nothing as he pulled off her boots then slowly peeled off her jeans.

Sexy.

Said nothing as he shucked his own boots and pants. He just watched.

Her.

Hot.

By the time he was completely naked, Rae had stripped off her tunic and bra. Sprawled on the bed, she held out her arms, sighing when he covered her with his warm, hard body.

She was naked and ready. So ready, she exploded on Luke's first thrust.

He froze, hard and deep inside of her, a bemused look on his face as she shuddered with a lingering orgasm.

"I'm sorry," she rasped.

"I'm not." He brushed a kiss over her mouth, smiled. "That was damn hot."

"Yeah, well . . ."

"And now I get to work you up all over again." He smoothed a hand over her face, over the curve of her neck, then down her body as he moved inside her—slow and deep.

Luke took his time and worked her up. Rae's body responded in wondrous waves, but the most exciting and erotic bonus was the way he held her gaze. Luke looked into her eyes the entire time he made love to her. As if she was the most captivating woman in the world. As if she was the center of his universe. As if . . .

Rae cried out with an earth-moving orgasm and Luke climaxed right behind her.

Her brain fairly shut down as her body rode a wave of intense euphoria. "Holy—"

"—hell," Luke finished as he collapsed beside her and pulled her into his arms.

Heart full, Rae struggled to find the right words to express what she was feeling. Description failed her, but words flowed all the same. "I love you, Luke."

He smiled into her eyes. "I love you, Reagan. Good and true."

THIRTY-ONE

No two ways about it. Rocky was irritated with the universe.

The relief she'd experienced after learning her dad's cancer hadn't progressed had morphed into anger that they'd been faced with that worry at all. Hadn't her dad suffered enough without having to deal with the fallout of that previous glitchy test? And what about her mom and the rest of the family? Everyone's nerves were stretched thin. Everyone was distracted. Not just with her dad's illness but now this thing with Rae. The media thing. The baby thing.

On the plane ride home all her mom talked about was the fact that she now had two grandkids on the way. All her dad talked about was his youngest son and how he'd grown up overnight. Luke buying out Dev and taking over full responsibility of the Sugar Shack was huge. Luke settling down and committing to one woman was enormous. At the rate he was moving, no one would be surprised if Luke ended up marrying Rae before spring. Which brought up talk of Dev and Chloe and their reluctance to commit to a wedding date, although Dev pointed out that if it was up to him they'd elope tomorrow.

It's not that Rocky didn't care about her brothers' lives. She adored them both, but it would have been nice if at least a portion of the family discussion would have centered on Rocky's impending wedding. She could have brought it up herself, but she was feeling churlish. Not that anyone had noticed. Well, except for Jayce. He'd noticed, but instead of explaining—because it made her feel petty—she'd blamed her grumpy mood on exhaustion.

Now, instead relaxing at home with Jayce and Brewster and putting together the last of her wedding favors, Rocky was immersed in an emergency Cupcake Lover meeting at Harper's house. A house Rocky had been struggling to redecorate and fully furnish because of Harper's indecisiveness. A quick look around showed that Sam had made more progress in three days than Rocky had made in three and a half months. His work on the staircase, several doorframes, and the kitchen in general was unmistakable. Pure quality. Pure Sam.

There was, however, little evidence of Rocky's influence. Not that she hadn't presented Harper with hundreds of ideas. Another bone of contention.

Just now everyone was gathered in the main living room. Harper and Sam had pulled in chairs from other rooms to create a circle of seating big enough to accommodate twelve people. She'd covered a couple of accent tables and a trunk with fabric samples, surfaces to accommodate paper plates and cups. No one cared that dinnerware was disposable. They were impressed that Harper had gone to the trouble of brewing tea and coffee as well as serving a batch of her own homemade cupcakes. Vanilla cupcakes with strawberry filling. Pretty damned tasty.

"I apologize for the cramped seating," Harper said. "This house is a work in progress and I'm not set up for entertaining. Obviously. But if everyone's comfortable—"

"We're good," Rocky said, speaking for everyone in order to get this ball rolling. Almost all of the members had arrived within minutes of one another, with the exception of Rae and Luke, who'd been five minutes late.

Considering this had once been the home of one of the original Cupcake Lovers, there'd been a lot of chatter about Mary Rothwell and the fact that she supposedly haunted this place. Not that Rocky had ever seen her ghost, but there was a definite vibe in the house even if only in her mind because of the legend.

Chatter of Mary had naturally segued into the history of the Cupcake Lovers, which segued into talk of the memoir/recipe book, which segued into whether to self-publish, which is when Rae and Luke had arrived, hand in hand, looking ridiculously happy. Since Luke was still a member of the club, he had every right to be here and even more so, Rocky supposed, given his personal relationship with Rae. But Rocky sort of wished her brother would've stayed away. Everyone, including Rocky, was keenly aware of Sam's crush or former crush on Rae. The tension was just plain awkward.

Regardless, everyone settled in and listened intently as Harper relayed what had been said in the media thus far regarding Rae and her humanitarian efforts, followed by Olivia Deveraux's attempt to sully Rae's reputation.

All eyes had turned to Rae as she explained in pained detail why she'd lied to her mother about her whereabouts last year and why she'd pretended to be someone else. She shared a little about her childhood and background—which garnered everyone's sympathy—and then her hopes and plans for the future regarding running Sugar Tots (to be renamed) as well as establishing a foundation that supported select charities.

Rae was composed throughout her explanation, but when she started talking about promoting education and helping people in need, she got all fired up. It was that passion that won over Rocky and everyone else in the room.

Luke looked plain smitten.

"Okay, this is great," Harper said as she paced around the exterior of the circle. "I mean I know certain aspects are uncomfortable for you, Rae, but I can spin this in your favor and I can do it with grace."

"Do you always text other people when you're in the middle of a meeting?" Daisy asked Harper.

Rocky knew everyone had noticed and it *was* pretty rude—shades of Tasha Burke—but leave it to Daisy to ask outright.

"Busy week," Harper said without offering an apology. "Don't worry. I'm a master at multitasking. Just so I'm straight," she said, still texting whomever. "The Cupcake Lovers have officially and unanimously decided to allow Rae to finance the self-publishing of your memoir/ recipe book. Correct?"

Everyone nodded.

"Based on reasons we've discussed to death," Rocky said as the president of the club, "yes."

"And based on Rae's defense, regarding her mother's attack, everyone believes and supports Rae."

Another round of nods and murmurs.

"Damn straight," Casey said.

"We know our Rae's heart," Ethel said.

Harper stopped texting and zeroed in on Rae. "Anything else I, *we*, should know? Any other incident that your mother could twist? Any secret she could possibly use against you if unearthed? Any—"

"I'm pregnant," Rae blurted.

The ensuing silence was deafening. Rocky, of course, knew. But clearly it was news to everyone else.

Harper looked a little blindsided by the overall tension in the room. Apparently she was unaware of Sam's famous year-long crush on Rae. Because they'd been holding hands and sitting so closely, the publicist naturally assumed the baby was Luke's. "And this is, *was,* a secret because?"

"I'm not even at eight weeks," Rae explained, cheeks flushing. "The first trimester is unpredictable. I wanted to wait until I was further along before sharing."

"I felt the same way," Chloe said in Rae's defense.

"I would have felt that way," Monica said. "But you all know my history. When it finally happened I couldn't wait to shout it to the world."

"Hold on," Daisy said and Rocky instantly knew her grandma was doing the math like most of the other CLs. She pushed her glasses up her nose then squinted suspiciously at Rae. "You were living in California eight weeks ago."

"I went out for a visit," Luke said.

Daisy reached over and whacked her grandson hard in the back of the head.

Luke grimaced but didn't comment.

Harper sighed. "So are we happy about this news?"

"Yes," Luke answered for them both, his gaze firm on Sam.

Everyone was looking at Sam.

Rocky swallowed a huge lump of emotion when her cousin calmly stood and approached Luke.

Luke rose as well. "Be happy for me, Sam."

Sam pulled Luke into a bear hug, said something in his ear, then broke away, and pulled Rae into a warm hug.

Tension broken, the room erupted into a gabfest of

congratulations and baby talk as well Harper's idea on a spin on Rae's problem that would also afford free promo for Moose-a-lotta as well as the Cupcake Lovers.

Rocky wondered if anyone realized Harper's plan fell on the same day the CLs had planned to make Rocky's wedding cake.

Oh, yeah. She was irritated with the universe big-time.

NEED 2 TALK 2 U

Sam looked down at his phone then over his shoulder at Harper. For Christ's sake he was standing in the same room. Still, the senior CLs had her cornered near the front door so she wasn't exactly free to speak her mind. Sam had lingered, relocating chairs back to various rooms, but now he was itching to leave.

CAN IT WAIT?

NO

Damn.

Sam hung back while Helen, Judy, Ethel, and Daisy finally said their good-byes. He glanced at his watch. Six thirty. Not knowing how long the meeting would take or how things would play out, Sam had hired a sitter to watch Ben and Mina until nine. He wasn't under the gun, but he was restless.

"*That* was interesting. Why didn't you tell me you had a thing for Rae?"

"Maybe you haven't noticed, but we don't talk a lot."

"What did you say to your cousin?"

"None of your business."

"Chill, Rambo. On another note . . ." Harper walked past Sam and into the kitchen.

He hated that he watched her ass as she went. What the hell was with her walk anyhow? She didn't slink or sashay exactly. It wasn't overt. Just a gentle sway of the hips, just enough to mesmerize him. Cursing his randy reaction,

Sam followed. "On another note, what?" he asked, almost tripping on a puddle of red dress near the threshold.

Wearing nothing but a matching silky bra and thong, Harper lounged against the counter in her funky heels, holding a white cupcake in a red foiled baking cup. "Why won't you try my cupcakes?"

"What?"

"I sent you home with almost a dozen the other day. You didn't try one. I baked these fresh for tonight. Everyone in the club had one. Everyone but you."

"I wasn't hungry." Sam's heart rammed against his chest, his cock throbbed. He wasn't sure why he'd avoided Harper's cupcakes. Something psychological. He hadn't given it thought. He would now.

Harper's blue eyes twinkled with an ornery gleam.

Sam knew that gleam. She was about to torture him with some sexy deed.

Sure enough she stuck her thumb in the center of the strawberry filled cupcake. Gaze locked on Sam's, she licked then sensuously sucked the red goo from her thumb. One brow raised, she taunted, "Hungry now?"

Sam was randy and moody and not up for games. He moved in—swift and sure. He took Harper in his arms and ravished that luscious mouth. Sin and strawberries. Hell, yeah.

Her hands worked his belt and buttoned fly while he unclasped her bra. He had her naked and writhing in his arms, kissing her, touching her, just rough enough to rev her senses.

Her damn phone rang. Incessantly.

Sam broke the wild kiss long enough to toss the cell on the top shelf of the fridge. Slamming shut the door, he spun Harper around, bending her over the counter. He splayed his hands down her back, over her ass, her thighs.

He kissed the back of her neck, made her sigh, then entered her from behind, and made her squeal.

It was hot.

It was fast.

And it left them both limp and gasping for air.

In the aftermath, Sam was shocked that he'd been so urgent, so selfishly dominant. But when Harper smiled over her shoulder at him, the guilt slid away. He started to speak, but she shushed him.

Right. No talking after.

Screw that.

"What was that for?" he asked as she stepped back into her dress, no undies.

"I was wound up. Also I sensed you could use a distraction."

With that she shoved her tousled hair out of that beautiful face, grabbed her phone from the fridge, and cast him a parting, enigmatic glance. "See you tomorrow, Sam."

THIRTY-TWO

Luke had never asked a girl to sleep over in his house. Let alone sleep over every night for, well, hopefully the rest of their lives.

After putting in a full night bartending and hosting at the Shack, he'd returned home around two in the morning to find Rae fast asleep in his bed. She was bathed in a soft wash of moonlight and he could see just enough of her face to know she was sleeping peacefully. She looked content. He liked that a lot. Sam's words had been ringing in Luke's ears all night.

"I wish you the happiness I had."

Just thinking about it choked Luke up. Sam's years with Paula had been the happiest of his cousin's life. What's more, the wish had been sincere.

Luke had climbed into bed with Rae, knowing he'd turned a corner in his life. There was no going back. He'd had a hard time getting his mind to shut down. A lot of unsettled issues. The thing with her mom. The beef with Geoffrey, something Luke still wasn't clear on. Sugar Tots would require a lot of Rae's time and Luke would be taking on new challenges at the Shack. They'd have to settle into a new routine, somehow juggle their professional and personal lives. He knew he had to attack his dyslexia in a new way. Learning to conquer rather than cover. He wanted to be able to read stories to his kid without stumbling. He wanted to handle the books and inventory at the Shack without having to rely on Dev or Anna.

He wanted to make Rae proud.

Luke drifted off fully expecting to wake up in a panic.

He woke up with Rae in his arms. He woke up content. "How long have you been awake?" he asked.

"A while."

"Why are you smiling?"

"I'm happy. I don't remember ever being this happy."

Luke kissed her forehead. "I'm glad." He glanced at the bedside clock. "Damn. It's late. What time did Harper say that film crew would be at Moose-a-lotta?"

"Noon."

"We best get cracking. You shower and dress and I'll start breakfast. Craving anything special?"

She smiled and his heart jerked. God, he loved that.

"Pancakes," she said. "With lots of butter and a ton of maple syrup."

"You got it, Champ."

She scrunched her brow. "Why do you call me that?"

"Because when life knocks you down, you get back in there swinging. Sam was right. You're a warrior at heart, Rae. I admire you for that."

"Thank you, Luke." She flushed then and bit her lower lip. "I hope I don't get knocked out today in that interview. I've never done well in the spotlight."

"You'll be fine. Harper's going to coach you beforehand and you'll have a huge cheering section watching from the sidelines. This mess will be behind us before you know it."

She nodded and swung out of bed. "That's incentive

enough to kick this Champ in the butt. Meet you downstairs. I won't be long."

"You look cute in my T-shirt," he said as she padded toward the bathroom.

She grinned. "I may never wear my pjs again."

"Speaking of," Luke said as he pulled on a pair of sweats. "I slid by the Pine and Periwinkle late last night like we talked about and I gathered all of your things." He nodded across the room. "Your laptop and suitcases are over there. Be warned. I'm not a neat packer."

She did a one-eighty and hustled over, thanking him with a brush of her lips. "I don't care about neat."

He thought about his overall housekeeping skills. "Remember you said that."

Twenty minutes later, Luke was adding a sixth flapjack to a serving plate when he heard a knock on the door. He wasn't expecting anyone. Wary of paparazzi, he peeked out a window before answering and was surprised to see his mom and dad standing on his front porch.

Frowning, he swung open the door. "You okay?"

"What kind of greeting is that?" Jerome asked while guiding Kaye inside just ahead of him.

"We wanted to meet Rae before this afternoon's filming," Kaye said as she shook off a chill. "To wish her luck."

"To tell her the family's behind her one hundred percent."

Luke dragged a hand through his hair, his chest swelling with emotion. "That's great. That's . . . I appreciate it," he said while taking his parents' coats and scarves. "I just wish you would have called first."

"Why?"

"So I could have prepared Rae. She's nervous about meeting you."

"Why?" Kaye asked.

While hanging the coats on the tree stand, Luke heard Rae galloping down the stairs. *Damn.*

"Luke! Help! Fashion crisis. I should know what color looks best on TV but I can't remember. I don't know which blouse would be best. I need . . ." She skidded to a stop in a skirt and her bra. ". . . your opinion." Red-faced, she crushed the two shirts she'd been holding at her side to her chest. "Hi."

Suppressing a smile, Luke placed his hand at the small of her back. "Rae, I'd like you to meet my parents. Jerome and Kaye Monroe."

Juggling the crumpled shirts to strategically hide her bra, she offered a hand in greeting. "Pleased to meet you. So sorry for my . . . disarray."

"I read somewhere that you should avoid pastels," Jerome said. "I'd go with that purple shirt."

"It's not purple," Kaye said. "It's eggplant and it does go nicely with your red hair, Rae."

Luke nodded. "I like the purple."

"Your mom's right," Rae said. "It's more eggplant. I do have a couple of other choices."

"If you'd like a woman's opinion, dear, I'd be happy to help."

Rae smiled, looking a little flustered but pleased. "Okay. Thank you." She backed away, still clutching the shirts to her chest until Kaye spun her and shielded her with her body as they climbed the steps.

Luke cleared his throat. "You're staring, Dad."

"Lovely girl."

"Yes, she is. Inside and out."

"Those pancakes I smell?"

Luke blinked at a man who'd lost several pounds over the last few months due to treatments and a loss of appetite. "You hungry?"

Jerome unbuttoned his wool coat. "I am."

If this was the sign of the day to come, Luke thought, we're in for a great one.

Rae knew there would be paparazzi on top of the film crew. She expected a few reporters, some local, some free-lance. But she wasn't quite prepared for the circus that awaited. At least three TV news trucks were parked along the street. Photographers were huddled outside of Moose-a-lotta, smoking cigarettes, drinking coffee, and trying to keep warm on a day when the temperature had yet to clear the teens. Then there were the curiosity seekers.

"Harper said it was pretty intense when she called a few minutes ago," Rae said. "but she didn't mention spectators. I don't understand. It's not like I'm famous."

"But your mother is," Luke said. "And this war she's got going with you made national gossip rags."

"You're being interviewed by Shawna Frost of *Vermont Today*," Kaye said. "She's a celebrity in these parts. Maybe the crowd is here for her, dear."

Rae swiveled and smiled at the woman who'd gone out of her way all morning to make Rae feel comfortable. "I'm really glad you and Mr. Monroe came with us although I'm sorry if it proves embarrassing in any way."

"Mr. Monroe makes me feel old," Luke's dad said. "Jerome or Jerry please. And it would take a lot to embarrass us. Our family has its own skeletons, trust me." He leaned forward then, gestured to the circus. "What's with the moose?"

"That's Gram," Luke said.

"What?"

"On special occasions, she appears as Millie Moose," Rae said. "The mascot of Moose-a-lotta. You didn't know?"

"I did not." He shook his head. "My mother the moose. Beautiful." He squeezed Luke's shoulder. "Maybe you should swing around to the alley, son. We'll take Rae in through the kitchen."

Luke looked at Rae. "Your call."

She peered through the windshield, blew out a breath. "I don't want to run from this and I don't want to make it any more of a show than it already is. Let's just do it."

"The direct approach," Jerome said. "I like your style, Rae."

"Me, too," Luke said. He squeezed her thigh and smiled. "Just remember everything Harper told you." He plucked up his own phone then. "Yeah, Dev? We're about a block and a half away. Looks a little dicey out here and we're coming in the front. Think you and Jayce could lend a hand? Thanks."

"Lend a hand with what?" Rae asked.

"Keeping you safe." Luke held her gaze a meaningful moment then rolled his SUV toward the action.

"It's kind of exciting," Kaye said.

"My mother would eat this up," Rae said. She got a weird feeling the moment the words left her mouth. A *bad* feeling. But Luke had already parked and suddenly she was in the thick of it. Rae was bombarded by the paparazzi. If she hadn't spied Dev and Jayce and Sam moving her way, she might have panicked. Along with Luke and his parents, the men shielded her as best they could. While several cameramen snapped away, questions flew at her from every which way.

"Is it true that you're engaged to a bartender, Ms. Deveraux? Is this the man?"

"What do you think of your mother's latest—"

"Why China—"

"Are these your bodyguards? Why—"

"Miss Rachel! Miss Rachel!"

A small voice broke through the chaos. Rae scanned

the crowd and saw one of her former students waving madly. She immediately broke from her protective pack and stooped in front of the small girl. Jill McBride. "Jilly! How are you sweetie?"

"Mommy says you're going to make our school be open again."

"Yes, I am." She glanced up at Mrs. McBride, a single mother who relied heavily on affordable day care. "Hopefully by the end of the month."

The woman smiled down at Rae then winced when photographers swarmed.

Rae shielded mother and child and cautioned the paparazzi in her most patient tone. "No pictures of minors please." To her relief they backed off, only to regroup as Luke and family steered her into Moose-a-lotta. Once inside all she'd have to deal with was crew from *Vermont Today.*

But then she felt a shift in energy and focus. She heard excited squeals.

"Is that—"

"It is."

"It's her!"

"Can I have your autograph, Miss Deveraux?"

And they didn't mean Rae.

It couldn't be but it was. Sick to her stomach, Rae turned and saw Olivia striding her way. Flanked by professional bodyguards, wearing an ankle-length fur coat and huge dark sunglasses, the has-been starlet looked like an older version of Jennifer Lopez.

She was in Rae's face in three seconds flat. "You thought you could avoid me by ignoring my calls?"

"Back off," Luke said.

"Easy," Dev said.

"After all I've done for you and this is how you treat me? If you think I'm one of those Hollywood mothers who's going to turn a blind eye to her kid's mental meltdown then think again."

Mental meltdown?

Suddenly Harper was at her side, whispering in her ear. "Don't respond in anger. Say nothing." Then she turned to Sam. "Get this inside." Then to the swarm of photographers. "Gentlemen of the press . . ."

Harper's words disintegrated into an indistinguishable buzz as Luke hustled Rae into the café.

Unfortunately, Olivia followed. "You ungrateful, sneaky bitch!"

"Whoa," Luke said. "That's enough."

"You're as bad as she is," Olivia said to Luke. "You came into my home, *my* home, pretending to be some mercenary from China."

Squeezing Rae's hand, Luke calmly stared down her mother. "I didn't pretend to be anyone. And I'm asking you nicely, Ms. Deveraux, please leave and don't come back."

Olivia barked a laugh. "What? Are you in *love* with my daughter? Do you actually think she has feelings for you? A *bartender*? She's an heiress, pretty boy. Wake up and smell the coffee."

"Stop," Rae ordered.

"That's enough, Ms. Deveraux," Jerome said. He glared at her bodyguards. "Dev, call Sheriff Stone."

"Does your boyfriend know about your boy toys?" Olivia pressed.

Rae palmed her forehead. "What?"

"Are the cameras rolling?" she heard someone ask.

"No cameras." Suddenly Harper was back in the mix, demanding control.

Rae tried to concentrate on Harper. On Luke. But she was keenly aware of an audience. Although the paparazzi and several reporters had been shut out, Rae was surrounded by the crew of *Vermont Today,* the members of the Cupcake Lovers and, most keenly, Luke's family.

"No wonder you refused to join me for several Christmas and New Year's celebrations," Olivia said as she reached into her ginormous designer purse. "You were too busy boffing boy toys. In *my* home," she emphasized while presenting Rae with several photographs.

The low buzz in Rae's ears had intensified to a roar. She flipped though the compromising photos—appalled. "This isn't me," she said in a choked whisper.

"And if that wasn't bad enough, you came on to Geoffrey! *My* husband. Your stepfather! Don't deny it. The one Christmas party you attended with me and you drank too much. Geoffrey drove you home and you made a play."

"No," Rae said. "That was last Christmas and it wasn't like that. Geoffrey came on to me. I refused. I—"

"You," Olivia said, "are a pathological liar."

Meanwhile Luke had taken the ugly photos from her limp fingers. "Not me," she said, dying inside as she saw the hurt in his eyes.

"You thought you were her one and only, Bartender Boy?" Olivia asked. "Days after she'd been with you she was screwing random men in my home. The pictures prove it."

"No comment," Harper said.

"My face, my room, not me," Rae said, feeling weirdly disconnected from her body.

"Photos are easily manipulated," Jayce said, taking the pictures from Luke.

"We're done with this," Jerome said. "Devlin? Jayce?"

Rae was vaguely aware of Dev, Jayce, and Sam ushering Olivia and her muscle from the café. Somewhat sensitive to the shock and curiosity emanating from the Cupcake Lovers. But mostly Rae was keenly and painfully aware of a moment of doubt in Luke's eyes. A moment in which he wondered if she'd screwed around, an intoxicated one-night stand like the one she'd had with him. A moment when he wondered if the baby was really his.

That moment shattered Rae's spirit far more than Olivia ever could. That moment closed her in and down.

THIRTY-THREE

Valentine's Day.

To think it used to be one of Luke's favorite days of the year. This time last year, he had three girlfriends. Pretty much his status quo. He'd lavished attention on all three. Flowers, candy, and a card. Champagne. He'd juggled three separate dates beautifully, devoted equal attention to all three ladies.

Luke Monroe had a lotta love to give.

Today, he had nothing. Just a big freaking hole in his chest where his heart used to be.

He'd screwed up. A split second of doubt had ruined a lifetime of happiness.

Rae had shut him out.

That damned stipulation.

"If even one of us is unhappy in this exclusive relationship . . . It only takes one to end it."

She hadn't ended it. Not officially. But she wouldn't see him. Wouldn't even speak to him. It sure as hell felt like the end because Luke couldn't see his way past the damage he'd inflicted. Rae had told him from the start that she rarely shared her feelings, rarely trusted, because she was always disappointed in the end.

She'd trusted Luke. Granted, for reasons he didn't fully understand, she'd withheld details regarding a sexual confrontation with her stepfather. But she had shared her carefully guarded feelings pertaining to her inability to trust. Her lack of genuine, meaningful relationships. Her lonely childhood. The hurt she'd experienced as an unwanted child and her hopeful efforts to somehow bond with her mother.

In addition to bearing her soul to Luke, she'd confided portions of her hardships with his family and with the Cupcake Lovers. She'd been ready to share a carefully worded version on television, all in an effort to quell a negative force and to do a lot of good.

Luke had shattered that trust with a split second of doubt. Those damned photos had done him in. Rae's face, that sweet, beautiful face . . . and those other men. Jealously had ripped through him like a wildfire, incinerating logical thought. He'd reverted to that moment when he'd felt used, when he'd confronted her in Bel Air, when she'd blown him off and thrown back shots of tequila in that bar. He'd allowed her mother's insults to attack his confidence.

The bartender and the heiress.

"Dammit."

Luke stumbled from his fridge to his recliner, beer bottle in hand. Several empty bottles cluttered the counter and the cocktail table. He'd started drinking late last night with Adam and Kane. He'd told them he was going to crash when they left around one in the morning. He'd lied.

Just as he dropped into his recliner, someone pounded on his door.

Luke ignored it. It wasn't Rae. Rae wouldn't pound. Or maybe she would. Maybe she was ready to tear him a new one. He'd welcome her fury to silence any day.

Bleary-eyed, Luke dragged his drunk ass to the door. Not Rae.

Fuck.

He could ignore them, but they'd only break down his door.

He twisted the knob, falling back as his dad, Dev, Jayce, and Sam shoved in.

His dad glared at the bottle in Luke's hand then glared at Luke. "It's eight in the morning, son. Little early to hit the bottle."

"He's still on a tear from last night," Dev said. He nabbed the bottle from Luke. "Adam called me this morning, worried about your state of mind."

"Why haven't you answered our calls?" Sam asked.

"Have you seen Rae?" Luke asked.

"She's staying with Casey," Sam said. "Harper spent time with her last night, devising a plan. Damage control. It's what Harper does, Luke, and she's good at it."

"Chloe spoke with Rae this morning," Dev said. "She's fine. Holding up anyway. I have a meeting with her later this morning. She's dumping her lawyer in L.A. and hiring me as her financial advisor."

Luke swayed a little on his feet, squeezed the bridge of nose struggling for a clear thought. "She's staying in Sugar Creek?"

Sam glared. "You thought she'd give up on her dream that easily? Don't you know Rae at all?"

Jerome growled in frustration. "I'll put on a pot of coffee. Jayce, fill my son in on what you learned. And Luke, for God's sake, focus."

Luke felt himself being hauled into the living room by

Dev and Sam. They dumped him on the couch then started clearing away bottles.

"The photos were definitely manipulated," Jayce said as he sat across from Luke. "Rae's head superimposed on another woman's body."

"Why?"

"I did some digging. Pretty confident this is part of a scheme Olivia and Geoffrey cooked up in order to gain control of Rae's fortune."

"Making her seem incompetent," Dev said. "Mentally unstable."

"Stein's loaded," Luke said. "Why would he need Rae's money?"

"With men like that," Sam said, "it's also about control."

"And maybe revenge," Dev added. "Rae reiterated to Chloe that Stein made the sexual advance. Rae spurned his attentions and he threatened to crush her if she outed him."

Luke's blood burned just thinking about it, mangling any semblance of clear thought. "She should have told me."

"So you could knock the bastard's block off?" Dev asked. "That's exactly why she didn't tell you. She was trying to protect you from Stein's wrath."

"As for Olivia," Jayce said, "it's about attention. That act she put on yesterday? You can bet she had an orgasm with all those cameras firing."

"The woman's whacked," Dev said. "And Rae's dealing with the fallout while you're getting trashed."

"I tried calling. I tried . . ." Chest aching, thoughts blurred, Luke dropped his head in his hands. "She won't talk to me. Doesn't want to see me."

"Oh, hell," Jerome said as he came back into the room.

"Coffee's not going to do it, Dad," Dev said.

"I got this," Sam said.

Next thing Luke knew, he was swaying in the downstairs shower stall. "Don't—"

Sam turned the faucet on full blast and pinned Luke against the tiles as the freaking ice cold water pounded Luke into lucidness. "Got your attention?" Sam asked.

"I love her, Sam."

"Then fight for her, dammit."

"How?"

"Patience."

THIRTY-FOUR

February 15

Rocky kicked off her morning, as was her routine, with a glass of OJ and a four-mile run alongside Jayce and Brewster. Unfortunately, the physical exertion did nothing to dispel the anxiety that had been building inside of her for the past few days. This was her wedding day and it wasn't like anything she'd ever dreamed.

Yes, everything was set. Everything was going according to plan. The Cupcake Lovers hadn't forgotten about making her cake. But instead of a joyful task, while baking up delicious perfection, they'd all battled the shock and sadness of seeing Rae humiliated by her whacko mother.

The next day, Valentine's Day, had been all but forgotten as family and friends pulled together, trying to comfort and help Rae. As for Luke, Rocky had never known her carefree brother to be such a mess. Jayce said he was pulling it together, but as of her wedding morning, Luke and Rae were still estranged and everyone was feeling the effect.

Most especially, Rocky.

Now, moments before taking her wedding vows, her composure shattered. She burst into tears.

Her mother, who'd been arranging Rocky's veil, swung around and cupped her daughter's cheeks. "What is it, sweetheart? What's wrong?"

"Can't do this."

"Of course you can. You've been waiting for this moment all your life."

Chloe moved in and squeezed Rocky's hand. "Just the jitters. Deep breath."

"Timing's wrong," Rocky squeaked out over a sob.

"I'll get Jayce," Monica said.

"No. Not supposed to see me."

"The timing's perfect," Kaye said. "You look beautiful. The church looks beautiful and all of your friends and family are waiting to share in your special day."

"Rae?"

"She's out there," Chloe said. "She's sitting with Casey and Sam and the kids.

"Luke?"

"He's with Jayce, dear. Remember? Your brothers are standing up with him."

"Have they talked?"

"Who, dear?"

"Rae and Luke?"

"I don't know. I—"

Rocky felt a warm, large hand squeezing her shoulder. "What's the trouble, Dash?"

Heart pounding, Rocky turned into the arms of the love of her life. "Everyone's supposed to be happy."

"I'm happy, baby." He smoothed tears from her cheeks. "I'll be damned delirious when you say 'I do.'"

"It's just . . . today. It was supposed to be magical."

Jayce kissed her with tender passion. "Then let's make some magic."

Rae sat in the pew, flanked by Casey and Sam, struggling with twisted emotions. She'd spent the last day and a half taking control of her tattered life. Harper had flown back to L.A. this morning but not before working miracles for Rae with the media and she'd promised to continue her PR efforts on Rae's behalf. In addition to Harper, Rae had also had the support of Sam and Casey, Dev and Chloe, Luke's parents, and Rocky and Jayce. So many people had stepped up to her defense.

Even Luke.

At least he had tried. Rae had shut him down. Shut him out. All because of that one moment of doubt.

She didn't blame him. Truly she didn't. She should have told him about Geoffrey's sexual advance. She should have trusted that Luke would have handled the news appropriately. If he'd had that heads-up, maybe he would have instantly seen through Olivia's twisted version. Those compromising photos hadn't helped. She *knew* she wasn't the girl in those pictures and even she had been rattled. Logically, she understood why Luke had lapsed. Logically, she knew the moment had quickly passed. She'd agreed early on to a paternity test if he wanted. She hadn't lied about the baby. Luke was the father. Logically, she knew he believed that. And she believed that Luke loved her.

Unfortunately, logic was no match for emotions and Rae had needed time to sort out her thoughts and feelings. Luke needed time, too, even if he didn't believe that at first. She knew through the grapevine that he'd taken their separation hard. Sam had been his greatest champion, although her friend hadn't told her anything she didn't already know. Most essentially, Luke was a kind man. A good man. Still, Rae had needed time. They hadn't spoken since that awful confrontation. She hadn't seen him.

Until now.

Casey reached over and squeezed Rae's hand as Luke entered from a side room and took his place beside his brother and Jayce.

Rae's pulse raced. He looked so handsome in his tuxedo and when he smiled over at his brother and Jayce, her heart did this funny dance. She knew he was hurting, but he was pulling it together for family. Just one of the reasons she loved Luke. He was all about family.

The bridal march signaled Rocky's entrance and everyone stood. Rae's eyes filled with tears as Jerome, looking more dapper than frail, escorted his daughter down the rose-petaled aisle. Rae tried to imagine what Rocky was feeling.

She couldn't.

When Jerome handed his daughter over to Jayce, Rae grabbed a wad of tissues from her purse.

Sam reached over and patted her knee then he shushed his daughter, who'd started to squirm.

Rae's pulse raced as the preacher started the ceremony, heart in throat along with everyone else in the church. This moment had been a long time coming for Rocky and Jayce. It was all so beautiful, so perfect . . . until Rocky stopped the preacher just as he reached the vow portion.

There was a stunned sort of silence as Rocky whispered into Jayce's ear. He nodded then kissed her cheek. She turned and addressed her wedding guests.

"As you all know, this is a very special day for me." She glanced at Jayce with a shy smile. "For us. We're about to say our vows, to pledge our forever love, and though it won't be official, I'd like to invite every couple, anyone who's in love, to stand and take these vows with us."

Rae stared, her chest exploding with wonder as, one by one, couples stood.

Rocky's parents.

Monica and Leo.

Daisy and Vince.

Dev looked at Chloe and, smiling, she moved from her bridesmaid position to stand beside her intended.

"Brace yourself," Sam said close to Rae's ear and then suddenly he was jostling her so she was seated at the end of the pew.

She blinked through confusion and tears to see Luke striding down the aisle.

He reached down and pulled her to her feet then, with everyone watching, he took a folded red paper from his pocket and gave it to Rae. "I made this for you."

"A valentine?" she whispered. Hands trembling, Rae unfolded the fairly large heart, her throat tightening as she noted the long, painstakingly neat handwritten message. She met his vulnerable gaze, swallowed, then looked back to the note. A note professing his love.

She imagined it had taken him as long to write the note as to gather his thoughts. He'd had to work hard to produce the beautifully written words. And he'd done it for her.

Words failed Rae, but she did smile. And she followed, when Luke took her hand and led her toward the altar to stand alongside Rocky and Jayce and Dev and Chloe. The moment could not have been any more perfect.

Until Rocky signaled the preacher to continue after smiling at her siblings and saying, "Magic."

HONORARY CUPCAKE LOVERS

Submitted Recipes and Tips from On-Line Members

RECIPE 1
RED VELVET CUPCAKES FILLED WITH VANILLA BEAN PASTRY CREAM
(submitted by JoAnn Schailey of Pennsylvania)

Vanilla Bean Pastry Cream
Ingredients
2 cups whole milk
½ cup sugar
1 vanilla bean, split along the length and scrape out the seeds
4 large egg yolks
¼ cup sifted cornstarch

Directions
- Combine the milk, sugar, vanilla bean pods and seeds and whisk mixture constantly over medium heat until it gently boils. Remove from heat.
- In a separate bowl, whisk the egg yolks and cornstarch about two minutes. Slowly add ½ cup of the hot milk

mixture to the egg yolks, whisking constantly until smooth. (Slowly stream the hot milk into the eggs to prevent the eggs from cooking). Add the egg yolk mixture to the pan of hot milk and whisk to combine. Return to medium heat and cook. Stir constantly until the mixture thickens. (The pastry cream may need to cook between 3 and 7 minutes to thicken.)

- Remove from the heat and strain into a clean container, scraping the bottom of the strainer with a spoon. (If the pastry cream is too thick to go through the strainer, return the contents of the strainer to the pot and whisk to remove any lumps. Strain the remainder of the pastry cream.) Discard the vanilla bean. Specks of the vanilla seeds will be visible in the cream.

- Press a piece of plastic wrap over the surface of the cream to prevent a skin from forming. Refrigerate until well chilled, approximately three hours. Vanilla bean pastry cream can be made the day ahead. Extra pastry cream can be kept for 2 days.

Red Velvet Cupcakes
Ingredients
1 package of Red Velvet Cake mix (moist) and the ingredients required to make the cupcakes

Directions
- Preheat oven according to the package directions.
- Line the cupcake pans with paper liners or use heart shape cupcake pans.
- Blend the cake mix according to the package directions.
- Bake according to the suggested cupcake baking times.
- Cupcakes are done when a toothpick inserted into the center comes out clean.
- Cool the cupcakes before filling.

Filling the cupcakes
Directions

- Use an apple corer or small knife to cut a plug about ⅔ depth of the cupcake. Remove the plug and trim off the excess cupcake to ⅛ inch, keeping the top of the cupcake plug intact. Put the pastry cream into one end of a plastic bag, cut a small hole in the corner of the bag, and squeeze the cream into the opening in the cupcakes to fill. Return top of plug to the cupcakes.

Cream Cheese Frosting
Ingredients

8 oz. cream cheese
1 cup confectioner's sugar
½ teaspoon pure vanilla extract
2 tablespoons of butter

Directions

- Mix all ingredients and frost the cupcakes.

Chocolate Shavings

Grate chocolate over the cupcakes. Serve. Refrigerate remaining cupcakes.

RECIPE 2
WHITE CUPCAKES WITH FRESH STRAWBERRY FILLING
(submitted by JoAnn Schailey of Pennsylvania)

Ingredients

1 box of "moist" Classic White Cake Mix and the ingredients required to make the cupcakes. If the cake mix gives a choice of using only egg whites, choose that option.

Directions

- Preheat oven according to the cake mix directions.
- Use paper liners for the cupcake tins.
- Blend the cake mix according to the package instructions.
- Bake according to the suggested cupcake baking times.
- Cupcakes are done when a wooden pick inserted into the center comes out clean.
- Cool the cupcakes.

Filling Ingredients

16 oz. fresh strawberries
4 teaspoons of sugar

Filling Directions

- Wash and lightly dry the strawberries.
- Trim off the green tops.
- Puree strawberries in a food processor.
- Strain pureed strawberries and reserve the liquid in a separate bowl.
- Combine the pureed strawberries with 4 teaspoons of sugar and cook until thick.
- Allow the thickened strawberry and sugar mixture to cool.

Filling the Cupcake Center

- Use an apple corer or a small knife to remove a plug about ⅔ depth of the cupcake. Remove the "plug" and trim off the excess cupcake to ⅛ inch, keeping the top of the plug intact. Put a few tablespoons of filling into the point of a plastic bag and snip the tip. Squeeze the filling into the cupcake. Replace the "plug".

Strawberry Buttercream Frosting

8 tablespoons of butter (¼ pound)

3 cups of sifted confectioner's sugar
1 teaspoon pure vanilla extract
4 teaspoons of strawberry liquid (This is the liquid that has been strained after the strawberries have been pureed)

Directions
- Combine butter, confectioner's sugar, vanilla extract and beat at medium speed until creamy. Add 4 teaspoons of strawberry liquid and beat until well mixed. To obtain a deeper color frosting, add 1 to 2 teaspoons of strawberry puree. (The icing will have small pieces of strawberry.) Frost the cupcakes.
- After serving the cupcakes, refrigerate any uneaten cupcakes.

RECIPE 3
CHOCOLATE COVERED BANANA SUPREME
(submitted by Dawn Jones of New Jersey)

All Ingredients
1 box Duncan Hines Signature Banana Supreme Cake Mix
1 whole Banana
1Can Dark Chocolate Frosting

Cake Directions
1. Preheat oven according to cake mix
2. Line a muffin pan with paper liners
3. Follow directions on box
4. Pour or spoon batter into prepared liners
5. Bake according to cake mix, cake is done when it springs back to the touch or when a cake tester or toothpick inserted in center comes out clean

Center Directions
- Using a steak knife cut out a plug (piece of cake) from the center of each cupcake and put it aside, then slice the banana and put a piece of the banana and a teaspoon of frosting into the hole then add the plug (piece of cake) and frost with dark chocolate frosting
- Makes about 24 cupcakes depends on the cake mix